Free My Heart

By

Leslie Thompson

Freedom of Love Press

23 SWAINE PLACE
WEST ORANGE, NEW JERSEY 07052
(973) 736-4248
WWW.FOLPRESS.COM

Thank you to my preview reading ladies for taking time out of your busy schedules to help me organize what flows from my imagination onto these pages.

❧ PROLOGUE ❧

Rió de Janeiro, Brazil
Autumn 1840

Rubina Arinzé Domingues sat atop a chocolate brown mare galloping towards the courtyard of her home in the distance. She laughed out loud as the wind whipped her dark curls from the confinement of a white ribbon. Her maid had tied the unruly locks back just an hour ago.

When she saw a wagon full of flowers bumping down the road towards the house she signaled for her mare to pick up the pace, excitement for what the rest of her day held in store urging her on. Rubina couldn't imagine feeling any happier than she was at that moment. Her parents were returning home after being away for two weeks, the flowers being delivered were for her 8th birthday party that evening and the mare she now rode had been a birthday gift from Aunt Luciana. She raced into the courtyard and came to a stop near a fountain in the center.

"*Perfeito*, Rubina, you ride just as well as I did at your age," her Great Aunt said proudly as Rubina dismounted.

"*Tía* Luciana, she is wonderful," Rubina said, throwing her arms happily around the woman's waist.

Luciana returned Rubina's embrace, placing a kiss atop her wind blown hair, which now framed her face in a riot of thick untamable curls.

"Yes she is and you must take very good care of her. She is bred from the finest stock," she said, smiling as Rubina fed the mare a carrot the stable hand brought to her.

"Unlike her new owner," said a bitter voice.

Luciana's smile wavered. She was hoping Rubina had not heard the comment. Turning around, she gave her sister an angry glare as she walked over to her.

"It is the child's birthday Maria, you will not ruin it for her," Luciana warned.

"You spoil her too much," she said in disgust as she watched Rubina tenderly stroking the mare's nose.

Maria could find no tenderness in her heart for her grandchild because she despised Rubina's mother. If it were not for fear of losing her son she would not be here to celebrate the child's birthday, as she did every year, by his request. At the thought of her daughter-in-law, all the hatred she felt for her began to rise up in Maria's throat like bile. Just as she was trying to get control of the emotion Rubina's gaze met hers.

She flinched as if Maria had physically struck her then looked away as her horse nudged her hand looking for more carrots. She could not understand why her grandmother seemed to dislike her so much and wondered what she could have done wrong to make her feel that way.

Luciana also witnessed the dark emotion in her sister's eyes, "It has been over eight years Maria, you must learn to let go of your anger. If not for your sake then at least do it for Reynaldo's. He loves Ifé and Rubina with all his heart."

"I am not the one that told him to marry an *escravo* and bring that *meia raça* into this world," Maria said bitterly.

Luciana fought back the urge to slap Maria, "He married Ifé because they loved one another. It did not matter to him that she was a slave and it should not matter to you either as long as your son is happy. You also seem to forget that that beautiful child you are calling a half-breed is your own flesh and blood."

"Father always did say that you were too soft-hearted when it came to the slaves," Maria said, refusing to acknowledge that what Luciana said was true.

Luciana sighed wearily, "I will not argue with you sister. Reynaldo and Ifé will be home soon and there is much to do before Rubina's party. If you are not here to help then I suggest you retire to your rooms until this evening."

Luciana walked back towards Rubina holding out her hand. "Come, little one, we can not have you greeting your parents looking like a street urchin," she said, smiling at the dirt smudged on Rubina's face and the torn lace hanging from the hem of her dress.

Maria quickly stepped aside when they walked past her. As if she were afraid Rubina would accidentally brush up against her and pass along some undetermined illness. The slight saddened Rubina even more and made her wonder if her grandmother would ever love her.

As Luciana helped Rubina get dressed the usually rambunctious child was uncharacteristically quiet.

"Why such a serious expression on such a happy day?" she asked as she adjusted the collar of Rubina's dress.

"*Tía* Luciana, why does *Avó* Dominquez not like me?" she asked sadly.

Luciana hesitated before answering, not sure what to tell her niece. She loved her as if she were her own grandchild and couldn't bear hurting her with the truth on what was supposed to be a happy occasion for her.

"I'm sure your grandmother cares for you very much," she said, the lie burning its way down her throat.

Rubina shook her head, "I do not think so. She does not look at me the way you, *Mãe* and *Pai* do?"

"What do you mean?" Maria rarely visited and when she did she never stayed longer than a few days. Had her feelings been so obvious at those times that the child even noticed?

"When you all look at me I see a happy light in your eyes, but when *Avó* looks at me I see something dark that scares me sometimes."

Luciana hugged Rubina to her, "Oh *querido*, you have nothing to fear from anyone as long as you have your *Mãe*, *Pai*, and me to take care of you," she said, her heart aching at the sadness in her great-niece's voice.

If only Maria would look past her snobbish ideas of social status and see how beautiful and special her grandchild was. Rubina was a happy and bright child whose lack of fear and rambunctious behavior continuously gave her parents many worries and reminded Luciana of herself as a child. She was also free-spirited and outspoken, traits that both parents encouraged. To look at the child was like looking into the face of a cherub with her wide round hazel eyes, pert nose, ruby red bow lips, for which her father had aptly named her, and smooth dark cocoa skin. Luciana believed that if Maria would just take the time to get to know her grandchild, she would not be such a bitter woman.

The sound of a commotion out in the courtyard drifted up through the open terrace doors of Rubina's room.

"Ah, it is time," Luciana said cheerfully, hoping to sweep away the blanket of sadness that had spread over them.

She stood and took Rubina's hand, "Let's go and welcome your parents home. I am sure they will have armfuls of birthday wishes for you."

Worries about Rubina's grandmother's dislike for her were pushed aside and replaced by the joy of her parents return home. Rubina adored her mother and father and at 8 years old, couldn't imagine a world without them being there to love and care for her and keep her safe.

As they made their way down the staircase, an eerie silence had settled over the household. Whenever the Dominguez's returned from a trip there was normally a flurry of activity with some of the staff rushing through the front doors with their baggage and the housekeeper giving directions to the busy staff, but when Rubina and Luciana reached the bottom of the staircase they saw that the front doors were thrown open and the household staff were standing quietly in the courtyard.

Rubina came to a halt and her eyes widened with fear. "Mãe...Pai?" she whispered anxiously before dropping Luciana's hand and running out to the courtyard.

Luciana hurried behind her, feeling the same sense of dread as Rubina must have felt. The older woman gasped in shock as she saw that the Dominguez carriage had been led into the courtyard by a farmer's wagon and that two bodies lay beneath woolen blankets on the carriage's leather seats. When Luciana reached the vehicle, Rubina was scrambling up into it gazing tearfully at the still bodies of her parents.

"What happened?" Luciana asked no one in particular, her voice thick with emotion.

A shabbily dressed man stepped forward, ringing his battered hat in his hands, "*Desculpe-me Senhora*, I work a farm near *Senhor* and *Senhora* Dominguez's land. I was returning from town when I came across them on the road. It looks as if they were set upon by thieves. I could do nothing for them," he said, looking sadly down at his shoes.

Luciana nodded in understanding and placed a gentle hand on his arm, "Thank you for bringing them home," she said.

Rubina sat on the floor of the carriage hugging her knees to her chest with tears streaming down her small face and pain and confusion clouding her usually bright hazel eyes.

"*Vindo, querido*, we must take them inside," Luciana said, reaching for the distraught child. Luciana's pain was like a knife in her heart, she could only imagine how Rubina felt.

Suddenly a wail pierced the quiet courtyard. Everyone turned to look back at the house just as Maria Dominguez collapsed upon the ground. Rubina rushed into Luciana's arms, truly afraid for the first time in her young life and feeling that that was the only place she would ever feel safe and secure again.

A week after her parent's funeral, Rubina lay in her bed gazing up at the lace canopy surrounding it. This would be her last week in the only home she's known before going to live with her Aunt Luciana at the family's sugar plantation.

Rubina felt a tear slide down the side of her face onto her pillow. She had rarely cried since the day her parents were brought home. She remembered her mother always telling her she would have to be stronger than most because of who she was. That she could not show weakness because there would always be someone who would use it against her. She wiped away the tear, taking a deep breath as she did so.

"I will be strong *Mãe*, I promise," she said as she pressed her mother's cameo to her chest. It had been a gift from her father on their last anniversary. He said that the woman in the cameo looked so much like Ifé that he had to buy it for her. As she and Luciana were packing away her mother's jewelry, Rubina had asked if she could keep the cameo.

She soon fell asleep but awoke a few hours later feeling as if someone was in her room. Opening her eyes, she sat up. "Carlotta?" she called out, as she squint into the darkness thinking her maid had come into the room to check on her.

She started to cry out as she noticed a dark figure standing in the doorway of the terrace off of her room, but a rough hand covered her mouth before she could make a sound. Just as quickly, an arm wrapped around her like an iron band, trapping her arms to her sides, preventing her from struggling. Rubina bared her teeth behind her captors hand and bit the fleshy part of his palm. He swore, snatching his hand away, but before she could release a scream he shoved a wad of material into her open mouth, almost gagging her in his attempts to quiet her. A rope was wrapped tightly around her body then the intruders took her from her room just as quietly as they had entered.

They traveled for some time before finally coming to a stop in a forested area. Rubina was placed on the ground up against a tree in a clearing. She had no idea how far they had gone, it had been too dark and they were moving too fast for her take note of her surroundings, but she did know that they were no longer on Dominguez land. As the two men spoke quietly to one another, the sound of a distant horse's whinny caught everyone's attention. The men pulled guns from their waist bands, pointing them towards a copse of trees in front of them.

A slim figure dressed in a peasant skirt, blouse and cape with the hood pulled low over her face stepped into view with three horses in tow. Rubina's eyes widened in surprise when she recognized the animals being led by the woman, they were her parent's horses and the mare Aunt Luciana had given her. She did not understand how the woman had managed to get a hold of them, especially since her parent's horses did not take to strangers well.

The men withdrew their weapons and walked over to look the horses over, nodding their heads in satisfaction. The woman handed the lead man a small bag. He opened it, pouring part of its contents into his hand. Rubina could see they were gold coins. He nodded, putting the small treasure into his saddle bag.

The woman walked towards Rubina, kneeling down before her and pushing the hood of her cape away from her face. Rubina squeaked, shocked at the site of the familiar face.

"Are you surprised to see me?" Maria said sarcastically.

Rubina could only stare in disbelief. She could tell by the cruel smile on her grandmother's face that she was not there to rescue her.

"You and your mother ruined everything," Maria told her. "Because of you I lost my son and now a fortune that should have rightfully gone to me."

Her smile turned into a vicious sneer, "And if I can not have it, I sure as hell will not let you."

Maria had a blackness within her that twisted her usually beautiful features into an ugly mask. She reminded Rubina of the wicked witches in the fairy tales her mother had read to her. She willed herself not to be afraid. Her grandmother was one of those people her mother had warned her about, the kind that would use her fear against her.

Suddenly a genuine smile appeared on Maria's face transforming her features back into the beauty she appeared to be.

"Ah, I see the de Souza spirit in your eyes. It is a pity you inherited your mother's dark skin, things could have been so different if you did not look like a slave."

Rubina wished her hands weren't tied to her sides because she truly would like to have scratched her grandmother's eyes out. Since that was not possible she turned her head away, snubbing her just as the woman had done to her many times before.

Maria's face contorted in anger once again. She stood, placing her hood back over her head, "From this point on, our business is done," she told Rubina's captors.

"You should have no problem obtaining a high price for her. She comes from excellent stock," she said cruelly.

❧ ONE ❧

Atlanta, Georgia
Summer 1851

Ruby stood in the marketplace where her life as a slave began over ten years ago. All she has to do is close her eyes and she could still feel the fear of that day. The press of bodies and the smell of sweat and sickness permeated the slave pens she'd spent a night and the better part of a day in. She came to the marketplace often and although the memories were stronger on some days more than others, she was not sure how much longer she could endure the pain of being reminded of what she had lost. With the memories of her time at the slave market, came the memories of her life before she was brought to America. She ached to have her family and life in Brazil back. She would not allow herself to think they may have gone on without her or that her Aunt Luciana was no longer alive to help reclaim her past.

A few years ago Elizabeth, Ruby's owner, had promised that when Ruby reached 18 years of age, she would be given her freedom. Ruby had anxiously waited for that day. The past year had been the most difficult. Right before her 18th birthday, Elizabeth's beau proposed and she asked Ruby to give her another year before she signed the papers. She claimed she couldn't possibly plan her wedding without Ruby's help.

Ruby had to physically shake off the lingering memories before turning away from the auction block in search of Elizabeth. Close on her heels was Joseph, the family's coachman, or as Ruby called him, the family's watchdog with his hanging jowls and dower expression. John Elder had put

Joseph in charge of escorting Elizabeth and Ruby when ever they left the house. He claimed it was for their safety. Ruby knew the real reason was to keep an eye on her. There had been a large number of slave escapes in the area over the past year and he was not taking any chances of losing his daughter's prized possession because of talk of a secret underground route to freedom. Ruby didn't know why they worried so much. She trusted Elizabeth would keep her promise to set her free so there was no need for her to run off in the dead of night.

"Ruby, you must see this beautiful cameo," Elizabeth said as Ruby reached her side.

"Miss Lizzie, I think you already have far too many cameos. I couldn't possibly find space in your jewelry box for another," Ruby teased.

"Not for me Ruby, for you."

"The only money I have is from the needlepoint I do that your father allows me to sell and I'm saving that to use when I'm granted my freedom. I'm not going to waste it on jewelry I do not need."

Because Elizabeth's back was to her, Ruby didn't see the frown that came across her mistress' face.

"Oh, but Ruby, this one is different. It sort of resembles you," Elizabeth told her as she handed her the cameo, her frown quickly replaced by a smile.

Ruby's heart skipped a beat, as she gazed down at the cameo. *"Meu Deus."*

Elizabeth gazed at her curiously, "Are you alright? You look as if you've seen a ghost."

Ruby ran her fingers softly over the profile in the cameo. Her mind was reeling. She wasn't sure if she wanted to laugh or cry. The cameo Elizabeth had placed in her hand was the very image of the one she had lost the night of her kidnapping. A feeling of joy overwhelmed her. Was this a sign that it was finally time for her to reclaim her past? That her family was waiting for her?

"Ruby," Elizabeth said worriedly.

"I'm sorry Miss Lizzie, it's just that the cameo reminds me of someone," Ruby said in amazement.

Elizabeth sighed in exasperation, "You aren't going to start talking about your life in Brazil are you? It was entertaining when we were children but I thought you would have out grown it long ago."

Ruby ignored her, walking over to the vendor, an old, white-haired, Colored woman with a weathered, kind face and wizened eyes.

"Excuse me, where did you get this?" Ruby asked.

The woman smiled broadly, her teeth yellowed and crooked, "I used make and sell them at market before I came here but that was a long time ago. Now my hands were too swollen and my eyes too weak. My granddaughter makes all this now," she said indicating the cart full of jewelry and trinkets.

"How much would you like for it?"

The old woman stood, leaning on her weathered cane, squinting closely at Ruby then shook her head, "I woke up one morning from a dream of an angel telling me my time here is about to pass. My fingers were no longer swollen and my eyesight was a little bit clearer. I knew it wouldn't last for long so I got to work and didn't stop till I finished. You remind me of that angel. Being able to do just one more piece like that before I go is payment enough."

Ruby reached into her purse, taking out enough money to buy two cameos and handed it to the woman, "This is part of the money I was going to use to help get home to my family. You have brought me one step closer so, please, accept this as a token of my gratefulness for all of your beautiful work."

The old woman nodded, taking the money, tears of gratitude in her clouded eyes. "God bless you child."

"And you," Ruby said, feeling as if she were walking on air.

She turned and was startled to find Elizabeth blocking her path. She was so caught up in the excitement of finding the cameo she had forgotten that her mistress was there.

"What's wrong?" she asked in response to the bewildered expression on Elizabeth's face.

"Do you realize you and that woman conversed in Portuguese?"

It was Ruby's turn to look bewildered, "Did we?" she asked, trying to remember what was said, knowing that she could switch from English to Portuguese and back again without even realizing it sometimes.

"I think I'd like to go home now," Elizabeth said, heading toward Joseph.

Ruby gazed down at the cameo, almost an exact replica of the one her father had given her mother. The very one she had dropped during her struggle with her kidnappers the night she was taken from her home all those years ago.

"Yes, it's time to go home," she said to herself, smiling as she followed Elizabeth to the carriage.

Two weeks later Ruby stood outside Elizabeth's door angrier than she could have ever imagined.

"There you are," Elizabeth said to Ruby as she entered her mistress' room.

"Robert will be here in an hour and my hair is still not finished."

Ruby picked up a hairbrush off of the dressing table.

"I still can not believe that I will be Mrs. Robert Englund in just two short days," she said excitedly.

Elizabeth chatted on about the wedding plans and her new home while Ruby quietly and quickly styled her mistress' blonde locks. Once she was finished, she looked up from her task and into the mirror, her gaze meeting Elizabeth's.

Elizabeth looked nervously away from Ruby's penetrating gaze and began rearranging her toiletries on the dressing table.

"Why are you looking at me that way?"

"I went to your father and asked about your promise to set me free. He told me you had changed your mind and that I would be staying on as your housekeeper. *Why*?"

The last word was said with a more force than Ruby had intended but she was so angry it was difficult to stay calm.

Elizabeth stood, gazing back at Ruby with the superiority of a master looking at a disrespectful slave. It was a look Ruby never thought she would see from the person she had considered her friend.

"You will not speak to me in that tone, Ruby," she said in reprimand.

Ruby was beyond caring about the consequences of her actions. Anger, hurt and confusion ruled her emotions at that moment.

"You promised you would not keep me here once you were married and now, for some unknown reason, you not only are denying me what you promised but did not even have the courage to tell me."

"I was going to tell you, I've just been so busy with the wedding and the new house that it slipped my mind," Elizabeth said petulantly.

"You never were a very good liar," Ruby said, walking over to the wardrobe and pulling out the dress she had pressed for Elizabeth's evening.

"Ruby, please don't be angry," she pleaded. "I need you. Robert and I will be starting a new life in a new home. I need someone I can trust to help me get the household in order. You would be in charge of an entire staff, just like Harriet is here."

Ruby lay the gown on the bed, "You don't understand. I don't want to be in charge of someone else's household. I don't want to live under someone else's roof not able to come and go as I please. I want to be free, Lizzie." The pain of Elizabeth's betrayal was obvious in her voice.

"Why? So you can go back to Brazil to a family that probably doesn't even remember or want you? To a country you probably wouldn't even recognize after all these years?" Elizabeth said angrily, ignoring the plea in Ruby's gaze.

"We have treated you as one of our own since the day we bought you off of that auction block. We never beat you, abused you or denied you anything —"

"Except my freedom," Ruby interrupted.

Elizabeth turned her back on Ruby, "I can't. I need you."

"But what about what I need Lizzie? Do you think that because I'm a slave I have no feelings? Because my skin is darker than yours that I don't have the same wants and desires as you? Why are you denying me the right to live as I choose?" Ruby asked desperately.

Elizabeth turned, giving Ruby that superior look once again, "You were bought and paid for and as your mistress I have every right to deny you whatever I feel may interfere with how you serve me."

Ruby gazed coldly at Elizabeth. They had been friends as children, but she was foolish to have thought that their friendship would continue as adults. She was, and always would be, a slave to Elizabeth and she should never have allowed herself to forget that.

"Forgive me, Miss Elizabeth, I've obviously overstepped my bounds. It won't happen again," Ruby said tiredly, continuing to retrieve the rest of Elizabeth's garments.

Elizabeth did not miss the fact that Ruby did not call her Lizzie, her childhood name.

"Ruby, don't be this way. I'm doing this for your own good. If everything you said is true about your grandmother, why would you want to go back? You are safe and cared for here."

"Will that be all Miss? Do you require anything else?" Ruby said, ignoring Elizabeth's words.

They glared at one another, neither willing to back down. Finally Elizabeth sighed in resignation and walked over to her jewelry box.

"I could use your assistance with the gown then you may have the rest of the evening to yourself."

Both knew that the closeness they once shared was now irreparably damaged.

Ruby sat in the kitchen drinking a cup of tea. It was late and the house was silent, but come morning there would be a flurry of activity as Elizabeth's wedding day finally arrived. Instead of feeling joy for her mistress, Ruby only felt sorrow for herself. She had been so close to going home. Now thoughts of Brazil, her Aunt Luciana and Uncle Amir only fueled the anger she tried so hard to suppress.

She gazed down at the cameo that lay beside her tea cup. It would not allow her to lose hope. Whenever she looked at it she heard the old woman from the market telling her it was time. She hoped the woman's prophetic words were true because she was beginning to feel like a caged bird slamming her wings against the bars, trying to break free.

"Can't sleep?"

Ruby looked up to see Harriet, the Elder's housekeeper, standing in the doorway. She smiled at the round, thick, robust woman who had taken her under her wing and made her feel welcome when she had first come to live with the Elder's.

"Would you like some tea Harriet?" Ruby asked, refilling her own cup.

"I'll take a bit."

Harriet lowered herself into the chair across from Ruby, pulling a flask from the pocket of her robe.

She winked at Ruby's questioning glance, "For my rheumatism," she said, pouring a large portion of the flask's contents into her tea cup.

"I'm old, so I have an excuse to be wandering around in the middle of the night, what's yours?"

"Guess all the excitement about tomorrow has gotten to me," Ruby said with a weak smile.

Harriet snorted, "Child, I may be old but I'm not blind. You've been walking around here like a ghost for the past couple of weeks. What happened?"

"It's nothing Harriet. Probably just nerves over the new responsibilities I'll have after tomorrow."

"Duchess, look at me," the older woman insisted, calling Ruby by the nickname the staff had given her.

When Ruby gazed up and saw the sincere concern in the other woman's eyes she could no longer hold back the tears she had managed to keep at bay since her argument with Elizabeth. She told Harriet everything. It was the first time she had spoken to anyone about the promise that had been made to set her free. Mr. Elder didn't want the rest of the staff to know; afraid it would cause them to be jealous or angry that they had not been given the same opportunity. Ruby knew she could trust Harriet not to say anything to the others so she didn't worry as she poured out her disappointment and heartbreak to the older woman.

"So all those stories you used to tell us about your family and home before coming here were true?" Harriet asked. Ruby's stories of her grand life before coming to the Elders had been the reason the staff had nicknamed her Duchess.

"Yes."

Harriet nodded her head, "I always thought that there was no way a child could make all that up."

"Why didn't you ever say anything?"

"Well, I thought it would be easier for you to adjust to being a servant and not being served if we didn't treat you any differently."

"I believe my mother knew something like this was going to happen to me. By the time I was 6 years old I could do any of the jobs our servants did. I even worked in the sugar cane fields during harvest right along side her. She told me it was to teach me to stay humble."

"Well, she taught you good," Harriet said, impressed with Ruby's mother's logic.

"You never once acted better than any of us."

"That's because I'm not. I want the same things you all want, Harriet, to be free to live my life the way I choose," Ruby said in frustration, her heart aching and tears once again welling in her eyes at the thought of never being able to find her way back to her family.

"Your time will come, child, I can feel it. You just have to be patient and let God do his thing. You trust in him and he'll show you the way," the older woman said wisely.

One Year Later

Seth Grant leaned against the doorway of a livery stable, carefully watching the people passing by. He ignored the curious but appreciative glances of the women, unaware of how his brooding expression did nothing to hinder his dark good looks. He was more concerned about the time than how the dark brown color of his hair brought out the even deeper brown of his eyes and rich coffee skin tone, or how his trimmed mustache and full wide mouth looked as if he knew how to kiss a woman speechless. Seth's mind was on the fact that their contact was supposed to have met him at three o'clock and, judging by his pocket watch, the man was a half hour late. Although he had his day pass with him, he didn't want to stand around too long drawing attention too himself.   Turning to leave, the sight of a woman crossing the roadway several feet in front of him caught his attention.

He could tell by how well the tailored housekeeper's uniform she wore cinched her small waist and emphasized her full bosom and rounded hips that she had a curvaceous figure. Her skin was a smooth, rich, deep brown, and she wore her hair in a plaited crown that added to her height, giving her a regal appearance. Her eyes were wide with lashes so thick they looked as if they were lined with kohl makeup. Her nose was wide but small and her lips were full and so red that they surely had to have rouge on them. Her stance was tall and straight, full of pride and self-confidence. She was a strikingly beautiful woman.

She laughed at something the older woman said and Seth's heart skipped a beat. Her laugh had a rich, throaty sound, calling to him like an ancient siren's song, pulling him in her direction. It took him a moment to realize what he was doing. He didn't have time to stand there gawking at some woman like an inexperienced schoolboy, but he found himself rooted to the spot still gazing at her when she suddenly looked his way. Her gaze was curious, as if she possibly recognized him. She smiled, nodding her head in greeting. Seth managed to find the sense to tip the brim of his hat in response before quickly turning in the opposite direction and leaving the livery.

By the time he arrived at the hotel he and his partner Nicholas Collins were staying in, he was angry at himself for not only acting so foolishly at the sight of the woman, but for allowing her to distract him from his business. Seth headed towards the servants stairwell in back of the building. Although he was only posing as Nicholas' Colored servant, it was important for him to do whatever was necessary to keep up the appearance of his disguise.

When he arrived at the room they shared, Nicholas was already there.

"What took you so long?" Nicholas asked worriedly.

"He never showed. I ran into a servant in the hall delivering a message to you," handing Nicholas the folded paper, Seth sat heavily down in one of the large brocaded chairs in the suite.

Nicholas read it then tore it into small pieces, lit a match and burned it in an ashtray on the side table. They could not afford to leave any evidence of their true reason for being in Atlanta. It had been from their contact letting them know that he had to reschedule their meeting.

"Maybe we shouldn't make this trip," he said worriedly, "I've got a bad feeling about this one."

Seth closed his eyes, laying his head on the back of the chair, "It's too late. We've already got the passengers and the train will be leaving in two weeks time no matter what."

"Do you ever want to quit, Seth? Do you ever get tired of putting your life on the line?"

Seth sat up, gazing at his friend, "Is that what you want to do Nick?"

Nicholas sighed heavily, "Lately, I've been wondering if we're fighting a losing battle."

Seth had known Nicholas Collins since they were children. He'd never seen the jovial man look so tired. His usually perfectly coifed blonde hair was mussed, as if he had worriedly run his fingers through it, and his steel blue eyes seemed to have lost their light.

"We've been friends for a long time, Nick, so I know you believe in this cause just as much as I do, but I'll understand if it's becoming too much for you," Seth told him. "But you'll have to understand that I can't quit, not now. This has become more than just a search for my brother, it's now a necessity."

Nicholas nodded in agreement, "You know I would never abandon the cause, but I have to think of Melissa and the children if something were to happen to me during one of these missions. The Fugitive Slave Laws have made this almost as dangerous for the conductors as it is for the fugitives. There's no telling how they would be treated once word got out that I was a conductor for the Underground Railroad," he explained.

"That same law is what brought me here, Nick. Even if I find Thomas, it will continue to bring me back," Seth told him.

The Fugitive Slave Law was originally enacted in 1793 and gave White Americans permission to turn in Blacks they thought to be escaped slaves to their owners in the south. But in 1850 the laws became harsher, putting bounties on fugitives' heads and forcing them to prove their free status, not to a jury, but to a special commissioner who was paid ten dollars for finding them guilty and returning them to their owner and only five dollars for setting them free. The law encouraged slave hunters, or "kidnappers", as they were also know as, to flood the northern states and seize Blacks, free or fugitive, and sell them back into slavery. The harsher enactments of The Fugitive Slave Law and the high bounties put on a runaway's head made every White person a probable slave catcher. Seth's brother, Thomas, had become a victim of this new greed.

Seth and Thomas owned a blacksmith and livery stable handed down from their father. Thomas' fine quality of work was well-known in the area, so when two White strangers arrived in town, needing new shoes for their horses, they were directed to Grant Blacksmith and Livery. Seth was away purchasing another horse for their growing livery so Thomas was working alone. When he finished shoeing the men's horses he gave them what he knew was a fair price for the work done, but the men didn't think it was and refused to pay. Thomas refused to return their horses until he was paid so the men left angry.

Later that night, the two men were overheard at a bar in town talking about how they were going to get that "uppity nigger" for trying to cheat them. Thomas was warned and decided to stay at the livery for the night in case they tried to return for their horses. When his wife, Jenny took him breakfast the next morning the lock on the livery stable was broken and Thomas and the stranger's horses were gone.

Upon Seth's return that afternoon, the sheriff was waiting and told him what happened and that a search party had been sent out as soon as Jenny informed them of what she discovered. Unfortunately, if the men Thomas dealt with were slave catchers, then he knew the search party would not find anything. Seth also knew that Thomas was worth more alive than dead and that his only chance was to escape on his own or for someone to go south to bring him back.

When the search party returned with no news of Thomas, Seth refused to standby doing nothing while his mother and sister-in-law wept from the heartbreak of another life being stolen by the Fugitive Slave Laws. He joined up with Nicholas, who had been a conductor for the railroad for several years by that time, disguising himself as his manservant, heading south on missions in the hopes of finding or getting any word of his brother.

That was over a year ago. He and Nicholas were now in Atlanta to bring another group of passengers north and to follow up on a possible lead on Thomas' whereabouts.

"Do you think the lead on Thomas will be another false one?" Nicholas asked.

"I don't know, but whether it is or not, I have to follow it."

A knock at the door interrupted their conversation. Their visitor was a Colored messenger boy. Seth accepted the envelope from him, handing him a fifty cent piece in return. The boy looked at the coin in confusion.

"You sure this what you wanna give me mister?" he asked Seth.

Seth knew the tip was far more than the boy expected, "Why? Do you think you should have been given less?"

The boy hesitated only a second before answering, "No sir, this here is just fine," he said smiling broadly and sprinting down the back stairway.

Chuckling, Seth watched the boy's retreating figure.

"You're still as soft-hearted as ever," Nicholas said.

"Just helping the cause," he handed Nicholas the envelope addressed to him.

"It's from our contact," Nicholas read. "He was called away on a medical emergency last night and just arrived back in town. His son had been the one that sent the message over to the hotel letting us know about the need to reschedule."

"Did he say when?" Seth asked.

"Tonight at a party he's attending for a local attorney. I'm going as his guest."

"That's too public a place to talk railroad business," Seth said skeptically. He did not want to chance getting caught or have their mission derailed when he was possibly so close to finding his brother.

"I agree but we have no choice. He's leaving first thing in the morning for a medical conference, that's the only time he has. He assures us that it will be safe."

As Seth watched Nicholas burn this note just as he did the previous one to cover up any evidence, he didn't feel as assured as his friend but Nicholas had been doing this much longer than he, so all he could do was trust him.

Ruby stood next to Harriet, watching the party goers from the doorway of the dining room. They had just cleaned up the remnants of dinner and were taking a short break before they brought in the birthday cake. It was John Elder's 60th birthday and it seemed all of Atlanta had shown up to help him celebrate. Unlike the guests and other servants, Ruby could not find it in her heart to celebrate the occasion.

"Harriet, I need some air. I'm going to take a walk in the garden. I'll be back before the cake is presented," she told the older woman.

"Go on child. Take as long as you need," Harriet said in understanding.

Ruby made her way through the bustling throng of servants in the kitchen, heading out the back door to the small gated garden in back of the house. Once she stepped outside she took a deep, shuddering breath to ease the tightness in her chest, but it didn't seem to help. She walked slowly around the dark garden, needing no light to guide her. She and Elizabeth had traversed these grounds often as they were growing up. She knew the location of every bush, tree, flower and pathway by heart. Reaching out, she plucked a small rose from a trellis against the house and brought the flower to her nose, but her despondent mood would not allow her to enjoy its sweet scent.

Sighing, Ruby gazed up at the house that had been her home for ten of the last eleven years and knew she could no longer live this way. Since Elizabeth's wedding a little over a year ago she had been the perfect servant, running her mistress' household flawlessly. But there was no longer the warmth of friendship that they once shared. That all changed when Elizabeth broke her promise. Ruby went about her day to day duties without any hint of the anxiety she felt over possibly never making it back to Brazil and reuniting with her family.

Memories of her life before coming to America were vivid as if it were yesterday. All she had to do was close her eyes as she did now, and she could see her parents, her Uncle Amir and Aunt Luciana with such clarity it was as if they stood before her and it brought a pain to her heart that she was afraid would never go away. Time had not faded her memories. She felt as if there were a constant pull on an invisible cord that kept her attached to the past and the family she was stolen from. Time only made the cord tauter, making the pull towards Brazil stronger.

The sound of voices interrupted her thoughts. She peered into the darkness, hoping she wouldn't be caught out in the garden alone by a male guest who may have had one too many glasses of wine and was looking for entertainment. She heard about it happening far too many times and there was nothing the women could say or do because they were property, they had no rights. She breathed a sigh of relief as she realized the voices came from the open window of John Elder's study, but her relief was short lived when she remembered that she had to go pass the window to get back to the kitchen door. Peering into the window, she hoped the only people in the study were servants, but it was the family's doctor, Dr. Clark, and a man she'd never seen before. She leaned back up against the wall trying to figure out how to get by the window without being seen. She didn't want to be caught and accused of eavesdropping. Her only choice was to circle the outer path of the garden to another darker one that led back to the house.

Ruby moved to step away but had to stop when one of the men in the study moved towards the window. She stood completely still, praying that he didn't seen her. When the conversation continued she stepped back further into the shadows, quietly letting out the breath she had been holding. She hoped their conversation ended soon because she would surely be missed if she was out here much longer. Her worries were quickly forgotten when she overheard Dr. Clark mention the Underground Railroad. She listened more intently even though she knew that if she were caught and accused of eavesdropping, she would not be able to deny it now. Her heart beat rapidly within her chest as the two men spoke. She didn't hear much of the details but she heard enough to know that they were making arrangements for a group of runaways going north.

Learning that Dr. Clark was an abolitionist was as big a shock to Ruby. Her way home had been right in front of her face all of these years. This was her chance, she thought excitedly. This was what she'd been waiting for, she just had to find a way to approach Dr. Clark and be one of those passengers in the group going north.

The men's conversation was brief and as soon as Ruby heard the sound of the study door closing she moved to rush back up the path toward the entrance to the kitchen but her progress was halted when she was suddenly grabbed from behind. She was pulled roughly up against a hard body and a calloused hand quickly covered her mouth.

"I don't know what you're doing out here or how much of that conversation you heard but if I hear about anything

happening to either of those men, I'll come back here looking
for you," a man whispered harshly in her ear.

It was obvious he was a part of what Dr. Clark and his
associate had been planning. If she could let him know she
wasn't a threat she could try to convince him to take her with
them.

"Duchess."

The sound of Harriet's voice calling Ruby startled both she
and her captor. She was quickly released but by the time she
turned around to stop him from leaving he had disappeared
into the darkness.

"Wait," she whispered desperately

"Duchess!" Harriet called out more urgently.

"Coming Harriet," she squinted once more into the
darkness, and then rushed up the path towards the kitchen.

Harriet stood in the doorway, her hands on her broad hips,
"You better hurry up on in here. Miss Elizabeth was about to
send a search party out for you."

"I'm sorry Harriet, I guess I lost track of time."

The older woman gazed at her curiously, "Guess that fresh
air done you some good. You look a little flushed."

Ruby smiled, "Yes, I think fresh air was just what I needed."

Seth stood at the edge of the two dozen or so servants that
had gathered on one side of the room while the party guests
stood on the other side to sing "Happy Birthday" to the guest of
honor. He thought the lack of light in the garden had been
playing tricks on him when he saw the woman standing in the
light of the window outside the room Nicholas and their contact
had met. But as he watched the women wheeling out the
birthday cake there was no mistaking that the younger one was
not only the same one that had been out in the garden but also
the same woman he had seen while he was at the livery stables
earlier that afternoon.

She was just as beautiful as he thought, but he refused to
allow that beauty to distract him as it did previously. He
needed to find out why she had been outside that window, how

much she'd overheard and if she was a threat to their plans. He refused to let anyone get in the way of this particular group of runaways because, if what Nicholas told him was true, Thomas would be joining them for the trek back home.

❧ *Two* ❧

Ruby sat dejectedly in the kitchen waiting for the pot of water she put on the stove to boil. Elizabeth had not been feeling well since her father's party a few days earlier so her husband had sent for the doctor. Ruby had been trying to find a way to get in touch with Dr. Clark and thought that this would be her chance, but her luck had not held. Clark Jr. came in place of his father who was away and wouldn't be back for a week.

Ruby sighed heavily as she placed a tea kettle, a cup and a small plate of biscuits on a tray to take up to Elizabeth. As she made her way upstairs she wondered if the son knew of his father's activities. The only way to find out would be to ask him. She would not think about the risk she was taking or the fact that she could be endangering not only herself, but also the Clarks. What was important to her right now was that if she did not escape from this life soon she never would.

When Ruby arrived Elizabeth watched her intently as she set the tray on the bedside table, prepared her tea just the way she liked it and handed her the cup.

"Ruby, are you happy here?"

Ruby was not surprised by the question. In fact she had been expecting it for quite some time.

"No, I am not," she answered honestly.

The two women gazed at one another, both thinking of how much their relationship had changed. Elizabeth sighed, setting her tea cup back on the tray.

"I don't understand you Ruby," she said in frustration. "You have everything a slave could ask for, far more liberties than any in this household, yet you are still unhappy. Why?"

"Because I don't have my freedom," she said, not bothering to lie.

A look of sadness crossed Elizabeth's face, "I had hoped you had given up that silly dream by now."

"Will that be all Miss Elizabeth, I still have to go to market this afternoon," she said, ignoring Elizabeth's comment.

"No, there's one more thing. I'm with child and I've decided that I want you to be the child's nanny," she said, sounding almost satisfied with herself.

Although she appeared calm, Ruby was seething with anger. There was no end to Elizabeth's selfishness. Well, Ruby thought to herself, it was her turn to be selfish. She would not be here when that child arrived. If she couldn't find a way to join Dr. Clark's next wave of fugitives north, she would find her own way.

"Yes, ma'am," was her only response.

Elizabeth sighed heavily, dismissing Ruby tiredly. She had hoped that the change in household positions would please Ruby, but it was obvious that there was only one thing that would make her old friend happy, and it was the one thing Elizabeth could not bring herself to give.

Elizabeth and Ruby normally went to market together but on those rare occasions that Elizabeth couldn't join her Ruby was given a day pass. Unfortunately she was also given a time limit on that pass. If she went over that allotted time someone was sent out to look for her, which was one of the reasons Ruby had not tried to escape before. Today, Ruby's pass allotted her just a couple of hours to go to market, get what she needed and come home. Only that was not what Ruby had intended to do. She walked to the marketplace, picked up a few items just in case she was questioned once she arrived back home, and then immediately headed for Dr. Clark's office a few blocks away. Fortunately, because she didn't linger in the market place she made it to the office in good time, but an "out of office" sign on the door put a halt to her plan.

She knew she couldn't chance waiting to see if any one would return soon. Her wait could be a few moments or a few hours. She needed to get back to the house before Elizabeth became suspicious. If she hurried, she would make it home with time to spare.

As she wove her way through the crowded marketplace, Ruby's arm was gently grabbed from behind.

"What's the rush?" someone whispered into her ear.

Her heart nearly jumped into her throat. She slowly turned to see who would be so bold.

"Excuse me?" she asked, yanking her arm from the grasp of a man she didn't know.

"I asked what the hurry is," he repeated with a grin.

"Do I know you?" she gazed at him in confusion.

"Not yet, but you will."

Ruby waited for an explanation but he said nothing more, just stood gazing down at her. She met his gaze directly with her own, taking note of his neatly cropped hair, deep brown eyes, brown complexion a shade darker than her own, wide nose, trimmed mustache over a full, wide mouth, and clean shaven chin. The scent of soap, leather and sunshine emanating from him enveloped her. It was a sensual and comforting scent that gave her an unexpected thrill.

Seth didn't realize that being so near to her would affect him this much. His body reacted to her beauty and their close proximity in a way that excited and frustrated him. Nicholas and five runaways were depending on his usual clear head, he could not allow it to be clouded by this woman.

Ruby wondered at the change in his expression. He suddenly looked as if she had done something he didn't like.

"You have obviously mistaken me for someone else," she told him, turning and heading back into the crowd.

"Do you make it a habit of sneaking outside windows listening to private conversations?" he asked her retreating figure.

Surprise then realization registered on Ruby's face.

"You're the man from the garden," she said excitedly.

Happiness was the last reaction Seth had expected. She confused him even further when she grabbed his hand, looking pleadingly into his eyes.

"Take me with you," she whispered desperately.

This was not going at all the way Seth had planned. He'd been wondering for days how to find a way to get to this woman and learn how much of a threat she was to their mission. Then as he was returning the carriage Nicholas rented during their stay, he had seen her walking past the livery stables. He followed her to the marketplace, waiting for an opportunity to approach her. When she left shortly after, he continued to follow her all the way to Clark's office and knew then that she must have overheard too much about their plans.

When Seth didn't respond to her plea, Ruby gripped his hand tighter.

"You know I heard what was being planned. I want to go with you."

Seth looked around at the people walking nearby then pulled Ruby around the back of a nearby vendor's cart so they would not be overheard.

"What are you saying?"

"I want to go North with you," she said.

He looked down at her soft hands, clean nails, then up to her neatly coifed hair, pressed and spotless uniform and assumed that, unlike most of the runaways they lead north, she had never known a real day's labor in her life. She either would not make it through the arduous journey or she would only slow them down.

"No," he said without hesitation.

"I don't understand. Why not?" she asked in confusion, finding it difficult to believe she had gotten this close to her dream only to be denied.

"Because you're obviously a pampered woman who has probably never left her master's home with so much as a torn stocking, more than likely never picked anything from a field other than a flower and would only slow us down, and put us in danger." Seth knew he was being harsh, but he also believed in being honest.

Seth's refusal was more than Ruby could handle. She spent the past ten years of her life waiting for the time when she could leave this life behind and return to her family. Now once again she was being told "no". She had finally reached her breaking point.

"You don't know a thing about me or my life," she said angrily.

"You have not even bothered asking my name yet you think you know me. That's fine. I won't bother standing here trying to change your opinion of me. What I will do is walk straight to the sheriff's office and tell him everything I overheard if you do not agree to take me with you," she said with more confidence than she felt.

Seth looked ready to strangle her, "You wouldn't."

Ruby turned, walking away from him. He thought she was bluffing until she headed in the direction of the business district. He took off after her, grasping her arm to stop her.

Ruby breathed a silent sigh of relief. She was hoping he would stop her. She wasn't sure if she could truly follow through with her threat.

"You're serious?" he asked in disbelief.

"Yes," she managed to hide her relief behind a false mask of irritation.

"Why?"

"You aren't giving me any choice."

"You would jeopardize the chance for others to have freedom because you can't?" Seth could not believe she would be that selfish.

"I will do whatever is necessary to be free. If that means making threats, then that's what I'll do."

Seth could see the determination glowing in her beautiful hazel eyes. He had underestimated this woman. She said he had given her no choice, now she was doing the same to him. He sighed heavily, running his hand across his forehead in exasperation.

"Whatever decision you are considering should be made quickly. Joseph, the Elder family watchdog, is heading in this direction," Ruby warned.

"If you come along, how are you going to get pass this Joseph?"

"He works for John Elder, I am owned by Elder's daughter, it will not be a problem."

She gave him the address, "Come to the back door tomorrow morning around ten so we can talk more."

"And if I don't show?"

"I will assume you are more willing to take your chances with the sheriff than with me," she told him and walked away.

The following morning Seth stood at the back door of Elizabeth's home debating whether or not he should take his chances that the woman was bluffing or just bring her along. Either way could threaten the safety of the others in the group. Sighing heavily, he knocked. He did not like being backed against the wall which is exactly what this bold woman was doing.

"You took long enough," Ruby snapped as she yanked opened the door.

"I could leave," he said, turning to do just that. He sure as hell didn't need this kind of trouble on a mission that could be bringing him and his brother together.

"No! Wait, I'm sorry. I'm just anxious to leave here." Ruby had been on edge since she left Seth at the marketplace the other day.

Seth stopped and turned back around.

"Come, we can talk over there," she pointed to a bench in the walled garden.

"Aren't you worried about being seen talking to me?" he asked.

"Both Miss Elizabeth and Mr. Robert are out and the servants are doing their chores, but we do have to talk quickly because they will be returning soon."

"Why don't you start by telling me why you need to get away from here so badly," Seth asked.

"All right, as soon as you tell me your name."

"Seth."

"Seth, I'm Ruby," she held out her hand.

He accepted it, feeling a shock when their skin touched. She must have felt it also because they both gazed curiously down at their clasped hands then back up at each other. Clearing his throat, Seth slowly pulled his rough, calloused hand from the soft warmth of hers.

"You didn't answer my question," he said sounding irritated, not liking the effect she was having on him.

"Have you always been a free man Seth?"

"Yes."

"How would you feel if someone snatched that freedom away for no other reason than evil spite?"

Seth thought about his brother, Thomas, and how that was exactly what happened to him.

"I'd hate it and would do everything in my power to get my freedom back."

"Then you know exactly why I am doing this," she told him.

"Are you trying to tell me you were free once?"

"Yes. I was born a free person, lived as a free person until I was 8 years old and I plan on dying as a free person."

"Why now? You've obviously spent most of your life as a slave?"

"Just because I've lived as a slave all these years does not mean I've forgotten what it is like to be free," she said, desperation obvious in her tone of voice.

Seth understood, realizing that it must be the same feeling of desperation his brother was probably going through.

"How did you end up here?" he asked, curious to know more about this beautiful, well-spoken woman.

A look of sadness clouded her face, "It's a long story, one that we do not have time to go into right now."

Seth nodded. "We need to go over some details about the journey before I go."

"So you're taking me with you?" she said excitedly, her face lit up like a little girl that had just received a precious gift.

Seth chuckled. In a way, he guessed she had.

"Yes. You're to bring as little as possible, preferably just whatever clothes you are wearing at the time and an overcoat, if possible. Also, if you can get a hold of it, bring some dried food."

"We are constantly on the move until we reach Ohio and even then we're not completely safe," he further explained, "We travel under darkness and stay at safe houses or abandoned farms wherever we can find them. Although, since they added more restrictions to the Fugitive Slave Law, we haven't been as fortunate with the safe houses as we used to be. This means we have to make do with whatever we can, the ground, brush, caves, we're exposed to the elements often."

"If you are trying to deter me, it's not working. I'm hardier than you think," Ruby told him with a grin.

"Just want you to be aware of what you're in for."

She nodded in understanding.

"Do you have a plan to get away?" he asked.

Ruby hesitated in answering, "I honestly had not thought about it. This opportunity was unexpected."

"Well, you better come up with something soon. As you know, we're leaving in four days."

"Four days?!"

"Why do you sound so surprised? I thought you overheard all of the plans," he said suspiciously.

Ruby grinned sheepishly, "I had come out to the garden to clear my head. I ended up outside that window by accident and I barely heard a word, just enough to know what you all were planning, but not the details."

"So you were bluffing about going to the sheriff," he said.

"Yes. Without knowing where and when everything was supposed to take place, there wouldn't have been much to tell him. Also, I like Dr. Clark. I wouldn't want to get him in trouble for doing something so noble."

"You do realize that I still haven't told you where and when?"

"Are you going back on your word?" she asked nervously. She didn't know if she could bear being so close to escape and have it snatched away. It was too devastating to even think about.

Seth didn't answer right away. He stood, walking over to a nearby rose bush, gazing thoughtfully down at the flowers. After a moment, he turned back towards her. She was truly beautiful, he thought to himself. As her expectant gaze met his, he wondered what she would look like with dirt smudged on her face, her clothing ripped and snagged by bushes and her neat little braided bun scattered all over her head. She would probably still be as beautiful as she was now.

"Do you know where the Crawford farm is outside of town?" he asked, walking back towards her.

Ruby nodded. She couldn't believe it. She was finally going to be escaping this life. She had waited over ten years for this but it seemed as if it were all happening so fast. She was filled with excitement and trepidation all at once.

"We leave from there at midnight in four day's time. If you're not there, we leave without you. We can't afford to wait for anyone."

"I understand."

He nodded then headed towards the gated entrance.

"Seth."

He stopped, turning towards her.

"Thank you," she said, fighting back tears.

"Don't thank me yet," he warned.

❧ THREE ❧
Sergipe, Brazil

"I don't understand why you insist on going to see her," Amir complained to Luciana. She has brought you nothing but heartache and is now getting the punishment she deserves for being so selfish."

"Amir, she is still my sister and she has asked for me so I am going to her. You can either take me or stay here with my manager Franco and keep an eye on the plantation," Luciana told him.

Amir sat across from Luciana's desk watching her tally numbers in her account book. He had just returned from a business trip to Spain and had stopped at the plantation to check in on her. Upon his arrival she informed him that her sister, Maria, had taken ill and wanted to see her. As much as he disliked Maria, he understood Luciana's loyalty to her family, or what was left of her family.

"I will go with you but I hope you do not expect me to keep silent if the woman begins treating me like a servant."

Luciana finished her tallying and closed the book. "I do not expect you to be anything but your usual charming self," she said with a loving smile.

She could not imagine having gone through the past ten years without Amir by her side. He had become her closest friend and confidante. They shared the pain of first losing Ifé and Reynaldo, then Rubina's disappearance. In spite of the fortune she had spent searching for her great-niece they had no success in locating her. It was as if she dropped off the face of the earth. Her smile suddenly changed to a frown.

Amir leaned forward, reaching across Luciana's desk, taking her hands in his, "You're thinking of Rubina, aren't you? I see the sadness in your eyes."

"Even after all this time I miss her. I can feel that she is still out there somewhere."

"I dreamed of her last night," she told Amir. "I dreamed she was trying to come home."

Amir looked at her curiously, "I dreamed of Ifé last night as well. She told me that our family would soon be together."

"Strange that we should have those dreams right before visiting Maria," Luciana said thoughtfully.

"Do you still believe your sister had something to do with Rubina's disappearance?"

"Yes. Unfortunately I can not prove it."

"I think the proof was Reynaldo's stallion being lead away in the dead of night without making a sound. Espirito would not have gone quietly with a stranger. He would have made quite a fuss if a horse thief had tried to lead him and his mare out of the stable. There were very few people that he took to and Maria was one of them," Amir said suspiciously.

"Well, we will soon find out, for I intend on asking my dear sister about the night of Rubina's disappearance." Luciana said.

Maria sat in bed sipping tea, her thoughts also of Rubina, wondering if it was too late to try and find her. It had been over ten years and for all she knew, the child could have perished at the hands of the men she herself had paid to kidnap her.

She sat her tea cup on the bedside table. It didn't matter if it was too late for her to do anything or not, she still felt that she had to confess her sins. She didn't have much time left.

Maria thought back to that night so long ago when she had looked one last time into eyes so like her Reynaldo's. The child had an inborn strength that Maria had admired. She just wished she had not been so blind by Reynaldo's betrayal by marrying Ifé to get to know her grandchild. She realized, too late, that she had missed out on the very thing she wanted, her son's happiness. Luciana had told her the day of Reynaldo's funeral that Maria had been foolish to think she could be the only woman that truly mattered in his life. Her sister had been right. Maria had just been too stubborn to see that it was true.

She had lost her son twice because of her selfishness. Instead of learning from her mistakes and taking the time to get to know his child after he died, she had committed the unforgivable act of selling her only grandchild into slavery.

A knock at her bedroom door interrupted her thoughts, "Come in."

"Sister you look awful," Luciana said in her usual brusque manner as she entered the room.

"And I see you are still as tactless as ever," Maria responded.

"I would not say tactless, honest is preferable," Luciana placed a dry kiss on her sister's cheek.

Maria surprised Luciana by taking her hand and patting an empty space on the bed beside her, "Sit with me a moment."

Luciana nodded, doing as Maria requested.

"Amir," Maria said, acknowledging the man standing in the doorway.

"*Senhora*," he said with a slight nod, standing on the threshold debating whether or not to enter.

Maria made the decision for him. "Why don't you have a seat over there," she said, indicating a chair in the corner of the room.

With a pained expression, he did as Maria requested. He hoped he would be able to pay his respects and escape until Luciana was ready to leave, but it seemed as if he would not be getting off that easily. He began to wonder what she was up to. She had never shown the least bit of interest in him before this moment.

Maria focused her attention back on her sister, "Luciana, I asked you to come here because I do not have much time and I have something very important I need to tell you."

"Go on," Luciana encouraged.

"I must first apologize to you for being so heartless when we were young. I knew how you felt about Miguel yet I pursued him in spite of it. I was a selfish, spoiled young woman and I am very sorry I caused you any pain."

Luciana waved her a hand in dismissal, "That is all water under the bridge, but your apology is accepted."

Maria smiled gratefully, squeezing Luciana's hand. She then looked over at Amir.

"Young man, I also owe you an apology."

Amir looked around in confusion wondering if someone else had entered the room without his noticing. When he turned back to meet Maria's gaze, he realized she was speaking to him.

"Me, *Senhora*?" he asked in surprise.

"You did not deserve my spite. You were just a little boy and innocent to what was going on with my son. I am sorry and I would not blame you if you refuse my apology," she said.

It was a good thing she had not expected Amir to respond because he was speechless.

"Maria, you are full of surprises today," Luciana told her, just as shocked as Amir by her sister's apologies. This was a side of Maria she had never seen before. It made Luciana sad that it had taken an illness to make Maria see the truth of her ways.

"There is more," Maria said. "Everything you said about me the morning of Reynaldo's and Ifé's funeral was true. The only reason I hated Ifé so much was because I thought she had taken Reynaldo from me. She did not fit the image of the perfect wife I had wished for my son. She was too strong-willed and beautiful and it was obvious that Reynaldo loved her very much."

Maria looked down at her lap in shame, "Just as you said, I was jealous. I wanted to be the only woman Reynaldo truly loved. I wanted him to love his mother more than his wife and child," she admitted.

"I know it is too late to ask for their forgiveness but I hope it is not too late to make it up to someone else I have wronged," Maria said tearfully.

Luciana grasped both her sister's hands in her own, "Maria, you are alive. As long as you are here it is never too late to right a wrong."

Maria smiled sadly, "You may think otherwise after you have heard my confession."

"After the reading of Reynaldo's will, I was enraged and felt so betrayed that I wanted revenge. I felt I deserved far more than what I was given, so I decided that if I was not going to receive what I thought was fair, no else would, especially not the child of a slave," Maria hesitated before going on, wondering if she was making a mistake in admitting what she had done, but she knew she could not draw her last breath with such a deed kept secret.

"Luciana, I know you have had suspicions all of these years about my involvement with Rubina's disappearance. Well, you were right. In fact, the whole plan was my doing."

In spite of her suspicions, nothing prepared Luciana for hearing Maria confirm them. She would not have believed her sister was so cruel as to endanger a child out of bitterness, but Maria was about to admit she was and it was like a knife in Luciana's heart.

Maria let go of Luciana's hands and began fidgeting with the edge of her covers. She could not find the courage to look Luciana in the eyes so she focused on the fray she was causing in the blanket.

"I arranged for her to be kidnapped by slavers heading to America. I gave them Reynaldo's horses as partial payment," she admitted.

"That's why the horses didn't make a sound that night. They knew you," Amir said, his jaw clenched tightly in controlled anger.

Maria looked up in surprise. She had not noticed that he had walked over and was standing at the foot of the bed tightly gripping the post behind where Luciana sat. When she looked at Luciana the warmth she had seen in her sister's eyes moments ago had been replaced by a coldness that caused Maria to visibly shiver.

"All these years you knew where she was and did not say a word? All the time and money you knew I was putting towards the search for her and you knew all along that she was not even in the country?" Luciana asked with controlled anger.

Maria answered, "Yes," in a small, nervous voice.

"How could you sell your own flesh and blood into a god awful institution as slavery and feel no remorse over it?" Luciana asked in disgust.

"I do feel remorse, that is why I am telling you now," Maria cried.

"You are telling me so that you may clear your conscious in the hopes of being saved before you die," Luciana accused as she stood, looking disdainfully down at Maria.

"Well, sister, God may forgive your black soul, but I will not."

"But it may not be too late. There has to be a way to find her," Maria said desperately.

"You better pray that there is," Luciana warned her.

❧ Four ❦

Ruby had recited every prayer she could remember, despairing of ever being able to come up with a plan for her escape. It seemed God had finally heard her pleas when word arrived that Elizabeth's grandmother, who had been ill for quite some time, passed away. Ruby could barely contain her anxiety as she helped Elizabeth prepare for her trip to Alabama for the funeral. Elizabeth, her husband and parents left town the very morning of Ruby's planned departure.

They would only be gone for a week so Joseph was left in charge of keeping an eye on both Elizabeth's and the senior Elder's households since they were just a block away from one another. He was to stay at Elizabeth's. His room was located just steps away from Ruby's off of the kitchen but Ruby refused to let that deter her. She was too close to finally making her escape to allow him to interfere with her plans. She put a little of Elizabeth's sleeping powder in his dinner that night, not enough to render him senseless but just enough to ensure that he slept soundly.

Ruby waited patiently as the hours ticked by until long after everyone had turned in before preparing to leave. When the time came, she put on an overcoat she had taken from a pile of clothing Elizabeth's husband, Robert, had set aside for charity. She then wrapped several biscuits and apples she had hidden earlier in napkins and placed them in a potato sack with a few extra undergarments and an extra pair of shoes. After that she braided and tightly wrapped her hair in a large cotton scarf so that it would not become tangled in trees or brush along the way. The last thing she did was collect the cameo that she had purchased from the woman in the marketplace over a year ago. She refused to leave that behind. She wrapped it in a swatch of silk, put it in a small cloth bag and pinned the bag to her underskirt.

Once she was sure she had all that she needed, Ruby took a deep, shaky breath, quietly opened her door and crept down the short hallway that led to the kitchen. When she reached the door of the room Joseph slept in she listened intently for any sign that he may still be up and about. All she heard was his loud snoring vibrating through the door and relief flooded through her. She continued on to the kitchen towards the back door, unlocking and easing it open just enough for her to squeeze through. Unlike the Elder's garden, Elizabeth's only had one pathway which led right to the gate. Even in the darkness Ruby had no problem finding her way there, but to her dismay, when she went to open it, she encountered a chain and padlock holding the gate shut. Joseph must have put it on sometime during the evening without her knowledge.

Ruby refused to panic and took a moment to think. When an idea came to her she moved quickly, first pushing her bag of belongings through the iron grates to the other side of the gate, and then she hiked the hem of her skirt into the waistband and pulled herself up and over as quickly as she could. The block was patrolled nightly so she did not want to linger and take the chance of getting caught by the patrolman. As soon as she landed on the other side she grabbed her bag, immediately ducking behind a set of bushes nearby. She peered out between the branches and, seeing that the street was deserted, took off, making sure to keep to the shadows as she went along.

"How much longer do you think we should wait?" Nicholas asked.

Seth looked down at his pocket watch in aggravation as the minute hand glided to ten past midnight. They were supposed to be at their next stop within the next two hours. He couldn't wait for Ruby any longer. It would jeopardize the lives of the people he and Nicholas were responsible for leading north.

"Let's gather everyone up and move out," Seth said.

"Are you sure?"

"No, but we don't have a choice," he said, frustrated that he had risked them falling behind schedule for this woman.

Nicholas nodded, entering the abandoned barn where the runaways were hiding. Seth was just turning to follow him when he saw a flash of white out of the corner of his eye. Turning around he saw a figure running towards him.

The hem of Ruby's dress was still tucked into her waistband, giving Seth a tempting view of her long, shapely legs. His mind instantly drew an image of those legs wrapped around his torso and it made him even angrier than he already was. This was not a good idea, he thought to himself as she stopped, panting heavily, before him.

"I'm...sorry..." she managed to get out between breathes. "I...ran...the whole way."

"This will be the last time you jeopardize the safety of this group. Put us in danger like this again and I'll leave you on the spot," Seth said angrily, turning and heading into the barn.

Ruby followed close behind him wiping the sweat that pour down her face with the edge of the sack her belongings were in. She understood his anger and was genuinely surprised to see that they had waited for her.

"Are they ready?" Seth asked Nicholas as they entered.

"Has your lady friend shown up yet?" Nicholas asked. With his back to Seth he had not seen Ruby until he turned around.

"My God," Nicholas said when he caught sight of her standing in a pool of moonlight pouring through a hole in the roof of the barn.

Her skin was a flawless pecan brown and her hazel eyes, broad, straight nose, and deep red full lips told of her mixed heritage. Her features came together perfectly in her oval face. Her proud, straight stance and head wrap combined with the way she directly met his appraising gaze gave her the appearance of a regal and haughty queen. Nicholas thought she was breathtaking.

As innocent as Seth knew Nicholas' statement was, considering he had the same reaction when he first saw Ruby, to his chagrin he became jealous. He consciously stepped in line of his friend's view of the beautiful woman.

"Let's get going," he said in irritation.

"Oh, yes, let's go," Nicholas said, as if awakened from a trance.

Ruby was unaware of what was going on between Seth and Nicholas as she gazed at her fellow travelers who began moving from out of the shadows. The first was a young woman about her age with a small child of about 3 or 4 years old clinging to her skirt with one hand and sucking vigorously on the thumb of his other. The next one was a giant of a man who towered over Seth and his partner by at least a foot with biceps as big as the widest part of Ruby's thighs and a long, thick braid flowing down his back. The last person that stepped forward caused Ruby to gasp in surprise.

"Isaac?" she asked in disbelief.

The man walked towards her, grinning when he recognized her, "Duchess, is that you?"

When he reached her he laughed out loud, grabbing her in an affectionate embrace. Afterwards he stepped back, holding her at arms length.

"Look at you. All grown up," he said. "I haven't seen you in over five years."

Isaac had been the Elder's houseboy but had been sold off after being accused of stealing several rare books from Mr. Elder's study. He and Ruby had been good friends.

"Don't you think you've held us up long enough," Seth said angrily.

Ruby's smile vanished as she caught the look on his face.

"Yes, I apologize," she said guiltily, stepping away from Isaac to follow the others towards the doorway.

She didn't see Isaac's appreciative glance of her swaying backside as she walked away, but Seth did and he did not like it.

"I could care less about what is going on between you two but what ever it is will stop right now. As I told her, you will not jeopardize the lives of the others on this journey. Do you understand?"

"Oh, yeah, I understand," he said, ginning at Seth knowingly.

The group arrived at their next stop an hour later than was planned. Seth put the blame solely on Ruby and she knew it by the heated look he gave her when he checked his pocket watch upon their arrival. He stayed hidden in the brush with them while Nicholas went up to the small Tudor house in the distance. It was dark except for a single candle burning in a first floor window.

They had only been waiting for a few moments when a hoot owl called out. Ruby wouldn't have thought anything of it until Seth made the same sound and it was returned. He silently signaled for everyone to follow him in the direction of the house. They hurried through the brush and around the back to a small barn. When they entered the barn they were greeted by two elderly White women and given water, warm bread and a cup of warm honeyed milk for the child traveling with them.

Ruby had heard during whispered conversations amongst other slaves about the White abolitionists that worked from North to South to help runaways reach freedom but she had been hard pressed to believe that there were more than just a few south of the Mason Dixon Line. She accepted her cup of water and bread with a grateful thank you and received a warm smile in return.

Seth watched Ruby with mixed emotions. Although he did blame her for their being behind schedule, he was glad she had joined them. She had been of great assistance to the young mother and child that had come along. Ruby had volunteered to carry the sleeping child part of the way so that the mother wouldn't tire herself out during the journey. The woman had been tearful the whole time and only Ruby could keep her from completely breaking down. He also noticed that Ruby had not tried to make excuses for her late arrival. She had quietly followed the group, only speaking when she noticed the other woman lagging behind. She definitely was not what he had expected.

"I see you can't keep your eyes off of her," Nicholas said, standing beside him.

Seth frowned, "Just trying to figure out if she'll be more trouble than it's worth."

Nicholas smiled, "I see. Well, you think you can tear yourself away for a few moments? There's someone here I think you should see."

Seth looked at his friend hopefully. Nicholas nodded in response to his unasked question.

"Where?" Seth asked anxiously.

"This way," Nicholas led Seth towards a tack room in back of the barn. "The sisters thought you might want some privacy before we head out again."

When Seth walked through the doorway, his eyes immediately filled with tears of joy.

"Thomas?" he whispered.

Seth had come to expect the worst at the thought of finally seeing his brother again, but at first glance, Thomas looked no worse for wear. He and Seth came together in a tight familial hug.

"It's good to see you big brother," Thomas said with his broad, boyish grin.

Seth noticed the smile didn't quite reach his eyes, which looked terribly sad.

"How are you?" His question asking far more than it seemed.

Thomas' smile faltered, "I'm here."

Seth nodded in understanding. They would talk when Thomas was ready. "Well, let's get you on the road home."

"Home," Thomas whispered. "I feel like I've been gone a lifetime."

Thomas seemed lost in his thoughts for a moment then gazed at Seth as if he just remembered his brother was there.

"I can't believe you two found me," he said, his voice thick with emotion.

"I just wish it hadn't taken so long," Seth said bitterly.

"Better late than never," Thomas said with a grin, showing Seth a bit of his old self.

Ruby sat rocking and humming to the little boy in her arms while his mother dozed beside them. Her name was Esther and she seemed so lost to Ruby. She had cried as she told Ruby her story of having to leave her sister behind because she had taken sick right before they were to leave. Esther had not wanted to make the journey without her but her sister made her promise to get Esther's son Jessie to freedom and that she would follow later. Ruby felt compelled to befriend the woman, especially since they were the only females in the group.

Ruby glanced at the rest of her fellow travelers. They had all used the time they had during this stop to introduce themselves. They knew they had a long and difficult journey ahead of them and thought it best to get to know one another.

Esther was a small woman at barely five feet tall with a broad shapely frame, and a gentle, sweet nature. She had escaped a cruel mistress who hated Esther for being her husband's mistress and having his only child when she herself could not have any of her own. Jessie was that child, named after his father, Jessup.

Bishop's, seven foot frame, broad shoulders and a scar that ran from his right ear to his jaw line, aroused instant fear at first site. The group quickly learned that he was a gentle giant when Jessie, wanting to play after having his milk, walked over, plopped down right in front of Bishop and began chattering away. Everyone had held their breathe waiting to see what the big man would do. He simply smiled indulgently as he gently lifted Jessie onto his lap. Bishop had been a boy himself when he had been captured during a raid on his family's farm by a group of local White men who had been angry that his Black father and Indian mother owned so much land. They had lynched his father, raped and brutalized his mother and sold him to a tobacco plantation. He slaved there for fifteen years until a fever that ravaged the plantation took the life of not only his master but his wife and child also.

The last of the group of travelers was Isaac whom Ruby had known from the Elder household when she was young. He had been an inquisitive and bright little boy who wanted so much to learn to read and write that he would hide in the closet during Elizabeth's and Ruby's lessons. He had been caught when Ruby was sent to the closet to retrieve something and found Isaac sleeping there. Ruby felt bad that he had to result to such tactics to learn what she already knew so she volunteered to help him. She spent her Sunday afternoons hidden in a corner of an empty stall in the stables teaching him to read and write. But soon Sunday afternoons were not enough for Isaac's voracious appetite for learning. He began to sneak books from John Elder's library. He always managed to return them before anyone knew they were missing until he had borrowed one of Elder's favorite Shakespeare novels and didn't have time to return it before their master found it missing. There wouldn't have been such a fuss made over it if it hadn't been one of a set of original signed copies given to him as a gift from his wife. During the search it was found amongst Isaac's belongings. If there was anything John Elder did not abide, it was stealing. Isaac was sold to an associate of Mr. Elder's and had been working on a cotton plantation ever since.

When it came time for Ruby to tell her story she told them of being promised that she would have her freedom and then was denied when that time came. Since they wouldn't give it to her, she decided that she was going to have to get it herself. She didn't tell them of her life before becoming a slave and wasn't concerned about Isaac knowing because he didn't join the Elder household staff until after Ruby had stopped telling her stories because no one believed her.

Ruby knew that although they each had their own reasons for leaving their life of enslavement it didn't matter because they all shared a common need. The need to be free and live their lives the way they wanted without the rules of a master and the restraints of chains. It was a kinship that would bind them together during their difficult journey north and one that she was very glad to have.

As Seth walked out of the tack room with Thomas and Nicholas by his side, his eyes were immediately drawn to Ruby, his stomach fluttering lightly at the sight of her rocking Jessie in her arms. Her expression was soft and almost content as she hummed to the sleeping boy. She looked up, meeting his gaze, a slight frown marring her expression. He didn't like the frown and was tempted to walk over and smooth it away. As if reading his thoughts, a blush crept into her cheeks, but she didn't break the gaze.

"You keep looking at her that way somebody is going to think you actually like her," Nicholas said with a grin.

Seth ignored him, walking over to their hosts who were making small packets of dried beef for the group.

"I want to thank you both for finding my brother."

The older of the sisters squeezed his hand affectionately. "It was the least we could do. We lost our brother during John Brown's raid at Harper's Ferry. We couldn't very well stand by while you lost yours."

She turned, taking a packet from her sister and handing it to Seth.

"There's a little something extra in there for you and your brother. We know how you like Sister's dried fruit."

Seth smiled and kissed both women on the cheek, "You ladies keep spoiling me like this whenever I come through and my mother will get jealous," he teased.

The sister's blushed, giggling girlishly, "Good looking young man like you should have a wife spoiling him, not some old spinsters like us," the elder sister fussed.

"From your mouth to God's ears," he said, smiling.

"Well, we shall add that prayer to the ones asking for a safe journey for you all."

"Thank you ma'am," Seth said sincerely.

They nodded in unison then turned and began handing out their care packets to the others. It wasn't long before Seth and the group was back on the road. They would travel until daybreak and hopefully find shelter until they began their travels once again under the cover of darkness.

Just a few weeks into their journey, Ruby was wondering if she had bitten off more than she could chew. She realized Seth had been right, she had been spoiled. With her privileged life as a child and the privileges she was allowed as Elizabeth's personal slave, she had never known hunger or weariness and now she was getting a large helping of each. Their food supplies were low and they were still too far south to attempt to light a fire to cook any small game they could catch. The necessity of traveling under the cover of darkness had knocked her internal clock off schedule, and she had to adjust her body to rest at a time when it was used to being active. Then a few days ago, they had narrowly escaped walking right into a camp of slave catchers. If Nicholas had not decided to scout ahead they would have surely been caught. Ruby shuddered at the thought, still able to feel the dread and fear she and the others had felt then. The incident had forced them to continue on throughout the night and following day in order to put enough distance between them and the catchers so as not to run into them again.

Now they rested in an abandoned shack just pass the South Carolina border. Ruby was restless so she couldn't get comfortable enough to settle down for some much needed sleep. Peering out of the window, she spotted a copse of trees nearby. After looking back at her fellow travelers, all of which managed to fall right to sleep, she headed quietly for the door. As much as she had come to enjoy being part of such a close knit group, she needed some time alone to figure out what she would do once they reached their destination. Nicholas told them that most Freedom Seekers moved on to Canada but many had chosen to stay on in the Pennsylvania, Ohio and Southern New Jersey areas. Ruby was not sure where she would stay, but wherever it was it would not be for long. As soon as she was able to save up enough for passage, she was heading to Brazil.

She stayed close to the ramshackle building as she walked. Working her way around to the back, and looking carefully around to make sure no one lingered nearby. She took off across the short distance from the house to the trees she had seen outside the window. Once she reached her destination, Ruby crouched down low, listening intently the way their guides had taught them. She waited a full five minutes before deciding that there was no one around but the forest creatures. She sat up, took off her wrap, and then laid it on the ground to sit upon. Once she was comfortable, she leaned back against the trunk of a large oak and let out a calming breath to clear her mind.

She was considering what her options were upon their arrival in Pennsylvania. She knew she would have to get a job. Although she still had the money she made from selling her needlepoint while with the Elders, it would not be enough to get her passage aboard a ship. She also wanted to find a way to send word to her Aunt that she was heading home. She didn't want to just show up on her doorstep announcing who she was. Much had more than likely changed over the past decade. Her family may have accepted that she was gone and not coming back, they may not welcome her intrusion into their lives after all these years, or worse, the one person Ruby knew she could always count on may have passed away. Before she was kidnapped she was too young to know or think to care how her Aunt's health may have been. She just knew that she was always there for her and her parents, no matter what. Ruby shook her head, that was a thought she just couldn't bare thinking of. She had to focus on taking it day by day until she reached home.

Leaning her head back against the tree, Ruby smiled and closed her eyes. After all these years, Brazil was the only place she considered home. She knew she was fortunate to have been purchased by the Elders instead of a cruel master. She had not worked in a field or done hard labor since the last time she worked beside her mother during harvest at the de Souza sugar plantation. In spite of that, she had never been happy.

Ruby allowed her thoughts to wander into the past, to memories of her parents and the immense love she felt while growing up. It was not long before those memories lulled her to sleep, which is how Seth found her, dozing peacefully under the tree, and it made him angry. Not only because she could have gotten them all caught if someone other than him had found her this way, but also because her exotic beauty stirred his senses like no other. It wasn't the flirtation or blatant sexuality that normally drew him to a woman. It was her inner strength, her selflessness and her determination.

He had barely spoken a word to her since their journey began but he had watched her. Watched her become a friend to Esther, a second mother to Jessie, and a teacher to Bishop, who, after learning what she had done for Isaac, asked if she would help him learn to read and write. Even Nicholas and Thomas were impressed by her intelligence and sophistication and had become curious about her background. They believed there was far more to Ruby than she led everyone to believe. Seth didn't want to be but he was drawn to her. She was complex, mysterious almost to the point of aloofness, and exotically beautiful.

He squat down before her, studying her face, wondering what she could be dreaming that gave her such a peaceful expression. He gazed up at the plain cloth wrap tied securely around her hair, her high forehead which always seemed furrowed in thought, her wide but pert nose, her full, deeply red lips, her softly sculpted chin that was always raised haughtily, her long graceful neck and softly rounded shoulders. He refused to allow his gaze to go any further than that. He already felt a stirring of excitement over what little he had seen.

His gaze traveled back up to her face and was surprised to find her looking curiously back at him. He didn't look away or move from his position before her.

"We're leaving in a few hours," he told her.

"Alright."

"You mind telling me what you're doing out here?"

"I needed privacy to clear my head."

"You realize you could have given our location away?" he said, trying to sound angry but only managing mildly irritated.

"I was very careful and only meant to stay for just a few moments. I didn't realize I had fallen asleep. I'm sorry. I would never purposely jeopardize our safety," she said sincerely.

Seth sighed, "I know. The next time you feel the need to have a moment away from the others let Nicholas or I know."

Ruby nodded in agreement. Neither spoke for another moment, continuing to gaze at one another.

Ruby found herself studying him just as intently as she found him studying her moments before. In spite of the obvious dislike he had shown for her, Ruby found herself drawn to him and could not figure out why. Yes, he was a very handsome man, but something more drew her to him. It could be his strong and confident leadership, his boyish good-humor when interacting with his Thomas and Nicholas, or the sensitivity he showed to her fellow travelers' hardships. Whatever it was that attracted Ruby to Seth had her wanting to run in the other direction, and at the same time wanting to see where it would lead.

Seth felt as if he were losing himself in the intensity of her bright hazel eyes. His hand itched to reach out and touch the flawless skin of her cheek, wondering if it was as soft and smooth as it looked. His lips ached to feel the ruby red fullness of hers beneath them. As if reading his mind, the tip of Ruby's tongue appeared between her lips, wetting them nervously, not realizing how provocative the innocent gesture seemed. Just as the first time he saw her in Atlanta, Seth felt himself being pulled towards her, entranced by a siren's song only he could hear.

Ruby found she was unable to move as Seth's face came in close to hers. Her mind protested against the sensibility of allowing she and Seth's tenuous relationship to overstep the boundaries they were about to cross, but curiosity and an almost physical pull she had been feeling since they had met was overriding all thought.

Seth found himself on one knee with his face inches away from Ruby's when a bird squawked loudly in the tree branches above them. He and Ruby looked quickly away from each other, both confused about what was happening between them.

Seth cleared his throat loudly and stood, looking everywhere but at Ruby.

"I'm sorry, I don't know what I was thinking," he said.

"There is nothing for you to apologize for," Ruby reassured him.

Seth gazed down at her. Other than a dark tint to her usually light hazel eyes, nothing in her expression gave away that she had been just as affected by the moment than he had. Ruby continuously surprised him with how calmly she handled any situation, no matter how intense it was.

"What's your story?" he asked.

"It's the same as the others, a slave looking to be free."

"But you're not like the others. The way you carry yourself, the way you speak, the way you move, you're definitely different from the others."

"Just like the others, I spent most, if not all, of my life as a slave."

"Yes, most of your life, but what was your life like before that?"

Ruby gazed at him, seeing genuine interest and curiosity in his eyes. She wondered if telling someone her story would help her sort through what she needed to do. She had not spoken of her previous life since she was a little girl because no one had believed any of it was true. Would he be like the others and listen indulgently, thinking it was the result of a wild imagination?

"You have barely spoken to me other than to criticize or reprimand and now you are suddenly interested in hearing about my life?" she asked doubtfully.

Seth chuckled and sat beside her, "You're right and I apologize. To be honest, you surprised me. You're nothing like I expected."

Ruby smiled, "That bothers you, doesn't it? To be wrong and have to admit it, even to yourself."

Seth looked away from her penetrating gaze. It was as if she saw right into his heart.

"I guess so," he admitted.

She felt his honest admission deserved her honesty in return. She offered him a seat beside her and began her story.

"I was born Rubina Arinzé Dominguez. My mother was a slave on my father's family's sugar plantation when they met and fell in love. My great aunt, who managed the plantation, helped my father to free my mother so that they could marry. My childhood was filled with the love of my parents, Ifé and Reynaldo, my uncle Amir, whom my father freed with my mother, and my Aunt Luciana, who became my surrogate grandmother when my paternal grandmother disapproved of the marriage."

"Because of my family's wealth, I never wanted for anything. I was given expensive clothes, jewelry, a nanny, a private tutor, all I had to do was ask and it would be mine. But my mother made sure I was brought up aware of what my life would be like without the family's wealth. She believed that anything could happen and that I should be prepared for it. I think she must have had a premonition of what was to come of my life. My mother and I worked side by side with the slaves in the sugarcane fields during harvest and we frequently cleaned our large home from top to bottom alongside our own household staff.

"My father would protest every time he found my mother scrubbing the floor on her hands and knees, telling her that she no longer needed to work, that she wasn't a slave anymore. What he didn't understand, and what she explained to me, was that where she came from everyone worked. No matter what their wealth or status was they worked, believing it kept their village alive and thriving.

"She did agree on one thing with my father and that was that getting an education was just as important as working. She made sure I not only learned my father's culture, but also hers. She taught me the native language of her Yoruba tribe from Africa and helped my father to find a tutor that was versed in the English, French and Spanish language, art, history and even the running of a household. By my eighth birthday I could speak four languages, run a household, ride a horse as if I had been born on a saddle and break down a row of sugarcane almost as fast as a field worker who had done it most of their lives."

Seth was enthralled with Ruby's story. When she spoke of her privileged life it wasn't in a bragging manner, it was matter of fact, as if it were not important.

Ruby continued, "My life was full and happy. I was too young to imagine my parents not being there to shelter me from danger. My mother's lessons were a game for me, not preparation for where my life would lead. I had no idea that my own grandmother hated my mother and me so much that she sacrificed her relationship with her own son in disapproval of his marriage. I would never have imagined that her hate would touch me in such a life changing way and that the outside world would come crashing in on my happy childhood."

Ruby closed her eyes, trying to shut out the heartbreak the memories of her parents' death and her grandmother's betrayal brought forth.

Seth felt her pain seeping into his pores, enveloping his heart.

"You don't have to go on," he told her. "You've told me more than enough."

She gazed at him with tear-filled eyes, "I have never been able to talk about this to anyone and it pains me having kept this secret locked so tight within me for so long. I need to tell someone who understands what it is like to lose family and have to do whatever is necessary to find them again. Who better to tell than you?" she said, a small smile appearing in spite of the tears.

"Go on then," Seth encouraged, his heart reaching out to her in a way he had not expected.

Ruby nodded, taking a deep, cleansing breath, "On my eighth birthday my parents were on their way home from a trip when they were set upon by highway robbers and killed."

Tears clung to her lower lashes before falling to her cheeks.

"Right after the reading of my father's Will my grandmother was very angry. I didn't understand at the time all of what was said during the reading but she was not happy about what she was given and blamed me. Shortly before I was to leave to go live with my aunt who had been made my guardian I was kidnapped by slave traders who had been paid to do so by my grandmother."

"What?!" Seth said in disbelief.

"She met us in the woods to give the kidnappers their payment."

"I can't believe your own grandmother would do that," Seth could not imagine someone being so cruel to their own flesh and blood.

"I wouldn't have either if she had not been all too happy to tell me otherwise."

"You don't sound as bitter about it as I would have expected," he told her.

"Because I'm not. Yes, ten years of my life was taken away by a bitter woman's intolerance but I believe it happened for a reason. If she was cruel enough to sell her own grandchild into slavery, there was no telling how far she would have gone to get rid of me if her plan had not succeeded. She unwittingly saved my life, helping to prove that everything my mother had warned me about was true."

"Do you believe everything happens for a reason?" Seth asked.

"Yes," she answered confidently.

"So we have no control over our own destiny?"

"I believe you have control over the choices you make. Whether or not you choose to accept the path life lies before you or make your own way is up to you," she reasoned.

"I will not say that I haven't been angry over what happened, but if I spend my life focusing on it then I would become just like my grandmother, a bitter and lonely woman with nothing to show for my life but regrets."

"Do you honestly think she regrets what she's done to you?" he asked doubtfully.

"I honestly don't know," she said with a shrug, "but I do believe that there is no way she can be happy. What is a life without the love of family?"

Seth nodded in agreement. He could only imagine how empty his life would be without his family. He was here because he had risked his life to find his brother.

"So what are you going to do?" he asked.

Ruby smiled, "I'm going home."

"Home?"

"Yes, home to Brazil, to my family," she said without the least bit of reservation.

"You can't be serious?" he said, but the expression on her face told Seth that she was.

"You've been gone for over ten years, do you actually expect to show up on their doorstep and be welcomed with open arms?"

"Possibly," Ruby said optimistically.

Seth laughed out loud, "You can't possibly be that naive."

Ruby stood, "I thought you were different," she said, her expression suddenly turning cold. She angrily gathered up the wrap she had been sitting on.

"I thought you would take me seriously and not laugh in my face, but I guess I was wrong. You are just like everybody else," she said, heading back towards the house.

"Ruby, wait!" Seth called out.

Ignoring him, she kept walking but it wasn't long before his long strides caught up with her.

"I'm sorry," he said.

Ruby stopped but refused to look at him.

"I apologize for being so callous about your plans, but how do you expect people to react? You tell this grand story that could have been written in a fanciful novel then announce that you're going to traipse off to find a family, that has more than likely written you off, who are going to lovingly take you back into their lives. Does that sound realistic to you?" he tried to reason. He didn't understand how she could not see how farfetched it sounded.

"Yes, very realistic, because it is my life," she said proudly.

She had trusted only two people with her plans to find her family, Elizabeth and now Seth, and they both had laughed and regarded it as fanciful. Well she was tired of being laughed at.

"Tell me something Seth, did anyone say you were being unrealistic when you spoke of finding your brother and bringing him home?"

He had to admit, she had him there, Seth thought, looking down sheepishly.

"I thought so," Ruby said. "Now you know how I feel. That's why I thought you, of all people, would understand what it means for me to do this," disappointment was obvious in her tone.

Before Seth could respond, Ruby was walking away again. This time he didn't stop her.

Ruby entered the shanty to the loving reprimands of her fellow travelers. Esther had panicked when she awoke to find Ruby gone over an hour ago. Ruby had not realized how long it had been and apologized to the group. They readily accepted but Bishop made her promise never to go off again without him or Isaac with her. She doubted she would be doing it again, but agreed just to remove the worried expressions from their faces.

Walking over to the window she had gazed out of earlier, she saw that Seth was no where in sight. She turned around to find Isaac watching her curiously.

"Is there something wrong?" she asked.

"You tell me," he said with a grin.

"There is nothing to tell."

"What I saw out the window a few moments ago says otherwise."

"I don't know what you're talking about." Ruby realized he must have seen her and Seth arguing.

Isaac chuckled, "So that wasn't a lover's spat between you and our fearless leader?"

"I think you spend too much time reading that book of Shakespeare sonnets you carry around."

"Maybe," he shrugged, "or there's something happening between you two and neither of you wants to admit it."

Ruby looked at Isaac curiously, "You almost sound jealous."

"Maybe," he said with a shrug, "but I also don't want to see you get hurt."

Ruby smiled, gently patting his arm, "Thank you for your concern, Isaac. You are a good friend, but the only thing going on between me and Seth Grant is a mutual dislike for one another."

"Guess I'll have to take your word for it," he said hoping it was true.

Isaac watched her walk over to Ruth and sighed wistfully. He had developed a crush on Ruby the day he joined the Elder's household but he had been sent away before they were old enough for him to admit his feelings. Now, seeing her after all these years, it was like he was that young boy again, but this time he would not wait much longer before telling her how he felt. The moment their feet landed on free land, he was going to ask Ruby to marry him.

Early the next morning when they reached another "station", they were led to a wine cellar with a large secret room located behind one of the walls of wine bottles. The group was surprised to find freshly swept broad planked floors, four cots with clean blankets and an oil lamp that lit the windowless room with a soft glow.

To a daily visitor, it would have looked like the bare minimum but to the weary travelers who had not slept on anything but dirt floors or the cold ground, it was as like a suite at a fine hotel. They had learned over the past weeks that hiding places at these "stations", or safe houses, ranged from secret crawl spaces dug out of walls or floors that barely accommodated two people to rooms like the one they would be staying in that day.

Not long after their arrival they were given a meal of grits, biscuits, baked apples, sliced ham and cold cider. It seemed word had traveled quickly along the underground that their group was coming, so these particular "station masters" had food prepared for their arrival. With full stomachs and a warm, comfortable shelter, it was not long before the weary travelers were dozing off.

After the others had settled in, Nicholas, Seth and Thomas met in the main cellar room. They were a few weeks away from reaching the Ohio state line and things had gone rather smoothly, which worried Seth and Nicholas. Although they felt fortunate to have such an easy going group of travelers, even little Jessie had adapted to the hardships better than expected, the fact that they only encountered one close call so far south was unusual. During most missions, routes were changed frequently in what was known as a "drunken path" due to contact and station changes or slave catchers on their trail.

"You think they may be on to us and waiting at the end of the line?" Nicholas asked.

"They've done it before," Seth answered.

"I'll die before I let them take me back," Thomas said vehemently.

Seth and Nicholas gazed up at him from the map they had been looking over. Whenever Seth brought it up, Thomas had refused to talk about what happened to him over the past year. Seth didn't want to push him, but he also knew that it was eating his brother up inside. If he didn't let it out soon, it would lead to a breakdown.

"You know there is nothing you can tell us that will make us see you any differently than we always have," Seth assured him.

Thomas gazed at his brother then Nicolas, who had always been like another brother to them, and remembered when he had always been the easy going one of the three of them, making jokes, pulling pranks, walking around with a broad, jovial smile on his face. His happy-go-lucky nature also made Thomas a great target for bullies, but it didn't take long for him to earn their respect once he stood up to them. As he became an adult there were still those who didn't know and had underestimated him, but it only took one swing of his beefy arm and fist, muscled and hardened from years of working in the smith, for them to realize their mistake.

Other than those rare occasions, it was widely know that you did not mess with Thomas Grant. It was an image he never really paid attention to until now when his brother and oldest friend waited to hear what happened to him. How could he tell them that he wasn't the tough man everyone believed him to be? That he had been broken after only a few months and had become the good, docile, scrape and bow slave that earned nothing but pitiful stares from the other slaves.

Shame replaced the hollowness in Thomas' eyes and Seth couldn't stand to see that.

"Talk to me, Thomas. I'm your brother, I love you," he pleaded.

Sighing heavily, Thomas nodded, "Right after I was kidnapped I fought those slave catchers tooth and nail every chance I got. It didn't take long for them to start chaining my hands and feet together to keep me from running, then gagging me to keep me from telling anybody we came across from Pennsylvania through Ohio that I was a free man kidnapped by them. They had to stick to the back roads and sleep out in the open just to avoid running into people.

"They beat me, starved me, and even did their business on me while I slept to try and break me, but I refused to give in. When they got me to the plantation of the man they had told everyone I had escaped from I made sure that as soon as that gag came out of my mouth I told the man who I really was. You know what he said to me?" Thomas asked angrily.

"He told me he didn't give a damn where I had come from or whether or not I had been a freeman. All he cared about was that he needed a field nigger and I was just as good as none at all," he said in disgust.

"I knew the only way I was getting back home was to escape and I tried every chance I got, but somehow they always knew. No matter how well I planned it, they knew and were waiting. I soon found out that they had someone watching me. It was another field slave who was always shucking and grinning foolishly for the master and any other White man that came across his path. After three failed attempts they put chains back on me, but all that did was slow me down when they put me to work.

"The last time I tried to escape they made sure when they caught me that I would second guess that decision again," Thomas' voice broke.

"Have you ever been so close to death you could smell its foul breath on you?" Thomas asked no one in particular.

"You ever beg death to take you? To spare you the pain and just take you away from all of it?" he said, looking at Seth and Nicholas with a haunted expression.

"I was there and my request was denied," Thomas unbuttoned his shirt and undergarment, turning his back to Seth and Nicholas.

"My God!" Nicholas said in shock.

Seth couldn't speak. Tears of pain and anger burned his eyes, his hands clenching into tight fists as he looked at the lines crisscrossing Thomas' back.

A Choke Cherry Tree. Seth had heard of it from stories his mother had told them about her life in slavery but he had never seen one until now. Puckered, scarred skin ran from Thomas shoulders to his lower back, like the thick branches of a tree, tangling, gathering and branching out once again past the waist band of his pants like the tree's trunk and roots.

Thomas turned back around as he buttoned his shirt once again, but the image of the scars on his brother's back had burned itself into Seth's mind.

"They finally broke me Seth," he said shamefully.

"Not with the whipping, but with what they did afterwards," he took a shaky breathe to gather his emotions. He refused to shame himself further by crying.

"After they stripped my back, they refused to treat my wounds. They took me out into the woods, told me that if I wanted to escape so bad here was my chance. They left me with nothing but the pants I wore."

"My God," Nicholas repeated, anxiously running his fingers through his hair.

"I walked for half the night before the pain brought me down. I woke up the next afternoon face down on the ground, fevered, my feet bloody and swollen and my back covered in insects. I knew I couldn't go any further so I decided that I would rather lay there and die before I went back to that hell. So that's what I did. I lay there and let the insects make a meal of my torn flesh and welcomed the fever that came over me. I prayed the Lord would have mercy and take me but it seemed the devil was stronger that day. The next time I came around I was back at my slave cabin with that old shucking and grinning field slave standing over me," Thomas said bitterly.

"He happily told me that they thought I'd learned my lesson and brought me back. He had been sent to warn me that they would do the same thing again if I tried to run. That was the day I gave up being a free man and accepted that I was slave. I learned to 'no suh, yes suh, massa suh' with the rest of them," Thomas said sadly.

"You did what you had to do to survive," Nicholas reasoned.

"What I did was shame my family," Thomas said in disagreement.

"I shamed the memory of my mother's struggle to escape what I readily accepted. I shamed the memory of all the back breaking work our father did to keep food on our table. Most of all, I shamed my son who has a coward for a father."

Seth heard enough, "The only way you're shaming anyone is with the self pity you're showing right now," he reprimanded.

"The only thing Mama has been worried about is your safety. She's been on her knees everyday since you went missing praying you come home alive, no matter what it took. She's not going to give a damn what you had to do to stay alive. As far as Papa, you know just as well as I do that he had to scrape and bow just as much as you did to get the family's business off the ground. Neither one of them would fault you for what you did, including your son. I'm sure once he's old enough to understand what you went through he'll be just as proud of you as I am."

Looking up at Seth and Nicholas, Thomas didn't see the pitied or shamed expressions that he had expected. He saw only love and pride and it brought forth the tears he had so desperately been holding back.

Seth walked over to his brother and, taking him in to his arms, held him in a fierce hug, crying right along with him. The moment also brought tears to Nicholas' eyes, as he felt his friends' pain.

Once their emotions were in check, Seth had one last question for Thomas.

"If they were watching you so closely, how did you manage to get away this time?"

Thomas' expression turned cold. "After I was back on my feet the slave that had been my watchdog took every opportunity he could to tell me how lucky I was that they had let me live and that maybe now I would stop being so uppity and accept my life there. He was practically gloating that he had a hand in helping them break me. Then, one night, I decided that I'd had enough. If this was going to be my imprisonment for the rest of my days I was going to do something that deserved the lifetime of hell I would be living, so I made another attempt to escape, but this time I welcomed being followed.

"Once I hit the edge of the woods at the end of the property, I stopped and called out to the weasel because I knew he had been following me, but instead of standing up to me like a man, he went running back towards the plantation. The devil must have known what evil I had planned because he gave my feet wings that night. I didn't even give him time to call out before I twisted his neck, left his body lying at the edge of the property and went back to my cabin," Thomas said emotionlessly. He felt no regret over what he had done and knew he would go to Hell for it.

"After they found his body during patrol the next morning they pulled us all in from the field, questioning everyone. It wasn't said outright, but they all knew that I had been the one to kill him. With none of the other slaves having seen anything or refusing to say anything even if they did, the only thing the master and his overseers could do was guess. They didn't pursue it and I went on about my business. It didn't take me long to realize that I had actually done the other slaves a favor, no one had liked or trusted the man. They all seemed relieved that he was gone so when word filtered in through the surrounding plantations' slave quarters and into ours that a conductor was looking for his brother Thomas who had been kidnapped, a few of the braver slaves didn't hesitate to bring me the news. They also helped me to escape, spreading the word back through the other quarters to look out for me when I came through. The railroad connections through the quarters led me to the Sisters," Thomas said, referring to the two older women that had reunited them.

"I owe the Sisters much for keeping you safe," Seth said grasping his brother's arm.

"Amen to that," Nicholas said, just as emotional as the brothers were about their reunion.

"Well, I don't know about you two but I am bone weary. Seems confessing takes a lot out of a body," Thomas said with a weary chuckle.

They agreed to meet again later that afternoon when Nicholas returned from a quick trip to town with their hosts to map out alternative routes in case he received word of trouble along their currently planned route.

When Thomas and Seth entered the hidden room, they found two neat piles of blankets made up into makeshift beds on the floor. Looking over at the cots, Seth saw that everyone had blankets except Ruby who lay on a bare cot using her overcoat as a cover.

❧ Five ❧

Ruby sat on the cot she had slept on combing out her hair while watching the activity in the room. Isaac's nose was buried in a book their host had given him when they noticed him reading the book of Shakespeare sonnets he carried with him. Thomas and Bishop were seated at the small table in the room discussing the blacksmith business and Esther sat playing with Jessie on the floor.

Ruby had awoken earlier to find one of the blankets she had left for Seth and Thomas spread over her. Thomas told her that Seth had been the one to give up his blanket. His kindness touched her. When she asked of his whereabouts, Thomas told her Seth was out scouting the area and would return shortly. She had not realized how obvious her disappointment over not seeing him was until she saw Thomas' knowing grin.

As Ruby continued brushing her hair, she wondered how her attraction to Seth could have deepened in such a short time. She was not pleased with herself for letting it distract her so much. She had too many other things on her mind and did not have time to think about a man, especially one who obviously did not like her.

When Ruby looked up she found Seth standing in the doorway gazing at her curiously.

"Is there something wrong?" she asked worriedly.

A hush suddenly came over the small group as their gazes fell on Seth expectantly.

"Nothing we can't handle," he said with a reassuring smile.

All but Ruby and Thomas breathed a sigh of relief. Ruby could see that Seth's smile did not quite reach his eyes. Thomas had also seen the seriousness in them. Excusing himself from

Bishop, he walked over to his brother. Ruby watched as the two spoke quietly, then left the room. She laid down her brush, following closely behind them.

"There is something wrong, isn't it?" she asked.

"It's nothing," Seth said unconvincingly.

"If it was nothing you would have told us what it was. The fact that you are being so hush-mouthed about it means it's serious," she said.

"She has a right to know," Thomas said to Seth.

"I said we can handle it," Seth told him.

"The decision should be hers to make," Thomas argued.

"Would you two please stop talking as if I were not here," Ruby said in irritation.

Seth sighed heavily. Thomas was right, Ruby of all people, deserved to know what they were possibly getting into. Reaching into his shirt pocket, he handed her a folded piece of paper.

$500 REWARD

Will be given for the apprehension and delivery of my Servant Girl RUBY. She is dark brown with light, hazel eyes, 19 years of age, about 5 feet 6 inches high, of a slim and shapely habit, having on her head a long, thick covering of black hair that is worn in a crown of plaits. She speaks English, Portuguese and French easily and fluently, and has an agreeable carriage and address. She has been accustomed to dressing well and will probably appear dressed conservatively but fashionably. As this girl absconded from my daughter's home without any known provocation, it is probable she designs to transport herself to the North.

The above reward, with all reasonable charges, will be given for apprehending her, or securing her in any prison or jail within the United States.

All persons hereby forewarned against harboring or entertaining her, or being in any way instrumental in her escape, under the most rigorous penalties of the law.

JAMES ELDER.

Atlanta, Georgia

"Why will she not let me go?" Ruby said in frustration. It seemed Elizabeth refused to allow Ruby to live her life. She was like a dog with a bone that refused to let go.

"I take it you expected this," Thomas said.

"I did not expect it but I'm not surprised," she said, handing the reward notice back to Seth.

"Elizabeth Elder does not give up easily when she truly wants something."

"Well, it's very obvious from the reward being offered that she wants you back at any cost," Seth said accusingly.

He couldn't possibly believe this was her fault, Ruby thought.

"I told you that I would never willingly put the others in danger and I meant it. If our host will allow it, I'll stay on until tomorrow night to give you all a head start. The catchers are after me, not the others," Ruby told Seth.

"No," Seth answered.

"Seth, you know just as well as I do that it has to happen this way. She might as well have posted a sketch of me on that notice with the description she gave, it may only be a matter of time before they catch up with us," Ruby tried reasoning.

"You can't travel alone," Seth insisted.

"I can and I will, you have no choice but to go without me. I will not allow the others to be put in danger because of me," she argued.

Ruby didn't understand why Seth was being so stubborn on the matter. He had been making it quite obvious since their journey began that he was not happy with her being there. She thought he would be relieved to have her gone.

"Don't you think we should have a say about it?" Isaac asked. He, Bishop, Esther and Jessie stood in the doorway between the rooms.

"We started this journey together, so we'll finish it together," Bishop said.

"I already left my sister behind, I won't leave you too," Esther told her.

Ruby was touched by their concern and for the first time since she had left Brazil, felt as if she had a family, unconventional as it was. It gave her even more reason to separate herself from them.

"I truly appreciate all or your concern but I could not bear being responsible for you all getting caught. At this point, I stand out more than Bishop and his immense size."

"We aren't leaving anybody behind," Bishop insisted.

Esther handed Jessie over to Bishop and walked over to Ruby. Gazing up at her curiously, she reached up and touched Ruby's hair which hung in thick, long, waves midway down her back. Then Esther put her hands on her hips and smiled.

"It could work," she said.

"What could work?" Ruby asked hesitantly. She didn't like the determined gleam in the other woman's eyes.

"How bad do you want your freedom?" Esther asked Ruby.

"More than my life," Ruby answered.

Esther nodded, then, turning and looking at each of the men in the room, her gaze stopped on Isaac. Do you have another pair of trousers and a shirt?" she asked him.

"Yes, why?" he asked, just as confused as Ruby.

Suddenly Thomas laughed out loud.

"I think you're right. It could work," he said, grinning broadly and looking from Ruby to Esther.

"Ruby, how attached are you to your hair?" Esther asked.

"Why?" Ruby asked suspiciously.

Two hours later her question was answered. She stood before the group dressed in a pair of Isaac's pants and one of his shirts and a young man's vest, jacket and overcoat from a box of used clothing their hosts kept on hand. Esther plopped a hat on Ruby's shortened locks which now curled around her head like a cap.

"As long as she keeps her coat buttoned and the hat low over her face, she should be fine," Esther commented happily.

Everyone but Seth, who was leaning up against an empty wine rack scowling, nodded in agreement.

"You don't think this will work, do you?" Ruby asked him.

"Sure, as long as you don't walk or talk," he said irritably.

"I knew I shouldn't have let you talk me into this ridiculous scheme Esther," Ruby said dejectedly, taking off the hat and running her fingers through what was left of her hair.

"You look fine, besides, it'll grow back in no time," Esther said in encouragement.

"And we have at least an hour before we leave, that should be plenty of time for Isaac to show you how to walk like a man."

Isaac snorted, looking down at his feet when he received an admonishing glare from Esther.

"C'mon, we have work to do," she said, heading back towards the hidden room with Isaac, Jessie and a dejected looking Ruby in tow.

"I actually think she looks quite fetching with short hair," Nicholas commented.

"What's wrong brother, you look like you just ate a bitter apple," Thomas said to Seth.

"This whole plan is foolish," he complained.

"There is no way she is going to pass for a man, young or old. If anything, that ridiculous costume will make her stand out even more."

"Uh, huh," Thomas said with a grin.

"What?" Seth asked in irritation.

"You sure it's not more than that?" Thomas asked.

"What are you talking about?"

"I saw the way you were looking at her while she brushed her hair."

The image still stood out in Seth's mind. Even after seeing her in the men's clothing and shortened hair. She had been sitting on the cot, legs crossed Indian style, brushing her hair in long, gentle strokes. A feeling of contentment came over him as he had watched her from the doorway. He could see himself watching her do that simple task every night just before he ran his own fingers through the thick, curly locks as she lay in his arms. The suggestive vision made him realize how lonely his life was without the companionship of a woman. Ruby had begun affecting him in many ways and he was starting to like it. What he didn't like was the fact that they had cut her thick, beautiful mane of hair before he even had a chance to do what his imagination had so vividly drawn up.

Seth looked at his brother, knowing that Thomas could read him like book, but he was not ready to admit even to him that he had feelings for Ruby that went far beyond the conductor and fugitive bond.

"Seems you and Ruby are the only two who refuse to see what's going on," Thomas said, reading him just as Seth had known he would.

Nicholas and Bishop came over to join the conversation. Seth looked at both men and received knowing grins in return.

"We're all just waiting to see whose going to weaken first," Bishop said.

"And how long have you all been discussing my love life?" Seth asked in irritation.

"Since our first week on the road," Nicholas said.

"The first week?"

Nicholas nodded, "She's the only one in the group you barely say two words to except to complain about or reprimand her for ridiculous things."

Seth thought back through the past weeks and realized that he had singled Ruby out by the way he treated her. He had acted like a school boy going out of his way to make a girl think he didn't like her when he actually did.

"Thinking of how foolish you've been acting?" Thomas asked knowingly.

"Would you stop that?" Seth said, giving his brother a look of warning.

Thomas chuckled. "You know you have one major obstacle to overcome."

"What's that, the fact that she probably believes that I don't want her around?" Seth said sarcastically.

"There is that," Thomas said, "but what I'm talking about is her past."

Seth felt a sudden surge of jealousy. Had Ruby talked to his brother about her past and her plans after making him believe he was the only one she had spoken to about it?

"What has she told you?" he said angrily.

"Hey Thomas, I think he's actually jealous," Nicholas chuckled.

Seth ignored his friend, giving his brother a hard stare.

"Don't worry big brother, she hasn't told me anything different than what she's told everyone else, but she has asked if I knew how she could obtain passage on a ship bound for Brazil from Pennsylvania," Thomas told him.

"That woman is on a mission and I don't thinking anything, including a fine buck like you, is going to keep her from completing it."

Seth knew Thomas was right, especially since he knew Ruby's entire story, but something was pulling him in her direction and he was finding it very difficult to resist.

Meanwhile Ruby was in the other room silently praying that their farfetched plan would work. Isaac and Esther tried convincing her that she had gotten the walk and mannerisms he had shown her well enough to get by for now and that after a few more days no one would be able to tell the difference, but she wasn't convinced.

Days later, as far as the group knew, Ruby's disguise had worked at two station stops they had made so far. If their hosts knew she was a woman they had not commented on it. They were feeling good about their clever plan until they reached Maryland.

Ruby had gotten into the habit of leaving her hat on low over her face until they were safely in their hiding place so that no one would be able to get a good look at her. Unfortunately, the station master at this particular safe house wouldn't hear of it. Out of respect for the women in the house, all the men were to remove their hats upon entrance into his home. Ruby did as she was told but kept her face averted towards the floor. When the woman of the house began handing out bread to everyone Ruby continued to keep her head down, mumbling a timid thank you hoping that they would assume she was just a shy boy.

"Young man, I expect you to look at my wife when you speak to her. There is no need to keep your eyes downcast in this house. We are all equal in the eyes of God," the man told her.

"Yes, sir," Ruby responded, continuing to look down at her shoes.

"Come now, you are almost at freedom's door, you must learn to show pride in being one of God's creatures. Look at me," he commanded.

The rest of the group looked on nervously as Ruby hesitantly raised her head. There was no mistaking first the surprise, then recognition that came over the man's face once Ruby's light hazel eyes met his stern brown ones.

"You cannot stay here," he said, adamantly shaking his head.

"Sir, it's just for one night," Nicholas tried reasoning.

"No. I will not jeopardize my family's safety for her. The price is too high," he said regretfully.

"The rest of you can stay, but she must leave at once."

"Richard, you can not mean to put her out? It's almost daybreak," his wife pleaded.

"I do Maggie. There are slave catchers in the area as we speak searching homes for this young woman, desperate for the high price on her head. If we are caught harboring the others we may get off with a slap on the hand, but if we are caught harboring her, there is no telling what shall happen to us," he told his wife, his stern expression not leaving any room for argument.

"I understand Sir. I'll leave," Ruby told him. Relief over the fact that he would not turn her over to the authorities warred with the fear of having to take off on her own.

She was heading for the door when she heard the footsteps of the others move into step behind her. She stopped, turning to face them.

"No, please, all of you should stay here," she pleaded with her friends.

"Ruby you know we aren't separating. That was the whole reason for the disguise, so we wouldn't have to," Esther said.

"And it worked fine until now, but there was bound to be someone along the way who would recognize me. We were lucky that it was a friend of the cause and not a catcher or someone wanting the reward money," she said.

"Seth, you're not just going to let her walk out of here alone are you? We're all going, right?" Esther asked desperately.

"No, I'm not going to let her go out alone," he said, to everyone's relief.

"I'm going with her," he said without hesitation.

"What?!" Ruby exclaimed.

"Nick, you and Thomas stay with the others, we'll meet you at the committee headquarters," Seth said, and then he took Ruby's arm and led her out of the house.

"You don't have to do this. I can make it on my own. I've been on the road with you long enough to know what to look for and what to do along the way," Ruby said as Seth pulled her along. She was suddenly more nervous about traveling with Seth than traveling on her own.

Ignoring her, Seth continued walking towards a wooded area nearby.

"We'll have to keep going well past day break and into the night, heading towards New Jersey. It'll take us longer to reach Philadelphia but if we want to keep the rest of the group from getting caught we'll have to take a different route than they do."

Although she knew he was right, he didn't give Ruby a chance to argue. Once they made it into the woods he signaled that there would be no talking. They moved, swiftly but quietly, trying to get in as much distance and travel time as possible. Fugitives traveled through the daylight hours only in extreme cases. It was safer to travel under the cover of darkness because it lessened the chances of getting caught. When they traveled by day, they had to move along more slowly and carefully, taking the backwoods or staying close to rivers where it was difficult for dogs to track their scents.

Seth and Ruby made it through the next 24 hours without incident before taking shelter in a rocky cave alcove hidden by a copse of trees. Seth had to duck his head to avoid hitting it on the low ceiling. Ruby sat down moving over to make as much room as possible for Seth to sit. It was a tight fit. They sat shoulder to shoulder, their limbs grazing one another each time they moved.

"How did you know about this place?" Ruby whispered, her own voice sounding strange after not having spoken since they had left the others.

"It's one of many memorized by conductors for times like these when it's too dangerous to try and seek shelter at a safe house," he answered.

Ruby could feel the warmth of Seth's body and his natural scent enveloped her. They hadn't done more than a quick wash from a bucket of water in over a week and although his musky scent was pleasant to her, it also made Ruby wonder what she smelled like.

"What are you thinking about?" he asked.

"If I smell as bad as I think I do," she answered worriedly.

He chuckled softly, "You can't smell any worse than me."

Ruby spoke before she could stop herself from saying, "I like the way you smell," out loud. Then she quickly asked if he was hungry before he could respond to her comment.

"What's on the menu?" he asked, allowing her to let the compliment slide, silently enjoying the thrill it gave him.

"Unfortunately it's not a grand meal, but it should suffice," she said, handing him an apple and a strip of dried beef. They sat in companionable silence as they ate their meager meal.

"You should try and get some rest," Seth suggested once they finished eating.

"Alright," Ruby answered.

She wasn't the least bit tired, but she hoped that trying to go to sleep would take her mind off the warmth she felt from Seth's leg laying alongside hers.

"What about you? Aren't you going to rest?"

"In a bit."

"Seth, I want to thank you for staying with me. I would have been fine on my own though."

"I'm sure you would have," Seth said smiling. He was charmed by her need to be so strong and independent.

Ruby didn't have as much confidence in herself as he seemed to when she talked about traveling on her own, but she knew that separating from her friends was the best thing for them all. She was glad she didn't have to find out if she would have made it or not.

There wasn't much room to move around in their little space so Ruby just laid her head back against the rock wall, folding her hands in her lap. There were a few times during their journey that the group had slept in the falling rain using trees and bushes as shelter so she didn't think it would be too difficult to sleep where she and Seth presently were. Unfortunately, her body protested against the rocky floor, which definitely was not as soft as a leaf or pine needle covered ground. She was trying to subtly shift her bottom to find a comfortable position. Seth sighed shifting his position then placing his hand in the gap between her back and the rock wall. Pushing her slightly forward, he grabbed her around her waist. Before she could figure out what he was attempting to do, she was lifted onto his lap. When she tried moving off, he stilled her with a gentle squeeze around her waist.

"Relax," he told her. "I'm not going to do anything but be a cushion for you to sleep on. You're obviously not going to get any rest sitting on the hard ground and I'm not going to get any with you squirming beside me."

Ruby wanted to laugh. He actually thought she would be more comfortable on his lap when just sitting beside him affected her physically.

Seth also realized his mistake in putting them in such an awkward position. He felt his manhood stirring in response and knew that if Ruby moved just an inch to her right she would know how she was affecting him.

"Have I given you any reason not to trust that I have the best intentions in mind?" he asked.

Ruby didn't even have to think about that answer, "No."

"Good, because I'm too tired to argue with you," he said, closing his eyes with a heavy sigh.

Ruby willed herself to relax, moving just enough to lay her head on his shoulder. After a few moments she realized he had been right. His lap was more comfortable than the rock floor, although she did wonder for a moment how comfortable he could be sitting on that same rock floor with her added weight in his lap. It was not long before the warmth of his body and the comfort of being in his arms soon lulled her to sleep.

Seth, on the other hand, was wide awake. Ruby's body felt so right against his. It felt so natural holding her. It was as if she were made just for his arms. Everything he knew about this woman made her right for him. She was strong-willed, intelligent, caring, sweet-natured and beautiful. He enjoyed her independent streak and her refusal to be treated like a china doll that needed to be handled gently. She had yet to make one complaint about the hardships they had to endure during the journey so far, even when her glorious hair was cut off to help her disguise.

Seth sighed, content to let the warmth of her body envelope him. Pulling her closer, he wrapped his arms fully around her waist. Ruby moaned in response, curling up further into his embrace in response. Seth smiled as he drifted off to sleep.

❧ *Six* ❧

Ruby awoke slowly, not wanting to leave the comfort and warmth that surrounded her. She'd had the most wanton dream of Seth's hands exploring her naked body. Just thinking about the thrill it gave her made her blush and her body tingle as if it had not been a dream at all. What amazed Ruby was that she would not have minded in the least if it had actually happened, which was why she was in no rush to move out of the circle of Seth's arms. She wanted to hold on to that misty dream before reality came crashing in.

"Are you awake?" he asked.

"Mm hmm," she responded, enjoying the rumble within his chest as he spoke.

"Would you like to get up now?"

"No," she said, burying her face further into the crook of his neck.

A wave of intense pleasure shot through Seth as her lips brushed across his flesh.

"Ruby."

"Yes."

"I really think you should get up," Seth said hoping she wouldn't notice the evidence of his excitement beneath her hips.

Ruby sighed, shifting to her right, bringing her hip up against Seth's groin. She couldn't help but feel the hard bulge he had hoped she wouldn't notice. Ruby was more surprised than shocked. Other than that first time they had been alone earlier in their journey when it seemed as if he were going to kiss her, Seth had always given her the impression that he didn't care much for her. It could have been the position they were sitting in that brought his excitement on, but when she sat up to look at his face in the gray light filtering into the cave, she knew otherwise.

"Is that because of me or does every woman that sits in your lap get the same reaction?"

Seth was not surprised by her bold question. He would not have expected any less from a woman with such a strong personality.

"You," he answered honestly.

"I was under the impression that you did not like me very much."

"Well, you were wrong. I didn't want to like you but I guess I had no say in the matter."

"I didn't want to like you either," she admitted, "at least not in the way I do now."

"Quite a predicament," he said with a grin.

"So what do we do about it?" she asked.

"You tell me."

They gazed at one another. Their faces just inches from each other.

"I can not promise you anything," Ruby told him.

"I'm not asking you to."

"This is just the beginning of my journey."

"I understand," Seth said, reaching up and gently grasping her face in his hands.

"My heart is not free to share with any man," she said breathlessly. She didn't know if she was trying to convince herself or him of that admission.

"Ruby."

"Yes?"

"Be quiet," Seth said, guiding her lips down upon his.

Ruby's lips still tasted of the apple she had eaten earlier, only sweeter. Seth was softly nipping and flicking his tongue over her full lips as if tasting the delectable fruit Beginning their first kiss slow and gently, soon the attraction that they had tried for weeks to deny took over. The kiss became more passionate and demanding as Ruby responded by imitating his actions.

Ruby enjoyed the way Seth's calloused hands felt against her face. When they traveled up into the short curls on her head to draw her in closer and deepen the kiss, she moaned into his mouth. The dream she had awakened from just moments before was becoming reality and she never wanted to wake from it. She was trying to figure out how to turn her whole body toward him without breaking the contact of their lips when Seth suddenly pushed her away. She moved back toward him but he stopped her, placing a finger over her lips and cocking his head to the side, listening intently.

That's when she heard what had caught his attention, the sound of voices outside their hiding place. Ruby nodded her head to let him know she had heard them also and quickly slid from his lap. He reached into his bag and she saw a glint of metal and heard the click of his revolver being cocked. Neither moved, there was only one way in or out of the cave, they were cornered. Ruby closed her eyes, silently praying to every African God, Christian and Catholic Saint she knew of. Her prayers were interrupted when Seth took her hand in his. He must have felt her trembling beside him. She took comfort in his strong grip, willing her body to stay calm.

They could hear the voices clearly now, the men were slave catchers and they were on the trail of a fugitive. They believed he was held up in an abandoned barn nearby and were discussing the best way to approach him. They decided to camp in the area to keep an eye on the barn, figuring he would not start traveling again until after dark. The voices were soon trailing off as the men headed towards their destination.

Seth held Ruby still for a few more moments then leaned toward her. "Gather your things as quickly and as quietly as possible," he whispered.

Ruby did as she was told. She didn't have much so it didn't take her long.

"Stay here," he told her when they reached the opening.

"If I'm not back in 15 minutes, head northeast, staying off the main roads. If you need to find a safe house look for a white ring of bricks around the top of a chimney, a single candle is burning in a window or a quilt on the clothes line showing a house with smoke coming out of the chimney. Use the following phrase, 'The friend of a friend sent me.' Do you understand?" He quickly instructed her.

"Yes," Ruby said quietly, fear once again playing on her nerves.

Pulling out his pocket watch, Seth handed it to her, "15 minutes, no longer than that."

Ruby nodded. "Be careful," she told him, reaching up to stroke his face.

Seth turned his head and kissed the palm of her hand then took off through the brush to follow the trail the catchers took in order to find out what direction he and Ruby needed to travel to avoid them. Once he was close enough to hear their voices and judge which direction they were heading he turned back the way he came.

Ruby gazed down at Seth's watch, the fifteen minutes he had given her had come and it was time for her to leave. She was worried about Seth, but knew he would not want her to risk being caught waiting for him. Just as she was about to walk through the brush at the entrance of the cave, she heard the snap of a twig and held her breathe fearing it was not one of the catchers.

"Ruby," Seth whispered from the other side of the brush.

Tears of relief shone in her eyes as she made her way out of the cave. Seth saw them and ached to take her in his arms to reassure her but there was no time. He simply smiled and nodded to let her know it was alright then took her hand. They were off once again, having to travel with very little rest. Seth wanted to put as much distance between them and the slave catchers as possible. He also decided that it would be best not to stay at any safe houses for now. That would mean a tiring and rough journey ahead for them.

When they were finally able to rest for a day they stayed in an abandoned barn eating the last of Ruby's dried meat and apples.

"Seth?"

"Yes?"

"Do you pray?"

"My mother would say not enough, but yes, I do."

"Would you pray with me?" Ruby said, reaching out to him.

Seth smiled, taking Ruby's outstretched hand. It was warm and soft and fit well into his grasp.

"*Baba wa ti mbe li orun, Owo li oruko re. Ijoba re dé; Ife ti re ni ki ase, bi ti orun, be ni li aiye. Fun wa li onjé ojo wa li oni. Dari gbese wa jì wa, bi awa ti ndarijì awon onigbese wa. Ki o ma si fa wa sino idewò, sugbon gbà wa nino tulasin. Nitori ijoba ni ti re, ati agbara, ati ogo, lailai. Amin,*" she recited.

"Amen," Seth responded, only recognizing the last word of her prayer.

"It's the Christian Lord's Prayer in my mother's native language," she explained. "I sometimes recite prayers in Yoruba because it reminds me of my mother and comforts me."

"I've heard that prayer recited too many times to count, but never so beautifully," he said. She spoke the language so fluently. It sounded like music instead of words.

There was so much that Seth did not know about Ruby and wanted very much to learn.

"What religious faith do you practice?" he asked.

"I never really thought about it. I have gone to mass my entire life, my mother taught me the Yoruba faith and my father insured that my tutor taught me about other cultures and religions throughout the world so that I would have an understanding and tolerance of other's beliefs and way of life. So I guess it's not a matter of which religion I practice so much as if I have faith, which I do."

Seth chuckled, "You are a complex woman."

"I will take that as a compliment," she said with a smile.

"You already know so much about me and my life, as you once asked me, what's your story?" she asked, like him she wanted very much to learn more about who he was.

"It's definitely not as interesting as yours."

"It depends on who you tell it to. Yours could be just as interesting to me as mine is to you."

"I guess that's true," he said with a smile.

"My mother was born into slavery, the youngest of eight children, but grew up never knowing her brothers and sisters. They were sold off as soon as they were old enough to work. She had been the only one allowed to stay on with her mother, who had fallen ill after the loss of her ninth child and never fully recovered. My mother took her mother's place as the plantation laundress when she was just a young girl.

"She told me that even then all she wanted was to be free but she couldn't bring herself to leave her ailing mother. Her father had been sold off right after the loss of the last baby so she would have been left alone. Her mother knew that she was the only reason her daughter stayed so she talked my mother into running and leaving her behind. The Railroad wasn't what it is today. Most freedom seekers had to find their own way North without the benefit of conductors leading the way. They depended on the stars to guide their way. When my mother made it to Pennsylvania, a Quaker family helped her to get settled with a job working for Nicholas' family."

"Your mother sounds like a very strong and admirable woman."

Seth chuckled, "Obstinately stubborn is more like it."

"What about your father?"

"My father's family owned a stable of horses and Blacksmith business in Haiti before the Europeans came in and began pushing the native Haitians out. My grandfather and his brothers chose to sell everything and leave his homeland before it was taken from him and he was left with nothing. Unfortunately, life wasn't any easier in America for them because of the color of their skin. He and his brothers were able to get menial jobs as coachmen and stable hands but they weren't able to rebuild their stock of horses or their smithy, which bruised their pride.

"Although he was young, my father remembered how well life was for his family in Haiti and wanted to get back what his family had given up in their homeland. He began apprenticing under the local blacksmith when he was a boy, scraping and saving every bit of money he earned over the years doing small jobs around town then working for the blacksmith he apprenticed with until he had saved enough to start his own business. He brought pride back to the Grant family name and Thomas and I, with the help of our cousins, continue to try and maintain that pride."

"Your brother mentioned that you are also building up your stable."

Seth nodded. "It's been a long process but I've managed to purchase a few horses and just recently purchased our first carriage for renting," he said modestly.

"Your father must be very proud."

"I hope he is. I just wish he had lived long enough to see it all," he said sadly. "He died unexpectedly about ten years ago. Came home complaining of chest pains but refused to let my mother call the doctor. He died in his sleep that night."

"I'm so sorry," she said squeezing his hand, which she still held.

"Thank you. He lived a long and good life. I think my mother misses him more than anyone. She and my father were in love until the end."

Seth gazed at Ruby, "I think she would really like you. You share the same determination," he said, smiling.

"I would like to meet her. She must be an incredible woman to have made this journey alone. Was she the reason you became a conductor?"

"No, but she did inspire us to help the cause by donating much needed funds and supplies. Until Thomas was kidnapped, I had never thought about becoming a conductor. Even when Nicholas, who had been helping fugitives with legal matters, finding jobs and sometimes obtaining land, decided to start risking his life for the cause it was still not something I considered," he said, his tone filled with regret.

"Will you continue to make these trips after you and Thomas return home?"

"Probably, but I can't say for how much longer. I just know it's become more than trying to find Thomas. It's something I need to do. I've been fortunate enough to have a life that many only dream of having so it's only reasonable that I commit part of it to helping others achieve that dream."

Ruby admired his dedication, "I think that is not only generous but honorable."

"No, just the right thing to do," he said with a shrug.

They gazed at one another for a moment then Seth lifted her hand, placing a soft kiss on her knuckles. "You should rest. I'll do the watch."

"Only if you promise to wake me in a few hours to relieve you so that you can also rest."

"Alright," he agreed with a smile. He put his arm around her waist, pulling her close to his side so that she could rest against him.

Once again he marveled at how natural it felt to hold her in his arms. He tried his best to ignore his growing attraction to Ruby but this strong, beautiful woman had found her way into his imprisoned heart. A place Seth thought was closed forever to feelings of love and passion for any woman.

❧ Seven ❧

Seth and Ruby traveled over the next few weeks with little food or rest. He was used to the zig zag traveling done during most journeys, it was necessary to keep catchers from knowing exactly what routes the conductors traveled, but Ruby was not used to the hardships such a journey would bring. They were out of food and been able to rest for only a few hours a day and the temperature was dropping the further North they traveled.

They had just crossed the Delaware Bay into New Jersey and were a mile or so from a safe house when Seth gazed worriedly back at Ruby. She was trailing a few feet behind him looking ready to collapse any minute. He stopped, waiting for her to catch up to him but instead of slowing once she reached his side, she continued walking right past him as if she had not seen him at all.

"Ruby," he called out, but she didn't stop.

He rushed towards her, reaching her just as she began to stumble forward. He caught her in his arms.

"Ruby, look at me."

Her shoulders and head were slumped forward and her hat hid her face from view.

"I have to keep walking," she said wearily.

She tried shrugging out of his grasp but was too weak to fight him. Seth placed his hand under her chin, lifting her face up to his, and found her burning up with fever.

"Can you make it just one more mile?" he asked worriedly.

Ruby moaned in response then collapsed into his arms. Seth lifted her up, carrying her the last mile they had left to go. When they reached the edge of a small field fear for Ruby's

well-being gave him the added energy to run across the field
to a small house in the distance.

When he reached his destination he kicked loudly on the
door.

"Who the hell is banging down my door in the middle of the
night," a deep angry voice yelled from within.

"A friend with a friend," Seth said, a signal to announce the
arrival of a conductor with a fugitive.

The door opened just enough for the barrel of a shotgun to
fit through.

"Caleb, its Seth."

"Seth Grant?" the other man asked then opened the door
wider, shotgun still pointing at Seth.

"I need your help," Seth said, desperation clear in his voice.

Caleb Wilkes lowered the barrel, stepping aside so that Seth,
with his arms full with Ruby, could walk through.

"Put him on the sofa," Caleb directed.

Seth was so worried about Ruby that he did not realize his
friend had mistaken Ruby for a male. He lay her down,
removing her bag, hat and overcoat. She moaned painfully
with every movement her body made. He felt her flushed and
drawn face, sighing heavily when he realized the fever had
worsened. Caleb stood behind him looking curiously down at
her.

"That's not a boy, is it?" he asked.

"No and we need to get her fever down, fast," Seth said
anxiously.

"I'll get my poultices, you get her undressed. There are
blankets in the chest in the other room," Caleb told him.

Seth threw his belongings onto the floor, retrieved the
blankets Caleb told him about, and then began undressing
Ruby. He went about his task in a detached and brusque
manner, his attraction to her pushed to the back of his mind by
his concern for her well-being. Once he was finished, he placed
one of the blankets over her, dragged a chair from the corner of
the room and sat beside the sofa watching her chest rise and fall
with her labored breathing.

"Try to get her to drink some of this while I stoke the fire place for the poultices," Caleb told him.

Lifting Ruby's head Seth took the cup filled with liquid resembling dirty water, and brought it to her lips. Ruby took a sip, made a face, and turned away. He didn't know what was in it but if Caleb told him to give it to her then he would. The man was very knowledgeable in medicinal herbs.

"C'mon sweetheart, it'll make you feel better," Seth coaxed.

She groaned, weakly shaking her head. Seth put the cup back to her lips and she held them shut like a stubborn child. He knew it was the fever that caused her to act so disagreeable but he was too tired and worried to put up with it.

"Rubina Dominguez if you don't drink this, and I mean all of it, I'll put you back out in the cold," he threatened.

Her eyes fluttered open and a look of surprise shown through her fever glazed gaze. She obediently opened her mouth, slowly sipping the bitter brew he gave her, never once breaking her gaze on him until she had drunk it all. It wasn't long before her eyes fluttered closed once again and her breathing was less labored.

"She'll sleep through the night," Caleb told him. "In the meantime we need to wrap her in these poultices and the blankets to break the fever," He said, reaching for the blanket covering Ruby.

Seth grabbed Caleb's arm, "I'll do it."

Caleb studied Seth's face in the dim lantern light and smiled, "Alright, I'll go make us some coffee and get you something to eat. You look like you need it."

Seth had been surprised by the fit of jealousy that overcame him when Caleb reached to uncover Ruby. He had never been a jealous man. As a matter of fact, women he had courted accused him of being unemotional and insensitive, which was not the case. The truth was that it had been years since he'd found a woman that made him feel such passion. That was until now, he thought, gazing down at Ruby's sleeping form.

He pushed those thoughts to the back of his mind so that he could focus on helping Ruby get well. He would have plenty of time later to think about his new found feelings for her.

While Ruby rested peacefully Seth looked over at Caleb, thankful for his friendship.

They met 15 years ago while attending the Institute for Colored Youth, a higher learning school established by Richard Humphrey, a Quaker philanthropist, to instruct Black youths in the various branches of the mechanic arts, trades and Agriculture. Seth had been the best man at Caleb's wedding, the godfather to his daughter and, unfortunately, helped him to bury both his wife and child when they died of fever two years ago.

Caleb had been inconsolable, selling his dairy farm in Pennsylvania to retreat to this small cottage in Springtown, New Jersey a few months later. Seth had made it a point to visit his old friend as often as he could, but since Thomas' disappearance, his search for his brother and Railroad business took up much of his free time so the visits became few and far between.

"I haven't seen you for at least six months and you show up on my doorstep in the middle of the night with a sick woman, dressed as a man, in your arms using the code with your partner, Nicholas, nowhere in sight. What happened?" Caleb asked.

Seth chuckled, "You never were one to beat around the bush, were you?"

"Life's too short to be looking for the long way around anything. It's best just to forge straight on through," Caleb said with a grin.

Seth gazed over at Ruby in concern then looked back at his friend. "We found Thomas."

"Alive?"

"Yes, but he's carrying a choke cherry on his back."

Caleb shook his head sadly, "Hard lesson to learn for a freeman."

Seth went on to tell him everything that happened over the past few months. Caleb sipped his coffee, listening quietly. When Seth was finished he felt even more tired than the moment he arrived on his friend's doorstep.

"Well, you two stay here for as long as you need. I have to head into town soon for supplies so I'll stop by the Church to see if anything has come down the communication line about the others," Caleb told him, referring to Bethel African Methodist Episcopal Church, which was known by Railroad workers for providing a safe haven for fugitive slaves crossing over Delaware Bay into New Jersey.

"Thank you," Seth said gratefully.

"It's the least I could do after everything you did for Lucy and me. Before and after," Caleb said sadly.

"You don't owe me anything for that," Seth told him.

"Either way, you don't have to thank me," Caleb said, standing and collecting their empty cups to take into the kitchen. When he returned he dragged the large chair he had been sitting in next to the sofa.

"This'll be more comfortable than that rocking chair," he told Seth, then went into the bedroom and came back with a large quilt and extra blankets.

"After those poultices cool, take them off and wrap her in this quilt. I'll make another cup of that herb tea for her in the morning. You should also get some rest. You won't be of any use to her if you're dead on your feet."

Seth nodded in agreement, gratefully taking the blankets and quilt, "I will. See you in the morning."

After an hour Seth removed the poultices and wrapped Ruby in the thick quilt. He watched her for a few more moments, placing a soft kiss on her forehead before settling down in the chair for the night.

Ruby wondered if she had died and gone to heaven. She stood on the veranda of her family's sugar plantation gazing out towards the row upon row of sugar canes ready for harvesting.

She closed her eyes, taking a deep breath of the sugar sweetened air. When she opened them two small children stood giggling before her on the bottom step of the veranda. The girl seemed to be about two years old, with chubby dimpled fingers and face, skin the color of caramelized sugar, and thick black hair braided back in three neat rows resembling the rows of sugar cane in the distance.

Holding the girl's hand was a boy a few years older than her. His skin was chocolate brown and his squared, masculine face and deep brown eyes seemed familiar to Ruby. He smiled broadly, reaching a small but long fingered hand up to her.

"*Vem a mãe, vem jogo com nós,*" he beckoned.

Can you have children in heaven? Ruby wondered when the boy calling her mother asked her to play with them. Taking the boy's hand, allowing him to lead her into the yard, she also wondered who their father could be.

"May we also play?" a male voice said from behind her. Even though Ruby recognized the voice, she turned around just to confirm what she already knew.

Seth stood in the doorway of the house holding the hands of a young girl of about eight or nine who was almost the exact replica of Ruby's mother Ifé with one difference, she had the Dominguez eyes, a bright hazel that stood out prominently against the rich dark coloring of her complexion.

Gazing up from the girl to Seth's smiling face; Ruby realized why the little boy looked so familiar, because he had taken after his father. As she and Seth's gazes met, his was filled with such an intense outpouring of love that it physically enveloped Ruby within its warmth. If this were heaven, she thought to herself, she wanted to personally thank every God and every Saint she knew of for bringing her here. If it were a dream then she never wanted to awaken.

Unfortunately, someone else had other ideas. A cool dampness on her face began chasing away the warmth. She tried holding on to her dream which had begun slowly evaporating around her but the coolness pulled her away. She opened her eyes, blinking several times to focus on the figure leaning over her. When her vision cleared she was looking into the bearded face of a man she had never seen before.

"Ah, Sleeping Beauty awakens," he said with a grin.

"Are you supposed to be Prince Charming?" she croaked, her throat dry and voice horse from lack of use.

"Alas, fair maiden, I fear not," Caleb said with a grin. "Lowly Caleb Wilkes at your service, unfortunately, Prince Charming isn't here at the moment."

"Is Seth alright? Where is he?" Ruby asked in a panic, trying to sit up only to be knocked back down by a wave of dizziness.

"Whoa, take it easy," Caleb told her, putting the cloth pack on her head, trying not to chuckle out loud over the fact that she automatically associated Seth with Prince Charming.

"Seth is fine, he's out chopping wood."

Ruby sighed in relief and closed her eyes to stop the room from spinning.

"Here, drink this," he told her, helping to lift her head up enough to sip from a cup he held in front of her.

She sipped the warm liquid, "Milk, honey and cloves," she said with a smile. "My mother used to make that for me when I was sick. Thank you."

"You're welcome," he said, setting the cup down.

"Where am I?" she asked.

"You're in my home in New Jersey."

Her eyes widened, "New Jersey?! Then we made it? I'm free?" she asked, tears welling in her eyes.

Caleb smiled and nodded. He was almost thrown off balance when Ruby bolted up and threw her arms around his neck. He steadied himself, holding her gently in his arms as she wept.

"That's right, let it all out," he told her, knowing she wept with joy and relief that the journey was over. He and his father had done the same thing when they fled north after his mother died.

"Whew, that storm is going to be a...rough..." Seth stood in the doorway with an armful of chopped wood looking at the scene before him in shock.

"What the hell is going on here!" he said angrily. His jealousy at the sight of Ruby in Caleb's arms quickly overshadowed the joy of seeing her awake.

Caleb eased Ruby out of his embrace, trying not to laugh aloud at Seth's outburst.

"Ruby just found out she made it North and is a little emotional right now," he said standing up and clearing away the rags and cold water he had been using for her head.

"Now why don't you close that door and put some more of that wood on the fire so that she doesn't have a relapse," Caleb told Seth as he walked towards the kitchen.

Seth gazed over at Ruby who was sniffling and wiping tears from her eyes with the edge of the blanket. He did as Caleb suggested and closed the door, walking over to drop the wood next to the fireplace. He took his time adding more wood to the dying flames and removing his coat and gloves, trying to regain his composure. When he had walked in and seen Ruby in Caleb's arms his first instinct was to pull them apart and smash his fist in his old friend's face, but he had managed to resist the primitive urge and kept his anger in check.

Taking a deep breath, he walked over to Ruby, sitting in the chair Caleb had just vacated.

"How are you feeling?" he asked, placing his hand on her forehead, satisfied to find her skin cool to the touch.

"Tired, hungry, happy, sad, it seems to change by the second," she said with a small smile. She never imagined she could feel so much at the same time.

"Well, by the clanging coming from the kitchen, I'd say our host will at least be able to help with your hunger problem."

"How long have we been here? The last thing I remember was stumbling around in the woods."

"That was three days ago."

"Three days?" she said in disbelief. How could three days have come and gone and she not know it?

Seth nodded, "We were just a mile or so from here when I found out you were burning up with fever."

"You've been taking care of me?" The thought brought on the same warmth she had felt while she was dreaming of him.

"With Caleb's help."

"And which of you undressed me?" she asked a little worriedly.

"I did. The night shirt is Caleb's but I'm the only one who undressed and dressed you," he reassured her.

"Thank you," she said with relief.

"I'm just glad you're all right," he reached up, gently stroking her face.

They gazed at one another, both wondering where this relationship was headed. Seth started to speak but was interrupted by Caleb clearing his throat. He placed a bowl of soup and a plate of bread on the table in front of the sofa.

"Make sure she eats," he told Seth. "I'm going to stop and check on some elderly neighbors on the way into town to get more supplies."

"Be careful, looks like a major storm is getting ready to blow through," Seth told him.

"I'll stay in town if it gets too bad. There's plenty of food in the pantry and dried meat in the shed out back. I'll get back as soon as I can to let you know if I hear anything about the others."

"Thank you," Seth said.

Caleb nodded then smiled down at Ruby.

"Rest up Beauty and if the Prince here nags too much just throw him in the moat."

Ruby smiled, "I will and thank you for all your care and concern."

"You're welcome, now eat before it gets cold," he said gruffly.

"He seems to be a very kind and gentle man," Ruby said after Caleb left.

"He is. Now do as the doctor ordered and eat," Seth picked up the bowl of soup and handed it to her.

"I have a surprise for you once you're finished." He smiled boyishly and headed towards the kitchen.

Ruby began to eat, wondering what Seth was up to when she soon heard the sound of something scraping across the floor. As she ate, a dozen thoughts ran through her mind. The most prominent was the welfare of the rest of the group. She hoped that they had also made it to safety.

She still could not believe that she had finally made it North. She had dreamed of being free for so long that it was hard to believe she had actually made it and was another step closer to going home to her family. Her eyes began to fill with tears as she realized that her future was an open book now and she had no idea where to start.

Seth walked into the room to find Ruby weeping into her bowl of soup. Walking over to her, he took the bowl from her then, picking her up into his arms, carried her into the kitchen. His heart ached for this woman like no other before.

"I have something that will make you feel better," he told her.

The kitchen was just as warm as the living room with a fire burning in the potbellied stove. Sitting in front of the stove was a large porcelain bathing tub. It sat on four golden clawed feet and was decorated with delicately painted green vines and pink roses rising up the side and along the rim of the tub.

"It's beautiful," Ruby said breathlessly as Seth sat her in a chair nearby.

"It used to belong to Caleb's wife, Lucy. It was his wedding gift to her after she jokingly complained of all the splinters in her backside from bathing in a large wooden tub all her life while the White woman whose children she cared for bathed in a tub like this one. Caleb thought she deserved to have just as good a tub as that woman so he went to the general store and ordered this from a catalog."

Seth chuckled, "Lucy was mad as can be that he had spent his hard earned money on such a luxury."

"What a loving gesture. What happened to her?"

"She and their daughter died of fever a few years ago," he said sadly.

"He must have loved her deeply to have been this thoughtful," Ruby said, running her hand along the lip of the tub.

"He did. He was heartbroken when they died and has been in somewhat seclusion on this little farm ever since."

"That is so sad," Ruby said, tears welling up once again.

"Hey, I'm supposed to be cheering you up, not upsetting you. Allow me to draw your bath Madame," he said with a bow and grin.

He went over and took a large pot of hot water off of the stove, adding it to the cool water already in the tub.

"Let me know how that is, I've got another bucket ready to heat up when you're finished."

Ruby leaned over and tested the water with her hand. "It's perfect," she told him with a smile of anticipation. "I haven't enjoyed a bath in so long. I can't wait to get right in."

In her excitement she stood too quickly and a wave of dizziness rushed over her. She wove towards the tub and Seth rushed over before she toppled in.

"Hey, not so fast," he gently reprimanded. "You're still weak from being sick, take it easy."

"Guess I got a little too excited," she said weakly, holding tightly to his arm.

"Here, let me help you get undressed," he suggested.

Ruby didn't argue, after all, he'd been the one to undress her and take care of her while she was sick, what would be the difference now? She was awake, that's what the difference was, and a sudden feeling of modesty came over her.

Seth also battled with his own thoughts. Undressing her when she was sick and unconscious made it easier to detach himself from the task, but undressing her while she was wide awake and able to respond to his touch was difficult. He had to force himself to remember that she was still recovering and that he did not take advantage of women when they were weak and vulnerable.

He swiftly, but gently undressed her. It didn't take long because all she had on was Caleb's night shirt and a blanket. Once she was undressed he helped her step into the tub.

Ruby felt the warmth of the water envelope her and moaned with pleasure as she sunk into tub and closed her eyes. That moan did more to burst Seth's bubble of detachment to the situation than her lying naked and wet before him. It was a husky sound that was so sensual Seth's body reacted as if she had physically reached out and touched him. He had to leave the room before he made a fool of himself.

"There's soap, towels and a clean night shirt on the other chair beside you. I'll give you some privacy. Call me if you need anything." He hoped she didn't because he wasn't sure what he would do if he saw her naked body again.

Ruby nodded, barely noticing as Seth left the room. She lay for as long as she could before the water cooled too much then took the soap, lathered herself from head to toe, rinsed as quickly as possible. She stepped out of the tub, dried herself and dressed in the clean nightshirt Seth left for her.

When she was finished she sighed happily, gathered her blanket and went back into the other room. Seth sat gazing into the fire looking as if he had the worries of the world on his shoulder. She wanted very much to smooth away his solemn expression and see his smile.

"Seth?"

When he turned and looked at her, his heated gaze was one she had never seen before and it gave her an unexpected thrill.

"I started heating the water you left on the stove in case you would like to take a bath also," she told him.

He smiled but the heat never left his eyes, "Thank you, I think I'll take you up on that offer."

He stood and walked slowly towards her. "The storm has picked up. I don't think Caleb will be back tonight. Why don't you sleep in the bedroom? I changed the linen and lit a fire while you were bathing."

"Thank you," she said almost breathlessly as he stood directly in front of her. She met his gaze with her own, willing herself not to look away.

Seth reached up, laying his palm against her cheek, and ran his thumb over her full lips, "Ruby, Rubina. Your parents named you well. Your lips are as red as the jewel you're named after and, if I remember correctly, taste just as sweet as a red, ripe apple."

Although it had been some time, Ruby remembered their kiss in the small cave very well. She closed her eyes and leaned her cheek into his open palm. He leaned forward and Ruby could feel his breath caressing the side of her face.

"I want you so much right now that it hurts," he whispered. "My willpower is completely gone and I need you to walk away now before I do something we both may regret in the morning."

Ruby wondered what made him think that she was any stronger than he was. She wanted him just as much as he wanted her and also realized that as much as she wanted him, she knew that it would complicate things if she allowed their relationship to cross that line. She took a deep shuddering breath and stepped away from him.

Seth smiled weakly and nodded. "I'll let you know when supper is ready," he said walking past her into the kitchen.

❦ *EIGHT* ❧

Ruby lay in Caleb's large four poster bed staring up at the ceiling. She had too much on her mind to sleep. She not only had several decisions to make about her future but also her relationship with Seth. She vividly remembered the dream she had about him, their children and being back in Brazil. She couldn't help but wonder if there were some truth to if Seth would affect her future in more ways than bringing her North.

She may be physically free of slavery, to go wherever she pleased, but she was not emotionally free until she was able to see her family and know, one way or the other, if she would be accepted back into their fold. She couldn't have a future without settling her past. Her growing feelings for Seth would have to be set aside for now. If her dream foretold what was meant to be then she can only hope that they would somehow find their way back to one another.

Her priority had to be on finding a job once she arrived in Philadelphia so that she could save enough money for passage to Brazil. From what Thomas told her, she already had half of what she needed, she just had to decide what kind of work she wanted to do. It was still difficult for her to accept that she now could choose the work she wanted, whether it be a domestic or a teacher, it was her choice to make. Whatever she did, she only needed a year to save up what she needed for not only passage but also for a new life in the event that her family may not be so easily accepting of her.

Feeling as if she had accomplished something by making those decisions, her mind slowed its swirling and allowed her to finally drift off to sleep. She awoke a few hours later to the smell of biscuits and her stomach protesting loudly to not having been fed properly.

She climbed out of the bed and wrapped a blanket around herself. The fire had gone out while she slept and the room had grown chilly. Ruby made her way across the room and as she opened the door she heard whistling coming from the direction of the kitchen. She looked around the main room. Everything that had been out of place earlier had been neatly put back into place. Seth had cleaned and judging from the smells drifting to her from the kitchen was in the process of preparing dinner. She smiled, never imagining him to be so domestic.

Ruby sat on the sofa, curled her legs up under her and placed the blanket on her lap. She watched the fire and listened to Seth whistling an old spiritual she recognized that Harriet, the Elder's housekeeper used to sing while she worked. Ruby realized she missed the older woman and the camaraderie they had begun to share before Ruby left. Tears of sadness filled her eyes, but she closed them, refusing to let them fall. She had no time to think about the sadness of her former life. She had to concentrate on what her future held. She took a deep breath and released it slowly to ease the ache in her chest and opened her eyes again. Seth stood in the doorway of the kitchen with a tray of food in his hands.

"I was just on my way to bring you dinner. Are you alright?" he asked worriedly.

"I'm fine," she reassured him with a smile, "just still a little emotional about finally reaching this point."

He nodded, feeling that there was something more but not wanting to push her.

"Would you like to sit in front of the fire and eat?" he asked.

"That would be nice. I hope you plan on joining me."

"Are you sure?" he asked.

"Seth, judging by the wind and snow swirling around outside, we're going to be stuck here for some time. This is a small house. We can't keep trying to avoid one another."

"You're right," he said, placing the tray before her and going back to the kitchen to fix a plate of food for himself.

When he returned, Ruby had spread a blanket on the floor in front of the fireplace and was sitting Indian style. She looked so sweet and vulnerable in Caleb's oversized nightshirt.

"I thought this would be nicer," she told him as he sat beside her. "Like a picnic."

They watched the fire as they ate their meal, enjoying the warmth of the flames and the food.

"You cook, clean and take care of the sick, you'll be quite a catch for some lucky woman," she teased as they finished and he gathered up their dishes to take back into the kitchen.

"I hope so," he said.

He returned with two cups, handing one to her as he sat back down. The smell of spiced cider rose from the steam.

Ruby took a sip and chuckled, "Is there anything you can't do?"

"Make cider," he grinned, "that's Caleb's brew."

"It's very good."

"Especially when it's spiked with whiskey," he said, winking at her.

Ruby looked at the steaming cup and up at him questioning.

"It's only a taste," he chuckled, "Nothing too strong."

"Well, it definitely hits the spot. Although I've never even had more than a sip of wine so I'm not sure how much of this I should be drinking."

"I promise not to let you imbibe too much. I want you to keep a clear head."

Ruby didn't want to tell him that it was too late for that. She didn't know if it was the several large sips of cider she had already taken or a combination of that with a full stomach, warm fire and cozy environment, but her head was just a little fogged and she was feeling rather warm. She decided not to take any chances and handed the half empty cup back to Seth.

"I think I've had enough," she said, wondering if it was just her imagination or was her speech a bit slurred.

"I agree," Seth laughed, sitting their cups on the hearth.

Ruby stretched then lay on her side, supporting her head with her hand and looking drowsily at Seth.

"So, tell me why a woman hasn't snatched you up already?"

"How do you know one hasn't? She could be sitting at home pining away for me right now," he said trying to sound offended.

"Because you've made your attraction to me all too clear," she said boldly.

"You think you know me so well?" he said curiously. "I could be a practiced seducer for all you know."

"No, you're too selfless and gentle to be a seducer," she said confidently.

"Really?"

"Yes, that and the fact that Thomas told me you had no one special in your life right now," she said with a mischievous grin.

"Remind me to throttle my brother when I see him again," Seth chuckled.

Ruby didn't allow the thought of not seeing Thomas and the rest of the group again enter her mind. She was feeling too good and didn't want to lose the cozy cocoon that had wrapped itself around her and Seth this evening.

"You haven't answered my question."

"I guess the right one hasn't come along," at least not since Olivia, he thought to himself.

"Well, according to your brother, several have come along. You were just too busy to notice."

"My brother talks too much," Seth said in irritation.

"He just loves you and wants you to be happy. I wasn't fortunate enough to have siblings who cared so much about me," she said sadly.

"What type of woman are you interested in?" she asked, hoping to shake the melancholy that suddenly came over her.

Seth was quiet for a moment as memories of a dark-haired, caramel-colored beauty entered his mind, then just as quickly disappeared, as if in a wisp of smoke, when he gazed at Ruby.

"She would have to be intelligent, someone who will challenge my mind in a conversation, a generous heart, an independent and strong spirit, and a passionate, loving nature."

"Curious," she said, "you didn't mention her appearance."

"Because it doesn't matter," he said casually.

"Really?" she said doubtfully, "So if you met a woman with all those qualities but was short, stout, with bulging eyes, an eagle nose and a mustache as thick as yours, you would marry her?"

"Well, maybe if she didn't have the mustache," he said, looking as if he was seriously considering it.

They gazed at each other for a moment then laughed out loud.

"What about you?" he asked, "You didn't leave anyone pining away for you when you set out on this journey?"

"No. There were men interested in me, slaves of my owners' friends and family, even some Freemen. I was friendly to them but I made it a point to let them know that as sweet as they were, they would be wasting their time courting me. I was, and still am, more interested in getting to my family than finding a husband."

"What about Isaac?" Seth asked, hoping she didn't hear the jealousy in his voice.

"Isaac? He's just an old friend. I taught him to read at a time when it was frowned upon for slaves to have such knowledge, that's all. If he developed a boyhood crush he never had the chance to do anything about it before he was sent away. I'm sure he's forgotten all about it by now."

"I very much doubt it, especially when he looks at you the way he does," Seth said sarcastically.

"You almost sound jealous," Ruby said in surprise.

"And if I am?"

"Then I'd tell you that you have nothing to be jealous of. I'm not interested in anything more than friendship with Isaac or any other man for that matter."

"What if a man came along that did peak your interest romantically?"

"If he's the right man, he will know how important it is for me to complete my journey before making a commitment to anything or anyone else."

"What if he asks you not to go because you could be making the biggest mistake of your life?" Seth didn't know what was happening to him but he wanted more than anything to convince Ruby to stay in Philadelphia when they arrived.

"If it is a mistake, it will be one that I make willingly. I can not move forward until I know what I may be leaving behind," Ruby said in determination.

"I have never met a woman quite like you," Seth said, not sure if he was about to make the biggest mistake of his life, by revealing his feelings for her.

"I misjudged you from the moment we met and you proved me wrong every step of the way during this journey. I've come to respect your selflessness, strength and courage and admire your determination."

Ruby sat up from her lounging position. She could see in Seth's gaze that there was something more serious he wanted to say, and she wasn't sure if she was ready to hear it.

Seth moved towards Ruby, sitting directly in front of her but not touching her, "I also think you're intelligent, charming and beautiful and just the thought of kissing you again affects me physically. Every moment we're together I find it more and more difficult not to reach out, pull you into my arms and make love to you. And since, as you said, we're stuck here alone together because of the storm, I thought you should know how I felt."

Seth sat quietly, holding his breath as he waited for her response.

"I'm flattered and have an admission of my own to make," she said, deciding it probably was best to be open about their feelings so that there were no misunderstandings between them.

"I've also come to admire and respect you over these past few months. I've come to learn you are a warm, kind, understanding, gentle and passionate man who makes me feel more woman than I have ever felt before and I enjoy it very much," Ruby said, unashamed about speaking so bluntly.

Seth grinned, "Sounds like husband material to me."

"Only if you're willing to wait for me," Ruby replied with a teasing grin.

"What if I told you I would?"

Ruby wasn't sure if they were still teasing or if he was serious, "I'd tell you that it wouldn't be fair to ask that of you."

Seth pulled Ruby towards him so that she sat between his legs, "I'd say it would be worth the wait."

Ruby gazed into his eyes, which glowed like two dark pools with the reflection of the firelight, and saw that he was serious. Reaching up, she caress his face with her fingertips.

"Seth, I..."

"Ruby, I know, in spite of the weeks we've spent together, that we barely know each other and that's due to my own foolishness, but ever since we met in the marketplace I have felt a connection to you that has scared, and excited, me almost to distraction. I know you can't promise me anything right now and I'm not asking you to, but I also know, in my heart, that I want to be a part of your life and I'm willing to do whatever it takes to make that happen, including waiting for you to do what you need to do, or go wherever you need to go, to find your family."

"There is a chance that I might not return, Seth. If I find out that my family hasn't forgotten me and welcomes me back, I won't leave them again. I won't take the chance of losing them as soon as I find them," she told him.

Seth turned his head and kissed the palm of the hand she caressed his cheek with, "That's a chance I'm willing to take."

"Why? Because you think it's a fool's journey? That I'll find no welcome there and come running back here?"

She had not asked him the question in anger but honest curiosity and Seth could think of no answer. He couldn't find it in his heart to put down her dream of finding a home among a family who hadn't seen her in over ten years. Even if she had some kind of proof of who she was, ten years was a long time, people change. How could he tell her he thought she was setting herself up for heartbreak?

He didn't have to tell Ruby how he felt. She could see it in his eyes.

"Let's not talk about the future. Let's just worry about right here, right now," she told him, leaning forward and covering his lips with her own.

Her kiss began softly, then quickly deepened, urging him to forget, at least for a little while, what would happen to them once they left the safe haven of Caleb's cottage. Seth's response was to tease and explore her mouth with his tongue, the taste of cider and whiskey making the kiss even more intoxicating for both of them.

Ruby ended the kiss by gently pulling away and backing out of his embrace. She sat up on her knees and began unbuttoning the nightshirt she wore.

"Are you sure?" Seth asked.

"Yes," she said, never taking her eyes from his intense gaze as she reached for the hem of the shirt to lift it over her head.

Seth watched, mesmerized, as the hem eased up over her smooth thighs, rounded hips, soft belly, small waist and full breast. For the past two days he had avoided seeing her naked figure in a sexual way. There had been nothing sensual about his undressing her and wiping her body down with cooling cloths and compresses to ease her fever. Now she sat before him willingly displaying her voluptuous figure for his perusal.

"Is there something wrong?" she asked, laying the shirt aside. "You look strange, as if you aren't sure what to do."

"Oh, I'm very sure of what to do. You just took me by surprise."

"I've never done this before so I'm not sure what the niceties are," she said shyly.

"No, you're fine. I'm pleasantly surprised," he said, resting his hands on her hips and looking up into her face.

"You are so beautiful," he told her.

She reached up, touching her shortened hair, "I look to boyish," she complained with a slight frown.

Seth chuckled, "There is definitely nothing boyish about you," he said, his hands gliding up to her small waist, "You have all the right curves in all the right places."

Ruby smiled, taking his face into her hands. "Compliments will get you almost anywhere," she teased, placing a soft kiss on his lips.

"Almost?" he said in mock disappointment.

"I didn't say this would be easy." Ruby had always been bold and outspoken so she wasn't surprised to find herself that way when it came to love games.

"I love a challenge," he grinned mischievously.

Ruby felt a sense of rightness in her and Seth being together, in spite of the fact that they weren't married or had any intentions of getting married. She believed in dreams and the stories they told and if the one she had about Seth and their children were any indication, they were bound together and somehow, some way, if it was meant to be, they would find their way back to each other.

Seth knew Ruby was giving him all that she could right now. He told himself that it would be enough, that he understood what she needed to do and that he could wait for her. For that reason, he knew he couldn't be careless about this moment. As much as he wanted her, he would let her set the pace.

As if she had read his thoughts Ruby smiled as she leaned forward to kiss him. She began slowly, he matched her pace, letting her be the one to change the pressure and depth of their kiss. She parted her lips and ran the tip of her tongue along the outline of his mouth before delving in to taste him as he had done to her earlier. During the passionate kiss, Seth's hands didn't stray from Ruby's waist. He held back for her, but he wasn't sure how much longer he could continue to do so.

Ruby lost herself in the passion of their kiss. She felt fevered but not in the way she had when she was sick. This was a fever like no other that made her heart race, her skin tingle as pleasure began to build at the core of her womanhood, making her ache for more. When Ruby moaned into his mouth Seth could no longer hold back. His hands slid up her waist, caressing the sides of her breasts, slowly working his way to her taut nipples, gently circling them with his thumbs.

Ruby arched into his touch as Seth grasped her full, heavy breasts in his hands and pulled away from her lips. Her groan of protest was quickly replaced by an even deeper moan of pleasure as his lips covered her pebble hard nipples. The bolts of pleasure shooting through her from the heat of his mouth and the gentle flicker of his tongue over one then the other made Ruby gasp loudly for air. His lips left her breast and traveled upward to her neck, chin and ear where he gently nipped at the lobe.

"Seth," his name came out as a sigh.

"Hmm," he answered, placing soft butterfly kisses all over her face.

"You know, it's not fair that I sit here naked before you receiving all this attention and I don't get to touch you."

"Sweetheart, you are more than welcome to explore and touch to your heart's desire."

Ruby sat back on her heels, reaching for the buttons on his shirt. Seth's hands continued to wander over her body as she tried, unsuccessfully, to undo the buttons.

"It's very difficult to concentrate when you touch me that way," she complained breathlessly.

"Didn't say this would be easy," he grinned.

"*Touché*," she smiled and managed to finish unbuttoning the shirt, slipping it off of his shoulders.

His upper body was wide and muscled. She ran her hands along his shoulders, down to the thatch of hair that covered his chest and came to a thin line, disappearing into the waist band of his pants. His chest hair fascinated her and she spread her fingers into the soft curls. Other than artwork she had not seen a naked man before now. None of the sculptures or paintings she had seen could do Seth's body justice.

"You realize there is more to see than my chest," he said amused by her fascination.

"Do you mind if I undress the rest of you?" she asked, gazing at him in curious excitement.

"I am at your command."

"Famous last words," she said, playfully pushing him so that he would lay down.

Seth did as she wanted, laying with his hands behind his head, his nonchalant pose and manner belying his excitement and racing heart. He thought of the casual dalliances he'd had with experienced women skilled in the art of seducing men and knew that none of them were as genuine or entertaining as Ruby's innocent and playful seduction.

Ruby ran her fingers one last time through Seth's chest hair, following the line that led into the waistband of his pants. She loved the feel of his hard muscles rippling beneath her hand with his every breath. When she reached her destination she took notice of the bulge that had not been so obvious when he was sitting up. She tentatively ran her finger tips over the raised cloth, watching in fascination as it grew even larger beneath her touch.

"There seems to be more of you than I expected," she said, sounding a little worried.

"We can stop now, if you like." As much as it pained him to make that offer, he meant it.

"No, I'll be fine." Ruby reprimanded herself for being so naive. She took a deep calming breath and kept in mind that Seth wouldn't intentionally hurt her.

She reached for his belt, undid the buckle and the buttons of his pants, then grabbed the waistband and began tugging. Seth assisted her by lifting his hips as she slid them down. Ruby set his pants and undergarments aside and gazed at his naked form lying before her. The strength of his body shown in his well-muscled arms and chest, lean hips and long muscular legs, all from years of smith work and riding horses. His skin wasn't the smooth perfection of the statues she had compared him to moments before. His nicks and scratches here and there reminded her more of the carved wooden African statues she had seen when her parents took her to a market place in the town of Bahia near the plantation.

"Do I get to study you as intently?" Seth teased.

"If you like." The thought of him doing so thrilled her even more.

Seth sat up and pulled her into his arms. "I learn better hands on."

She sighed as he buried his face in her neck, gently nibbling and kissing his way down towards her breast. He lifted her up just enough to position her so that she straddled his thighs. Her sighs turned to moans as he paid loving homage to her breast while running his hands softly over her rounded curves and working his way back up to her lips. Their kiss was deep and passionate as they explored each other's bodies with heated caresses.

Ruby had never known such intense pleasure. Just as she began to think that there was nothing more wonderful than the pleasure she was feeling, Seth shifted her hips forward causing the nub at the juncture of her thighs to come into contact with the smooth, hard proof of his desire rising up between them. She cried out in ecstasy as she felt her inner walls contract in response and wrapped her arms around Seth's shoulders, moving her hips to apply more pressure to the sensitive point.

Seth didn't think it was possible but his manhood seemed to stiffen even more in response to Ruby's movements. The slow pumping was torture for him and was quickly pushing aside his idea of allowing her to set the pace. He moaned painfully into her mouth, grasping her breasts and flicking his thumbs across her erect nipples.

Their passionate kiss, the friction between her legs and Seth's fingers massaging her breast brought on a pressure so intense that Ruby could do nothing but let it flow through her until it exploded within like a volcano's eruption. She threw back her head and cried out as wave after wave of pleasurable sensations washed over her, her body quaking in response. Her nails dug into Seth's shoulders as if he could keep her from floating off as the tide slowly subsided.

Seth could no longer hold back, lifting her up, he tried as gently as possible to ease her over his erection but as the tip of it was swallowed within the moist heat of her womanhood it was too much, he found himself unable to control the urge to impale himself within her sheath.

"Forgive me," he whispered hoarsely, bringing her quickly down upon him.

The contractions of Ruby's inner walls were just beginning to subside when suddenly her pleasure turned to pain. She tried shifting to relieve the discomfort but he stilled her.

"No, I'm not fully within you, you need to adjust to me or you'll only feel pain," he said through gritted teeth.

"You said that I could set the pace, did you not?" she asked.

"I know and I'm sorry..."

She heard the regret in his voice and, covering his mouth with her own, began moving her hips in a seductive dance that only a woman would know. Seth forgot about being careful, forgot about not wanting to hurt her, all he could think about was the hot, moist sheath that was inching down the length of his erection and enveloping him with each movement Ruby made of her hips.

Ruby quickly forgot about the pain as she adjusted to the feel of him within her. It felt so natural, so right to be with him this way. Seth was thinking along the same lines as he was comforted by how perfectly they seemingly fit together, as if they had been made for one another.

She felt so tight and warm, he thought he could stay this way with her forever, but his body had other ideas when Ruby's slow movements became more rapid and her arms tightened around his shoulders. Her inner walls contracted around the length of him and he pulled her close as they cried in unison with their release.

They sat dazed and satisfied, trembling in each other's arms. Seth lay back, bringing Ruby down with him, not wanting to let go of her just yet. She lay with her head on his chest, listening to the rhythm of his heartbeat.

"What does *você é meu amor* mean?" Seth asked.

"It means 'you are my love'. Why?" she asked drowsily.

"No reason," he said smiling. She didn't even realize the very words she just translated for him, were words she had cried out during her passionate release.

Ruby awoke curled up on her side in Seth's arms feeling a little tender but content. They were lying in Caleb's four poster bed with a warm fire burning in the hearth. She vaguely remembered Seth carrying her into the bedroom but she had quickly fallen back to sleep as soon as her head hit the soft pillow. She gazed up at the window and could tell by the bright natural light coming through that it was late morning. As far as she could see the snow had stopped and the sky was clear, which meant Caleb would probably be back late that day.

Ruby snuggled closer to Seth wishing that they could stop time and stay right there in the cozy cottage alone for just a few more days. Unfortunately she knew that they couldn't. In spite of what just happened between them she was still determined to go to Brazil. She told herself, once again, that if she and Seth were meant to be together, they would find a way. She didn't want to believe that she could be walking away from the love of her life. She would make the most of the time they had together. She had been honest with him and he had accepted that she could not make him any promises. What they shared now was all that she was free to give to him.

Ruby eased herself out of Seth's arms, trying not to wake him. She knew he had to be tired after staying up and caring for her while she was sick because she only received a groan in response as she left the bed. She was now going to return his kindness by taking care of him.

When Seth awoke the entire cottage was filled with warmth and the aroma of griddle cakes, fried ham, and coffee. He got up, dressed and made his way to the kitchen. He stood in the doorway quietly watching her flit from the table to the stove and back looking very content in doing her tasks.

Ruby saw Seth out the corner of her eye and turned toward the doorway. Butterflies fluttered in her stomach at the sight of him leaning against the frame dressed in nothing but a pair of trousers.

"Hungry?" she asked.

"Famished," he answered, not moving from the doorway.

"Well, come eat before it gets cold."

"I wasn't talking about the food." His was voice filled with husky passion, his gaze on her promised he would definitely take his fill of her if she allowed him.

Ruby's nipples hardened in response to his lustful gaze. "You need food to keep your strength up in order to satiate those other hungers," she teased.

Seth walked towards her and took her into his arms, "Will you at least give me a taste to hold me over?"

Ruby wrapped her arms around his neck. "Just a taste," she warned playfully.

He ran the tip of his tongue along the outline of her mouth, before easing it between her lips. The kiss was slow and light but filled with just as much passion as the deeper kisses they had previously shared. When Seth pulled away Ruby stood gazing dazedly at him.

"I believe my hunger has been appeased for now," he grinned and sat down at the table, heaping food onto his plate.

She wondered how she could be so affected by a simple kiss yet he seemed so calm. Then she looked down and noticed that his hand was trembling slightly, proof that he had also been just as affected as she. With a pleased smirk, she turned back towards the stove and poured them coffee.

After finishing their meal and cleaning up, Seth took Ruby's hand and led her into the other room. He sat on the sofa, pulling her into his arms as he did so. They quietly watched the flames dancing in the fireplace.

"Did I hurt you last night?" he asked in concern.

"A bit, but it was brief."

"I'm sorry," he said placing a kiss on the top of her head.

"There is no need to apologize. I was a virgin, I knew to expect some pain," she said in a matter-of-fact manner.

Seth chuckled, "Have you always been this blunt and outspoken?"

"Yes. My nanny used to tell me that little girls were made to be seen, not heard. I don't think she actually believed it. She probably hoped it would help to curb my tongue," she said laughing.

"What do you think you would be doing right now if you had never left Brazil?" he asked.

Ruby smiled, "Getting ready for the plantation's spring planting and helping the slaves prepare for Market Day."

"Market Day?"

"Twice a year, after planting and harvest, *Tía* Luciana allowed the skilled artisans and craftsmen on the plantation to sell their wares at market in the town of Bahía, where many of the freed Africans and slaves settled," she explained, smiling at the memories.

"Readying for Market Day was as festive as Christmastime. Those going to market would be up for hours before departure putting finishing touches on their items to sell. There was furniture, clothing, quilts and toys. Carved wood, clay and stone sculptures, and intricate paintings done on mud cloths and if my aunt thought someone was particularly talented she would give them genuine artist's canvases and supplies."

"Oh and Seth if you could have seen my uncle Amir's flutes, *meu deus, bonito*," she said, excitedly reverting to her native Portuguese. "Such detail carved into such a small piece of wood."

Seth marveled at how beautiful she was in the glow of her excitement. There was no trace of the longing and loneliness he would usually see when she spoke of her family.

"Your aunt must have made a nice profit from what the slaves sold."

"Not at all. Everyone was encouraged to keep any profit made so that they would have money saved for when they were set free. My uncle Amir was the only one who didn't keep the money he made from selling his flutes. He would give it to my aunt for the plantation's orphans," she said with much pride.

"Your aunt freed her slaves?" Seth said in surprise.

"Yes, she was not an advocate of slavery. She tried, for many years, to convince her father to free his slaves and offer them wages for their manual labor but he refused. Once she inherited the plantation, she considered doing just as she tried to convince her father to do. Then she thought of another way that she could make more of a difference. In payment of at least two years of good service she offers her slaves the opportunity to learn a trade, save money and receive a basic education so that when the time came for them to live as freedmen they would have the necessary knowledge to survive."

"How does she manage a plantation if she frees her slaves?" Seth asked.

"With every slave she frees she purchases a new one and gives them the same choice. My aunt told me once that as much as she despised going to slave auctions and paying for human beings, she felt that it was worth it because every slave bought by her was another person saved from the hardships that most go through on other plantations."

"Your aunt sounds like an amazing woman," Seth said.

"She is that," Ruby said, smiling. "That's how I know she hasn't forgotten me and that I will see her again."

"How long do you think you'll stay before you head to Brazil?"

"It shouldn't take more than a year to save the money I need for ship passage."

A year, Seth thought. A year to show her how much he cared for her and hope that it would be enough. Standing, he pulls Ruby up with him. Lifting her into his arms, he carries her back to the bedroom, lays her on the bed and does what he wanted so much to do the previous night. He makes slow sweet love to her.

❧ NINE ❧

Caleb walked into the cottage to find it quiet with the fire in the fireplace almost burned out and no sign of his guests in the front room or kitchen. Thinking Seth must have moved Ruby to the bedroom where it would be more comfortable Caleb thought nothing of just walking in to see how she was doing, but stops short when he opens the door. Seth and Ruby lay wrapped in each other's arms sleeping peacefully beneath the blankets. Grinning, Caleb quietly backs out of the room and closes the door.

A few hours later Seth comes out to find Caleb sitting before the fire drinking a cup of coffee.

"Coffee's on the stove," Caleb tells him without turning around.

After getting a cup for himself, Seth joins him.

"How long have you been back?"

"Since late afternoon. I didn't wake you. Figured you two needed the rest so I went out and hunted some small game for supper."

Seth nodded, still gazing into the fire.

"I see our patient is doing much better," Caleb grinned.

"Yes, she is," Seth said, looking down into his cup of coffee, avoiding Caleb's gaze.

"Guess you'll be back on the road soon."

"In another day," Seth said, sounding a little sad. He dreaded leaving because of the possibility that he may never see Ruby again once they reached Philadelphia, but they had no choice.

"Any word in on the rest of the group?"

"No one's heard anything about a group being captured recently and you know word of a white conductor being caught would have spread down the line pretty quickly, so they more than likely made it through," Caleb told him. "You should know though, the reward on Ruby's capture has gone up to $800."

"Damn," Seth sighed heavily.

"Someone is real determined to get her back," Caleb said.

"Yeah, well, she's just as determined to get away."

"You know the road isn't going to be easy, don't you?" Caleb asked.

Seth knew he wasn't referring to the road to Philadelphia.

"I know, but I love her," Seth said sadly.

"I could see that the night you landed on my doorstep. You tell her that yet?"

"No, and I'm not going to. It wouldn't be fair to her. She's got something she needs to do and I don't want to be responsible for holding her back."

"You told me she's searching for her family, you think telling her how you feel will keep her from doing that?" Caleb asked doubtfully.

"No, my ego isn't that big," Seth said, chuckling. "I just don't want her to leave feeling as if she's obligated to me in any way."

"I think you're underestimating her strength."

"Maybe I'm overestimating my own," Seth said. "If I tell her how I feel, I'll only be setting myself up to be hurt."

"I believe, with all that the two of you have been through, you were brought together for a reason. If it's meant to be, you'll be together again."

"But at what cost?" Seth asked. "It would be unfair to ask her to stay and I can't go with her. It's ultimately her decision and I won't make her choose that way. Telling her I love her would be doing just that."

Both heard the bedroom door open and turned to see the subject of their conversation walk out dressed in her men's trousers and shirt.

"Caleb, you're back," she said with a smile.

Both men stood as she walked over and placed a kiss on Caleb's bearded cheek.

"You're looking good as new," Caleb commented.

"I had a very good care giver," she said, glancing at Seth.

"I see," Caleb said, grinning at his old friend. "Maybe I should have stayed away a little longer."

"I was just telling Caleb that we'll be leaving in another day," Seth said, changing the subject.

"Has there been any word of the others?" she asked in concern.

Caleb repeated to her what he told Seth, including the information about the reward for her.

Ruby shook her head sadly, "I had hoped Elizabeth would have given up by now."

"Once we reach Philadelphia it'll be more difficult for her to reach you. The city is populated with so many freedman and fugitives that you should have no problem losing yourself in the crowd," Seth tried to assure her.

"You think so?" She couldn't imagine that being true with such a high reward being offered.

Seth walked over to her. He couldn't stand to see the worried frown marring her beautiful face. "I guarantee I won't let anything happen to you," he said, gently brushing his knuckles along her cheek.

They gazed intensely at one another, saying with their eyes what neither could put into words.

Caleb cleared his throat loudly, "I guess I better go put supper on the stove."

"He knows about us, doesn't he?" Ruby asked as Caleb left the room.

"Yes. Does that bother you?"

"No. I trust him if you do."

"I'll go help in the kitchen. You sit down and relax," he said, brushing his lips lightly across hers.

"A woman could get used to all this pampering," she teased.

Seth chuckled, heading towards the sound of banging pots.

Alone, Ruby went over in her mind all that had taken place over the past few days. Caleb's little cottage had become a wonderful retreat for her and Seth, but soon reality would be crashing in on their secluded world. Although she was anxious to get back on the road so that they could meet up with the rest of their group, she also felt sadness over leaving the warmth and comfort of Seth's arms. After they left Caleb's home, they would no longer have the intimacy they shared during their short time here. Although she would not tell Seth, Ruby had admitted to herself this morning that she was in love with him, which was even more of a reason to put an end what they had begun. It would make it much harder for her to walk away when it came time for her to leave and she refused to even consider not continuing on to Brazil. She had to know, one way or the other, if she still had a family to go back to.

Sergipe, Brazil

"Rubina is in America."

Amir had barely walked through the door of Luciana's study before she made her announcement.

"America? You located her?" he asked, taking a seat in the chair before her desk.

"Not exactly. I found the ship that transported her there," she said.

"It's been over ten years, how did you find that information?" Amir asked.

"I made arrangements for our family attorney, Juan Pablo, to go through the logs of the ships that departed at the time of her disappearance. There were three transport ships that day that carried human cargo, all three were heading to America, and only one of them carried a child." Luciana said excitedly.

"And you verified this information?" Amir asked doubtfully.

"Yes. Do you think I would be foolish enough to take that as my only evidence?" she said in reprimand.

"Forgive me Luciana. I know how determined you have been to find Rubina, I want very much to find her also, I just don't want you to be led on a wild goose chase." Amir loved Luciana dearly but she was like a bulldog with a bone when she got her teeth into something and that something had been locating Rubina over the past 10 year.

"I know that you worry because you care but I have been a business woman longer than you have been alive, I'm quite capable of knowing when I am being taken for a fool," she told him. Every fiber of her being was telling her that their search for Rubina was coming to an end. She would not let anyone, including Amir, who was like a son to her, stop her from proceeding further with the information she had obtained.

"Now, as I was saying, the one ship carrying the child stopped in Atlanta, Georgia to drop off their human cargo."

"So will you be sending Juan Pablo there?"

"Yes, and we will be joining him," Luciana said with a grin.

Amir looked at her as if she had finally lost her mind in her determination to find her great-niece, "You can not be serious?"

"Very much so, so get your business affairs in order, we depart at week's end."

"Luciana, I have been to the American South. It is not the safest place to go announcing that you are looking for your niece who you believe is a slave," he said, hoping to sway her not to go.

"You have no faith, dear boy. Our Rubina will be home with us soon. I can feel it," she said confidently.

Philadelphia, Pennsylvania

With Caleb's assistance, Ruby and Seth arrived safely in Philadelphia less than a week after their departure from Greenwich, New Jersey, where Caleb lived. He brought them in his wagon knowing three Black men in a wagon full of supplies on the main road, would less likely be questioned by patrolman or catchers than two men on foot in the woods. In case they were stopped and questioned, Seth and Caleb carried their

Certificates of Freedom as proof of their freedmen status and had obtained a forged copy for Ruby from a "friend" in town before they started on the road.

Greenwich had originally been settled by Quakers who, in later years, sold small tracts of the land to free Blacks. The town was not only an important center of support and employment during the freedom seekers transition from slave to free person, but also a way station for freedom seekers crossing the Delaware on their way to New York and Pennsylvania. There were many friends of the Railroad there who housed and assisted fugitives, including one resident who was very good at forging certificates of freedom but only as a last resort. Seth and Caleb felt, in Ruby's case, it was a last resort.

When they arrived in Philadelphia, the principal center in the East for the Underground Railroad, the streets were busy with the hustle and bustle of it's morning residents heading home from church or running errands. Ruby looked around at all of the many hued Blacks strolling freely alongside Whites. Many dressed as well as the Whites they socialized with.

"Are all these people free?" she asked Seth in awe.

"Yep, every one of them. Some were once freedom seekers like you while others, like me, were born free," Seth said, smiling at her wide-eyed gaze.

"This is it," Seth said as Caleb brought the wagon to a stop in front of the Lebanon Seminary, "our final stop, home of the Philadelphia Vigilance Committee."

"What is the Philadelphia Vigilance Committee?" Ruby asked.

"They're like a welcome committee for fugitives when they arrive in the city. They provide them with clothing, money, transportation and for those moving on to Canada, a place to stay before the difficult crossing from upper New York to Canada. It's also the main office most of the conductors work out of," Seth explained.

"I had no idea the abolitionist movement was so organized," Ruby said in amazement.

"Many people south of the Mason Dixon line don't realize how strong and organized we truly are," Caleb said. "They believe the movement is run by either extremist like John Brown or pacifist groups like the Quakers, but the movement is far more than that. Just like the real railroad, it's a well oiled machine that reaches from Mississippi up into Canada and has more conductors and stations than anyone could imagine."

Ruby heard the pride in Caleb's voice and felt it herself. It was truly amazing what could happen when such a great many people worked together for something good. But as proud as she was of the Underground Railroad's work, she also prayed for the day when they wouldn't need such an incredible network.

After Caleb found a space for the wagon, he and Ruby followed Seth into the building to a staircase off to the side of the entrance. At the top of the stairs was an office where a Colored man sitting behind a desk looked up from a log book as they entered. His face lit up in a broad smile as his gaze set on Seth.

"Seth Grant," he stood, "You are a sight for sore eyes," he said coming from behind the desk and grasping Seth's hand.

"Will, how are you?" Seth said, shaking the other man's hand.

"I'm fine. You're the ones everyone is concerned about. Have you been down to the rectory yet?"

"No, we came straight to the office."

The man nodded and peered around Seth, smiling at Ruby.

"Miss Elder," he said, walking over and taking both her hands in his. "It's good to finally meet you."

"You know who I am?" she asked in confusion.

"Yes, I'm William Casey and you're well-known to the committee. We haven't seen the amount on a fugitive slave reward rise so quickly since Harriet Tubman came to us," he said, chuckling.

"I see," Ruby said, wondering if the price on her head would hinder her ability to find work.

William greeted Caleb, whom he'd also known for many years, then turned back to Seth.

"I'll fill you in on what's happened over the past few days as we go down to the rectory," he told Seth.

"Nicholas arrived over a week ago with the rest of your group and they have been anxiously awaiting your arrival ever since," William explained.

"Are they all alright?" Ruby asked as they reached the bottom of the staircase, heading toward the double doors leading to the rectory.

"They're all doing well, although they have been back here everyday, hoping for some word on your whereabouts. I was hard pressed to get them to leave at all when they arrived but Nicholas and I convinced them that it was best to get them settled as quickly as possible," he told them.

Seth hadn't realized just how worried he had been about the welfare of the rest of their group until he heard William's words. His whole body seemed to sigh heavily with relief. Ruby must have felt the same way because she reached back and grasped his hand tightly as William opened the doors to the other room. Seth responded with a gentle squeeze of her hand, moving up to stand beside her. As they walked through the double doors the group, kneeling in prayer at the front of the room, turned in unison. All was quiet for a moment until a squeal rose up and Esther ran down the aisle towards them. Ruby let go of Seth's hand and met her friend half the way. Tears were streaming down their faces as the two women flew into each other's arms.

"I knew if we prayed long and hard enough, the Lord would hear us and bring you two safely home," Esther said, holding Ruby tightly.

It was only moments before the men joined them, hugging and slapping one another on the back in greeting. Afterwards they all sat in the pews catching up on what happened during their separation. When Seth explained about their delay due to Ruby's illness and their having to stay on a Caleb's longer than expected due to the storm, she pointedly kept her gaze from his.

She didn't want anyone to see her blush at the memories of what he didn't tell them about their time alone. When Ruby looked up, her gaze met Esther's who was looking at her curiously.

Their conversation soon turned to what everyone had decided to do now that they had reached the Promised Land, as the North was called. They were all staying on in Philadelphia with Bishop working at Grant Blacksmith. And to Ruby's delight he had asked Esther to marry him and she had happily accepted. Isaac, with Nicholas and Thomas' encouragement, had decided to attend the Institute for Colored Youth to get a formal education in order to be become a teacher. It's the same higher education institute he, Seth and Caleb attended. They were all happy with their decision and excited to begin their new lives as free people.

"What about you Ruby?" Isaac asked. "Do you know what you want to do?"

She once again avoided meeting Seth's gaze. "I've been told that they are desperately looking for teachers for the Colored schools, so I've decided to take the teacher's exam."

"Excellent idea," William Casey said. "We could really use more bright and young folks such as yourself and Isaac educating our children. I have a contact that can get you set up for the testing within a few days if you like."

"Thank you, I would appreciate that. Could you also tell me if there is a boarding house nearby that I can stay?" Ruby asked.

"You won't need a boarding house," Thomas answered. "There's a room waiting for you at our mother's home," he said grinning.

"Momma is taking her in?" Seth asked in surprise.

"Well, since I knew Ruby was interested in teaching I told momma that she would be perfect for the school the Free Women's Committee is starting up."

Ruby knew Seth lived in that same house and that living together would not make it easier for them to keep their distance.

"Thomas, please thank your mother for me but I couldn't possibly inconvenience her that way. I'll be fine in a boarding house," Ruby said, hoping she didn't sound ungrateful for the offer.

Thomas chuckled, "You don't know our mother. Once she makes a decision about something she won't take 'no' for an answer."

"Of course, after you have some of her down home cooking tonight you won't want to leave. She made me promise to send word as soon as you all arrived so that she could make dinner for us."

Seth looked at his brother not knowing whether to thank him or wring his neck. Thomas had saved him from trying to figure out how to convince Ruby to stay but he had also put Seth and Ruby in a situation where they couldn't help but see each other everyday.

Ruby decided that if she made a big fuss about the living arrangements it would make everyone suspicious of what was going on between her and Seth.

"I would like to at least look more presentable when I meet her;" Ruby said looking down at her men's attire. "Is there a mercantile nearby where I can purchase a few things?" she asked.

"I'll take you," Esther offered. "It's not too far from here then you can come back to our house and change before dinner."

"Thank you. It'll be good to get out of these clothes," Ruby said, smiling. As convenient as it was to travel without worrying about skirts tangling in the brush or having to hike them up to run, she missed looking feminine.

"Well we better head on home Seth. Momma's been worried about you and she'll want to see for herself that you're alright," Thomas said.

Seth was relieved that Ruby wouldn't be going home with them right away. It would give him time to deal with the fact that they would be living under the same roof for an undetermined amount of time. Something Seth wasn't sure was a good idea under the circumstances but he knew there was no way of changing his mother's mind without telling her everything about his and Ruby's relationship.

A couple of hours later, parcels in hand, Ruby walked with Esther to her and Bishops home a few blocks away. With the Vigilance Committee's assistance, they were able to rent a small house in town, with Nicholas being kind enough to cover the first two months rent.

"I'm so happy for you and Bishop," Ruby told her friend.

"I never thought I would make it this far," Esther said, "let alone find a man to love me and my son along the way. I still can't believe I'm getting married," she said excitedly.

"Well, it's obvious he adores you and Jessie," Ruby said.

"What about you Ruby? Does Seth adore you?" Esther asked.

Ruby stopped mid stride, looking at Esther in surprise.

"How did you know?" she asked, not thinking to deny the truth. She and Esther had come too far together for Ruby to start lying to her friend.

Esther chuckled, looping her arm through Ruby's and pulling her back into step. "It's all in your face. I could tell the moment you two walked into the rectory that something had changed between you and it wasn't because you walked in holding hands. There's softness in your face and eyes when you look at one another."

"Is it that obvious?" Ruby asked, wondering if the others saw it also.

"To another woman it is. Men don't pay that much attention to notice," Esther said, smiling. "He's a good man, Ruby. Don't let him get away."

"Him getting away is not the problem. Me leaving is," Ruby admitted.

"Leaving? But I thought you were staying. Becoming a teacher," Esther said in confusion.

Ruby told Esther of her plans and that she didn't have time for love and marriage right at this time in her life.

Esther chuckled, "There's always time for love, Ruby."

"Maybe," Ruby said, shrugging her shoulders, "but there's no time for the life that comes along with it."

"You know, I believe God gifts us with things that he feels will make our lives complete. We just have to know when to recognize what or who that is and accept it for the blessing that it is," Esther said wisely, "I think he did that with me and Bishop and he's doing it with you and Seth."

"Well, I believe that if it was meant to be for Seth and I, then it will be. If so, no matter what the obstacles, we will find our way back to each other," Ruby countered.

The two women smiled at one another and agreed to disagree. They decided that Esther's wedding plans were a safer subject as they made their way down the busy street. When they reached the two-story townhouse, Ruby was impressed. It was small with two bedrooms, a small water closet upstairs and a sitting room and kitchen downstairs, but it was in good condition and modestly but comfortably furnished.

"Esther its lovely," Ruby said as they entered the foyer.

"I was so surprised the first time I walked in that I thought they'd made a mistake and brought us to the wrong house," Esther said, chuckling.

"When they told me it was the right one, I stood here balling my eyes out. I'd never lived in anything but a one-room shack in the slave quarters my entire life and never believed I would be living in house like this."

Bishop and Isaac, who was staying there until he registered for school, were in the sitting room. Jessie was upstairs taking his nap.

"Looks like you two found everything you needed," Bishop said grinning at the brown wrapped parcels tied with string in the women's arms.

"I did, but these are not all for me," Ruby said untying four of the parcels and handing each of her friends all but the fourth which was for Jessie.

"What's this?" Isaac asked.

"Open it." Ruby told them.

Esther looked at her curiously. She knew about the men's gifts but not about one for herself. She opened her wrapped parcel, removing a white lace and flower embroidered blouse and a simple deep blue skirt.

"I thought you bought this for yourself," Esther said, tears pooling in her eyes.

"I saw how much you liked it so I asked the store clerk for a smaller size while you were browsing."

"Thank you," Esther said giving Ruby a warm hug.

The men quickly opened theirs curious to see what their packages held. Within the brown paper lay crisp, white cotton shirts.

"Ruby, you didn't have to do this, but thank you," Isaac said placing a kiss on her cheek.

"Thank you," Bishop said, taking her up in a bear hug that took her breath away.

"You all are the closest thing to a family that I've had in a very long time. If I can't share what I have with my family, then there's no point in having it," she told them.

They all thanked her again, sincerely appreciating Ruby's kindness, knowing that they found a lifetime of friendship among their group.

When Seth arrived to pick them up they were all smiling and laughing, happier than they could remember ever being and enjoying their freedom and their friendship without the watchful eyes of a master. Seth enjoyed the joyous sound but only had eyes for one person, her beauty taking his breathe away.

Like the others, Ruby was laughing at something Esther's son Jessie said, her smile lighting up her features. Her shortened hair curled softly around her face, framing it in a pixie-like fashion. She wore small, delicate ivory earrings and a beautiful ivory cameo broach at the throat of her white blouse which was trimmed in lace at the collar and on either side of the buttoned front, and a soft, velvet black skirt that fit perfectly over her shapely hips. Seeing her dressed so simply, yet so elegantly, and walking towards him with such style and grace, no one could deny that she was born into a life of privilege.

It broke Seth's heart to realize how different Ruby was from all of them, a fact he had tried so hard to deny. There was no chance that she would settle for the quiet modest, life he could offer her with the possibility of going back to the life of comfort and wealth she had before becoming a slave.

Seth's smile was bittersweet when Ruby stood before him.

"You look beautiful," he told her.

"Thank you. Although I think I'm a bit overdressed but after weeks of wearing men's clothing, I needed to feel overly feminine this evening," she said. "You're looking rather fine yourself," she said with an appreciative smile.

Seth wore a pair of black trousers, a crisp white shirt open at the collar, and a gray jacket. He smelled of soap, sandalwood and leather, a combination that gave Ruby tingles of pleasure throughout her body.

"Thank you. You know," Seth said gazing at her intently, "there's something I've wanted to do all day."

"What's that?" Ruby asked. Her heart beat rapidly in her chest at his passionate gaze.

Not caring that the others stood just behind her, Seth took Ruby's face in his hands, and proceeded to kiss her in front of anyone who cared to look. He had missed the feel of her soft lips molding themselves to his. A thrill of excitement soared through him as she responded in kind.

Esther and Bishop grinned knowingly. Isaac looked on in disappointment. He had hopes of wooing her himself. The kiss was short but effective. If it wasn't known before, their friends knew now that Ruby and Seth had more than just a shared journey on the Railroad between them.

"Shall we go?" he asked, grinning at Ruby after their kiss ended.

"I think so. We've already put on enough of a show for everyone," she said, chuckling, not the least bit embarrassed.

Seth took the wrap Ruby held in her hand and lay it across her shoulders, then placed her arm through the crook of his as he led the way to the wagon waiting out front. Ruby enjoyed the attention he was paying her. She had never been treated in such a gentlemanly manner before.

As they rode through the heart of the city to the neighborhoods lying on the outskirts of town Ruby noticed the homes weren't much different than the ones of the wealthy Whites in Atlanta, except that Colored people owned them as well, including Seth and his mother.

When they arrived at the Grant home, they entered a large, high-ceilinged foyer with a beautifully carved wood staircase to the right of the entrance that led up to a second landing which overlooked the foyer. To the left of the entryway was a sitting room, its French doors opened invitingly with a fire in the hearth to take the chill out of the early spring air. Another set of French doors opened off of the sitting room, leading to the dining room. Just down the hall from the main entrance was the kitchen where delicious aromas drifted toward the group. They all laughed out loud as Bishop's stomach growled loudly in response.

"Seth, is that you son?" a voice called from the kitchen.

"Yes ma'am and I have some hungry folks with me."

"Well, take them into the sitting room to warm up. I'll bring in a little something to hold them over till dinner is ready."

Seth led Ruby and the others into the sitting room. A few moments later Thomas arrived with his family, his wife Jenny and his son Thomas Jr., who was already best of friends with little Jessie. The two toddled off to a corner of the room where Thomas Jr.'s grandmother kept a trunk of toys for his frequent visits.

The group was full of laughter and lively conversation. It was the first time they were able to truly relax and enjoy each other's company as not only traveling companions, but also close friends.

Ruby sat beside Seth on a love seat, basking in the glow of his open affection towards her. Her hands had been folded in her lap when he reached over and took one of them in his, placing their grasped hands on his knee as they talked. When their gazes met, the message in them was very clear, right here, right now, was all that mattered. They would deal with the rest one day at a time.

"I see you all started the party without me," an older woman said as she entered the room carrying a tray.

"Now momma, you know there's no party if you're not here," Thomas said, placing a kiss on his mother's forehead as he took the tray from her.

When Seth and Thomas spoke of their mother, Ruby had the impression that she would be one of those strong, large, women she'd seen many times in the marketplace balancing baskets on their heads and making their own path as they moved commandingly along the rows of vendors, but that couldn't have been farther from the truth.

Abigail Grant was a slim, petite woman, no taller than five feet, if that, with salt and pepper gray hair secured in a neat bun atop her head. Her facial features were softly defined with laughter creases at the corners of her eyes and mouth. Ruby couldn't imagine this sweetly demure looking woman being the tough as nails mother her sons had described.

"Before you tear into my Johnny cakes there, I want to say a quick prayer, if you all don't mind," Abigail said.

They all stood, grasping each other's hands and bowing their heads.

"Dear Lord," Abigail began, "I want to thank you for the safe passage of these children on the road to freedom. Please continue to keep them safe within your loving embrace. In your heavenly name we pray, Amen." An echo of hearty "amen" circled around the room.

Still grasping her hand, Seth brought Ruby forward, "Momma, this is Ruby."

Ruby offered her hand in greeting to the older woman, "Mrs. Grant, it's so nice to finally meet you. I have heard so much about you from your sons."

"You can call me Abby," she said, taking Ruby's hand. "And I can see what Thomas said about you is true. I can tell just by your speech that you're educated. He also said you would be perfect for the school we're starting up, is that true?"

"Perfect is a strong word. I believe I have a lot that I can teach as well as learn," Ruby said, modestly.

"Well then, he was right. You'd be perfect," Abigail said with a nod and determined gleam in her eyes.

A few hours later, Ruby stood alone in the foyer with Seth after having said goodnight to their friends.

"I'll show you your room," he said, picking up the small valise she had brought with her.

She smiled, following him up the stairs to a room at the end of the hall. It was large and airy with a four poster bed that was twice the size of the one she had slept in before escaping. There was also a writing desk that sat beneath the window and a vanity table near the bed. The room was neither feminine nor masculine, but was tastefully decorated with blue and white curtains and bedding and simple wood furnishings.

"This used to be Thomas' room," Seth explained.

"I like it. It's very open and comfortable," she said.

He nodded, "I'll let you get settled in. My room is right next door and my mother's is at the other end of the hall. Don't hesitate to come to us if you need anything."

"Thank you, Seth. Not just for welcoming me into your home but also for taking me on board when you had your doubts and staying with me when I had to separate from the others. I owe you so much," Ruby said.

Seth brushed his knuckles softly across her cheek, "You don't owe me anything. You would have made it with or without me. You're too strong and determined not to."

"You mean I'm too stubborn," Ruby said, smiling.

Seth chuckled, "Well, that too."

They stood for a moment longer gazing at one another, neither wanting to say goodnight.

"If I don't leave now," he said, slowly stepping away from her, "I won't leave at all."

"I understand," she said, her heart skipping a beat at the thought of what would happen if he stayed.

"I have to return the wagon to the livery. I'll see you at breakfast."

"Alright."

Just as Seth reached for the doorknob he stopped, "Aw hell," he exclaimed.

He took three quick strides back to Ruby, took her in his arms, kissed her soundly but passionately on the lips, then just as quickly turned and left the room.

Ruby stood dazedly gazing at the door wishing they were still at Caleb's cottage. She sighed heavily and then went about putting her few belongings away in the dresser. Just as she was finishing up there was a light knock. Looking up from her task she saw Abigail standing in the open doorway.

"Miss Abby, thank you so much for your hospitality."

"You're more than welcome child. I did it more for myself than anybody else. It'll be nice to have another woman in the house," she said, placing a bowl of fresh yellow daisies on the dressing table.

"Figure these will brighten the room up some."

"Thank you, again. The room and the flowers are lovely. Far more than I expected," Ruby said gratefully.

Abigail sat in the chair by the vanity, "Come, sit down and tell me about yourself," she said.

Ruby sat across from her on a trunk at the foot of the bed. "There isn't much to tell. I was purchased by a well to do family in Atlanta as a child to be their daughter's companion and maid. Once we grew up she married and I became her housekeeper. I wasn't happy and was given the opportunity to escape when I met your son and here I am," she said casually.

"Mmhm, now tell me the real story," Abigail said with a grin.

Ruby wanted as little people as possible to know her background, but Abigail Grant had opened her home up to her without even knowing who she was and was ready to give her a job on her son's word that she was qualified. The least she could do was be honest. So she told the older woman everything about her life before and after being brought to America. The only part she left out was her and Seth's relationship. She wasn't sure herself where they were headed.

Abigail sat quietly listening to Ruby's story. She liked the young woman. Ruby reminded her of herself when she was her age, headstrong, independent and straightforward. Abigail thought she would make a good wife for Seth. From what she had seen during and after dinner, it was obvious her son was more than taken with Ruby. She hadn't seen him look at a woman the way he looked at Ruby since Olivia Wallace.

"So you're going to go look for your family?" Abigail asked when Ruby was finished.

Ruby nodded in response.

"That's good. If I could have gone back for my family I would've, but times were much more dangerous back then. Harriet Tubman, the Vigilance Committee and their Friends weren't around to guide our way. We depended on God and the stars to show us the way to freedom and keep us safe during our journey," Abigail said.

"I truly admire your courage Miss Abby, I don't know if I would have been able to finish the journey if it hadn't been for Seth."

"Oh, I think you would've done fine child. You're a lot stronger than you think," Abigail said knowingly.

Ruby smiled, "Seth said the same thing."

"Of course he did, he's my son so he's got at least some sense," Abigail said with a grin.

"Speaking of my son, does he know you'll be leaving again?"

"Yes, he does," she said with a frown, sad over the thought of having to leave Seth.

"Have you told him you love him yet?"

First Esther now Abigail, Ruby was beginning to think she wasn't doing a very good job of hiding her feelings for Seth.

"No ma'am, I haven't. It will only make it harder for me to do what I have to do," she explained.

"Maybe. You'll never know unless you do it. You don't know if you're family will accept you again, but you're willing to chance everything to find out. If you tell Seth how you feel about him you may not only find out he feels the same way but that he may do whatever it takes to make you happy, even if it means letting you go."

Abigail's wise words made sense to Ruby but she was still doubtful that revealing her feelings to Seth was a good idea.

"Ruby, I love my son. Seth's my oldest and because of that he's always going to hold a special place in my heart, and as much as I wouldn't want to see him get his heart broken, I believe your search is necessary. You can't give all you need to give to him if your past is holding you back. I also think Seth is strong enough to handle it."

"But am I strong enough?" Ruby said with a sad smile.

"That's something you need to work through," Abigail said with an encouraging smile of her own.

"Well, it's been a long, busy day and I'm ready to turn in," Abigail said, standing to leave.

Ruby nodded in agreement and walked the older woman to the door.

"You can come to me anytime if you ever need to talk," She told Ruby.

Ruby placed an affectionate kiss on Abigail's cheek, "Thank you."

"My pleasure," Abigail said, patting Ruby's cheek.

After they said goodnight, Ruby closed the door, leaning up against it with a heavy sigh. Over the past months she had found close friendships and love. She didn't know how she would find the strength to walk away from either.

❧ TEN ❧
Atlanta, Georgia

Luciana stood in the marketplace appalled at what she was witnessing. Children being torn from their mother's arms for the highest bidders, people being packed in cages like animals, most sickly and barely clothed, others beaten when they fought against the chains that bind them. It was the same scene at every slave market she had been to, but what made it even more heartbreaking was the acceptance in many of their expressions. They were third and fourth generations who had come to accept their life of slavery as if they weren't meant to do anything else.

Luciana inhaled the stench of sweat, sickness and fear that wafted over on the afternoon breeze from the slave pens. This was the world Marie had sold her own grandchild into, without caring for anything but her own need for revenge. Luciana's anger at her sister knew no bounds. Marie had finally done the unforgivable.

"If my sister is still alive when we return home I just may kill her," Luciana told Amir angrily.

"I won't stop you," he told her looking on at the scene before them in sadness. These were the children of his people. Their ancestors must be turning in their graves over what has happened to their country men. It had been many years since he himself had been on the block but he remembered it vividly. He and Ifé had been fortunate that Luciana had been the one to purchase them that day. But even then, the slaves on the block didn't have the hollow and complacent looks of these American slaves.

"Come," Luciana said, bringing him out of his reverie. "I see young Juan Pablo searching for us."

Luciana and Amir made their way through the crowded street toward a young man gazing through the crowd. He was the son of Juan Pablo de Santos Sr. and the third in line to handle the de Souza and Dominguez, families' legal matters. It wasn't long before the young man spotted them considering the striking pair Luciana and Amir made.

Luciana's tall frame was simply and elegantly dressed in a light grey riding suit with a white silk shirt ruffled at the collar and cuffs and a jaunty riding hat perched atop her salt and pepper gray hair that she wore in her signature braided and entwined bun.

Amir was dressed just as well as the rich planters strolling around the market place in his fawn colored riding breeches, chocolate brown polished leather boots and riding jacket, crisp white shirt and ascot at his neck. His manner of dress would not have mattered had he been home in Brazil, but he was in the American South where it was not common to find a man of his skin color dressed just as well, if not better, than a White man.

While Luciana received admiring glances for her deep honeyed complexion and earthy beauty, glances Amir's way were angry, if not downright hostile. His appearance, speech and status as a wealthy businessman may have gotten him respect at home, Europe and the various other countries he visited but it had no affect on the people here. They just saw his dark complexion and considered him an "uppity nigger", something he had been called many times since their arrival.

"Juan Pablo, what do you have for me?" Luciana asked as they met up with the young attorney.

"I may have found some information that is too much of a coincidence not to be connected to our search," he said, handing her the most recent posting for Ruby's capture.

This one offered a $1,000 reward and had a sketch of Ruby at the bottom. Luciana read the description and looked at the picture with a gasp. She turned towards Amir and handed the paper to him.

"Do you see it, Amir? Do you see the likeness?" she said excitedly. She had no doubt that their search was finally coming to an end.

Amir saw it and wanted very much to believe the same as Luciana but they had been disappointed too many times in the past. "I see a woman who is a very good likeness to Ifé," he said.

"Amir, you cannot be serious," Luciana said in frustration. "The age, the description, the picture and her name is Ruby. You cannot doubt that is our Rubina."

She took the paper from him and read it again, "This says to contact John Elder with information on the girl's whereabouts. We must locate this Mr. Elder."

"I've already taken the liberty of doing so," Juan Pablo said proudly. "His office is not far from here."

"You are your father's son, efficient as always. Lead the way my dear boy," Luciana said, excitement running through her veins.

They reached the Law Offices of John R. Elder, Esq. within moments and were taken directly to his office after telling the clerk that they had information on Ruby. John stood upon their entrance, offering them seats in front of his desk.

"Your servant may wait out in the front room if you prefer," he said, directing his gaze at Amir.

"Amir is not my servant, Mr. Elder, he is my nephew," Luciana informed him as they took their seats.

John remained standing for a moment looking curiously at the trio.

"Forgive me Miss..."

"Luciana de Souza and there is nothing to forgive," she said with a dismissive wave of her hand. "It's not surprising you would make that assumption with you being a Southern gentleman."

John grinned, at the backhanded insult and took his seat.

"My clerk said you have information on my escaped slave."

"I may," Luciana said, "but before I give you my information, I would like to ask you a few questions, if you do not mind."

John gazed at Luciana wondering what would these obviously wealthy foreigners have to do with Ruby? He considered telling them he wasn't interested in answering any of their questions but curiosity got the better of him. He sat back in his chair, steepling his fingers under his chin.

"Alright," he said.

"We are also looking for someone and believe your Ruby may be able to help us locate her."

"Well, Miss de Souza, as I'm sure you must know, Ruby is not here so I'm not sure how she will be able to assist you."

"I'm sure any information you can provide us about her will be enough," Luciana said. "How long ago did you purchase Ruby?"

"A little over ten years ago."

Luciana nodded, "Was there anything unusual about her?"

"No. She was alone, had no family being sold along with her."

"What I'm asking is, Mr. Elder, was she just like your average child born into slavery? Was there nothing different about her?"

John leaned forward, suddenly suspicious of why these people were here, "Miss de Souza, why are you asking questions about my slave when you have supposedly come to me with information about her?"

Luciana was a shrewd businesswoman. She knew when a deal was ready to be closed. She had hit on something with that question and it was time to lay the money on the table.

"One last question, Mr. Elder, truly," Luciana said.

"One question Madame, that is it, and then I will insist on some answers of my own," John said impatiently.

"Agreed," Luciana said. "Did your Ruby ever mention having another name, such as Rubina Arinzé Domingues?"

"How did you..." surprise registered on John's face and his question hung unfinished in the air as he began connecting what he thought was fiction about Ruby's past to facts of what he did know about her.

She had been very bright for a child her age, let alone a child born into slavery. He remembered hearing her singing while going about her duties, but what made it so unusual was that it had been in at least three different languages and for many years she had spoken with the same lilting accent as the woman before him. Realization suddenly set in and John wasn't sure what to think.

"You're her family from Brazil, aren't you?" he asked in disbelief.

Although, Luciana remained outwardly calm her heart beat rapidly in her chest with excitement. He had just confirmed what she already knew was true.

"If you're Ruby and my Rubina are one in the same, which I believe they are, then yes, we are her family," Luciana said, reaching into her purse. She slid a photograph across the desk toward John.

"This portrait was taken just a month before Rubina's parents' death and her own disappearance," she told him.

John hesitated a moment before picking up the photograph. He didn't need to see it to know that Ruby's stories had not been those of a very creative imagination, the people sitting before him was proof of that, but he forced himself to look at it anyway. There she was, Ruby, smiling brightly and happier than he had ever seen her. She sat on the lap of a handsome, distinguished looking gentleman who bared a strong resemblance to the woman sitting across from him. The gentleman held the hand of a woman standing behind them, a dark beauty with broad African features and a regal stance. Ruby seemed to have taken on the best features of both parents, something that made her a true, natural beauty.

"Yes, this is Ruby," John said, knowing he could no longer deny the truth.

He handed the photograph back to Luciana who could no longer hold back her emotions. Tears sparkled in her eyes and threatened to slip down her long dark lashes. It tore at John's heart to see such an obviously strong women show such tender emotion.

"Is there anything you can tell us that would help us to locate her?" she asked.

"All I know is that she ran away from my daughter's home several months ago.   Elizabeth has been heartbroken ever since," he said sadly. "We gave Ruby a good life, far better than most slaves dream of. She wanted for nothing," he said, hoping to reassure his visitors that Ruby had been treated well during her time with his family.

"Except her freedom," Amir said, speaking for the first time since their arrival. "She would not have run if she was happy with being a slave." His joy at finally finding a genuine clue to Rubina's whereabouts was overshadowed by frustration over the fact that as close as they had come to locating her, she was once again out of their grasp.

"I can't argue that," John said sadly. "I wanted to give Ruby her freedom as we had promised her but my daughter changed her mind when she realized how, after all these years, determined Ruby was to find her family. I'm ashamed to say we spoiled Elizabeth and, as a result, she has become a very selfish woman."

"You mean to tell us that you led her to believe she would be free then took that from her because of your daughter's selfishness?" Luciana asked in disbelief.

"You have to understand Miss de Souza, slavery is a way of life here. If we freed every slave that wanted it we would have no laborers to keep our economy going," he explained, as if it should have been perfectly logical to her.

"No, you would have no *free* laborers. You would have to pay them, treat them fairly, and treat them like humans beings instead of cattle to use at your whim," Luciana said angrily.

"How dare you think you can come and criticize our way of life when, from what I recall of Ruby's stories, you yourself have slaves. That her mother had even been one of your slaves," John said defensively.

Luciana sat forward in her chair, "That is true but the difference between my slaves and yours, Mr. Elder, is that my slaves are bound to me for no more than two years, are taught a trade and then are set free with a stipend in order for them to live productive, independent lives, bound to no one but themselves. The ones that choose to stay are given pay in addition to a roof over their head, food and clothing for themselves and their families and the opportunity to collect their papers and leave at any time."

The two stared at one another for a moment until Luciana sighed heavily and sat back in her seat backing down from any further challenge.

"Mr. Elder, I did not come here to criticize your lifestyle, I came to find my great-niece. If I have offended you in any way then I apologize. I can tell, by what you have told me, that Rubina was treated well. I thank you for that," Luciana said sincerely.

John's defensive demeanor slipped away as he also sat tiredly back in his chair, "I must also apologize for my rudeness. I'm concerned about my daughter. She is having my first grandchild soon and this obsession she has with finding Ruby is not good for her. If she could see that Ruby is safe and happy, I think it would finally put an end to all of this."

"Would it be possible to speak with your daughter?" Luciana asked. "She may be able to tell us something that would assist in our search."

"I think that would be a good idea. Meeting you may help her to realize that Ruby has not been chasing a fantasy," he said.

A short time later Luciana sat before Elizabeth. She had suggested Amir and Juan Pablo stay out front in the carriage so as not to intimidate the young woman.

"Father, what is so important that you had to rush over here in the middle of the afternoon?' Elizabeth asked, giving Luciana a curious glance.

John was sitting beside his daughter and took her hand in his, "Sweetling, I have some interesting news," he said, trying to find an easy way to tell her about Luciana.

"You haven't called me that nickname since I was a child, what's wrong?" Elizabeth asked worriedly.

"There's nothing wrong. Actually it's quite amazing," he said with an encouraging smile. "Remember those stories Ruby used to tell us about her family and life before she came to us?"

"Yes."

"Well, it looks as if they were true. This woman is Ruby's aunt and she has come all the way from Brazil to find her," he told her.

Elizabeth looked from her father to Luciana and laughed out loud, "Father, if this is one of your schemes to get me to call off the search for Ruby, then it's a very bad one."

"This is not a scheme, Elizabeth. This is Miss Luciana de Souza, Ruby's great aunt."

"I don't believe it. If you're not up to something then obviously this woman is," she said accusingly.

"I assure you, Mrs. Englund, I am not up to anything except finding Rubina," Luciana said calmly.

Elizabeth gazed intently at Luciana at the sound of Ruby's birth name, "You have obviously made a mistake. I don't know anyone named Rubina."

"There is no mistake," Luciana said handing her the photograph of Ruby and her parents.

Elizabeth gazed at the photograph sadly, "She looks so happy," she said quietly, then realizing she had spoken her thought out loud, looked angrily at Luciana.

"Nothing we did for or gave to her was enough. She just wouldn't be satisfied with the life she had here," she said bitterly.

"As my nephew mentioned to your father earlier, you did not give her the one thing she asked for. Her freedom," Luciana said.

"Freedom? Freedom to do what?" Elizabeth spat. "To follow scores of Coloreds escaping north to some imaginary

Promised Land only to end up poor and hungry or doing the same work they were doing here? Freedom to turn your back on a friend that needs her so that she could go run off to a family where her own grandmother cared so little for her that she sold her into slavery? What kind of freedom is that?"

So, Rubina did know it was her grandmother who had betrayed her, Luciana thought. She could only imagine what her niece must have been thinking when she found that out.

"It's the best kind Mrs. Englund. It's the same freedom you and I experience everyday, the freedom to choose how you want to live your life. Rubina did not choose to have her parents die, she did not choose to have a cruel bitter woman for a grandmother and she never chose to become a slave," Luciana said.

"Until the day she was taken from the only home and life she had ever known, she had the same rights and privileges that you have had your entire life. Imagine all of what happened to her happening to you. Imagine, for just one moment, that you are Rubina and tell me you would not run the first chance you had. Stop being the selfish, spoiled child for once and imagine yourself in her place," Luciana said, not meaning to sound cruel but knowing that there was no other way to get through to Elizabeth.

Elizabeth's face turned a mottled red, "How dare you come into my house and speak to me that way."

"How dare you dangle freedom before my niece like a piece of candy then snatch it away when you realize it's not what *you* want her to have. Rubina comes from a strong and determined people. She would have run sooner or later. You would not have been able to hold her forever."

Luciana leaned toward Elizabeth, looking directly into the younger woman's eyes, not holding anything back so that she could see the pain and desperation there.

"Rubina's mother and father meant the world to me. It was heartbreaking losing them so suddenly, but the pain was bearable because I still had my little *querido* until she was cruelly taken from us just a few short weeks later," Luciana said sadly.

"I've spent years and a fortune searching for her and now I sit before you doing something I have never done my entire life, beg. I'm begging you to please help us find her. I'm asking you to not do as her grandmother did, to let bitterness and anger rule you. Help me to find not only my niece but your friend," Luciana pleaded.

"She was my friend," Elizabeth admitted tearfully, "my closest and dearest friend. None of my peers could understand that. They would tease me about being so close to my slave. They would say that it wasn't normal for a White person to want to spend so much time with a Colored. But Ruby understood me, as if she were another part of me, the brave, outspoken and unselfish part of me. I felt whole with her by my side," she said, accepting the handkerchief her father offered and wiping the tears flowing down her face.

"I have done her such an injustice," Elizabeth said, sighing heavily.

"You can right what you have done," Luciana said.

"How? If I knew where she was, she would be here now."

"Call off your search," Luciana suggested. "She's not safe as long as you have that price on her head. If she has traveled through this underground network I have heard about then it will not be easy getting information if it looks as if we are out to get a reward."

Elizabeth nodded in agreement, "Father, will you take care of it?"

"Yes, but it will be difficult. I'm sure word of the reward has spread quickly and with the Fugitive Slave Laws being enforced, many may try and capture her anyway for the amount you're offering," John said.

"I have one other request," Luciana said to Elizabeth.

"Anything, I just want this to be over," Elizabeth said tiredly.

"Free her."

"Free her? Why? What difference would that make if she has already run away?"

"It would mean that she could stop running and looking over her shoulder. You may not have physically put chains on her, but as long as you have papers saying you own her, there will be emotional chains. She will never truly be free of you, whether she is here or in Brazil with us," Luciana reasoned.

Elizabeth sat quietly gazing down at her lap. Luciana was asking her to let go of her last connection to Ruby, the one thing that could bring her friend back to her.

Luciana knew what she was thinking, "If you refuse then I will pay whatever price you determine she is worth."

Elizabeth looked up aghast at Luciana, "You would put a price on your niece's head?"

"No, but I will pay whatever price you have put on her head if that is what it takes to find and free her."

"And if I refuse to free or sell her to you?"

"Then you will have to live with the guilt of what you have denied her for the rest of your life," Luciana said in a matter-of-fact manner. She refused to let this young woman's selfishness keep her from finding Rubina.

"I see where Ruby gets her bluntness," Elizabeth said with a slight frown.

"I do not have time for subtlety Mrs. Englund when Rubina's life is at stake."

John Elder had kept quiet during their exchange but he felt that he had to speak up now, "Lizzie, you have to do this, if not for Ruby then for yourself. You have this baby to think of," he said, taking her hand and placing it on her round belly to remind her of what was more important right now.

"We're all concerned that this whole matter has taken over your life. Robert told me you haven't even decorated the nursery because you want to wait for Ruby to return and help you. The baby is not going to wait for something that is not going to happen and neither can you," he tried to reason with her.

Elizabeth nodded. Tears once again in her eyes, she looked at Luciana, smiling sadly, "Father will draw up the papers and I will sign whatever you like," she said, rising to leave.

"You are doing the right thing," Luciana said, grateful that they were able to get through to Elizabeth.

"Miss de Souza, if you find her please tell her how sorry I am. For everything," Elizabeth asked.

Luciana nodded and gently hugged the younger woman.

Philadelphia, Pennsylvania

Ruby watched the neighborhood children playing as she sat rocking in the Grant's porch swing. She was enjoying a few days of laziness before the school term started and she began her teaching position. She had taken the Teacher's Exam the week of her arrival to Philadelphia. Because she had no formal training the testers didn't think she would pass, but, to their surprise, not only did she pass but she scored in the top five. When they asked how she had done it, she simply told them she read a lot. She refused to tell them of her many years of sitting beside her mistress during her classes with her personal tutor. Ruby felt even that bit of information was best left private since she only trusted a handful of people with information about her life.

Ruby had kept busy during the past months getting to know the city, helping Esther plan her wedding, and running around helping Abigail with her Auxiliary Committee's meetings, charity events and socials. She had been welcomed with open arms by Abigail's friends and their daughters whom the older woman suggested Ruby spend time with since they were all about the same age. Ruby took her up on her suggestion, attending sewing circles, teas and social events for her peers. She truly enjoyed those times with the other young women. Other than Elizabeth, Ruby never had friends her own age while growing up. The Elder household had a small staff, none of which were children except Isaac who had been sent away when he had been accused of stealing John Elder's books. Now she had several friends and acquaintances that she would get together with whenever possible.

She also enjoyed the time she and Seth spent together. Although they lived under the same roof, they rarely saw each other for more than an hour during breakfast or dinner. His days, and many nights, were spent at the smith and livery. When he did have a free evening or afternoon, he made it a point of spending it with Ruby. He took her to shows, dinner, dancing and introduced her to the elite and middle class of the Philadelphia Free Colored community. The Grants were well-known and doors were open for him not only in the Colored community but many Whites as well.

The times Ruby most enjoyed with Seth were when they would simply take long walks, talking about anything and everything that came to mind. Sometimes he would take her to the stables and saddle two of the horses so that they could go riding together. Then there were the times when they would relax in the sitting room reading a book, knowing that it was enough just to be together.

Other than a discreet kiss every so often, they had not been intimate since leaving Caleb's home. They grew closer with each passing day, getting to know each other in a deeper way than they could with physical intimacy.

She and Seth rarely spoke of her leaving, but she knew it was on both of their minds and that the more time they spent together the more difficult their parting would be.

Ruby gazed up, feeling Seth's presence as he leaned casually against the doorframe.

"You look very deep in thought," he said, sitting beside her on the swing.

"Not really, just enjoying the afternoon breeze," she said, smiling.

"We don't have to go to the Wallace's for dinner if you would rather stay home this evening," he offered.

"Oh, no, I want to go. Besides, you said Cornell Wallace is one of your best connections for obtaining more horses for your stable. This dinner is too important for you to miss."

"Alright," he said, smiling. Ruby had a way of making those around her feel as if they could do anything as long as she believed in and supported them. Seth enjoyed how important it made him feel.

"You know, you're mother was not too happy to hear that we were going to the Wallace's. I thought you said that Cornell Wallace had been a good friend of your fathers."

"They were. My mother and Lucille Wallace are also good friends. It's their daughter Olivia that my mother has concerns with."

"What happened with their daughter?"

"It's something that happened a long time ago," he said tensely.

"In other words, not a good topic of discussion," Ruby said, noticing the slight frown on his face.

"No, it's just something that would be better left in the past. My mother is not one to easily forgive when she feels someone close to her has been wronged."

"I'll have to remember that," Ruby said.

"You have nothing to worry about, she adores you," he said, smiling again. "You've become the daughter she always wanted."

"Miss Abby has come to mean a great deal to me as well," she said sincerely. Abigail Grant reminded Ruby so much of her Aunt Luciana. She had become a surrogate mother to her since she had arrived in Philadelphia.

"What about me?" Seth asked.

"I better go up and start getting ready," she said, turning away from his penetrating gaze.

As she stood to leave Seth also stood and grasped her hand.

"You know we're going to have to talk about where this is headed sooner or later," he told her, reaching up and gently stroking her cheek with the pad of his thumb.

"But not tonight," he said with a grin.

Ruby smiled gratefully and made her way into the house. She had managed to avoid the discussion of her and Seth's relationship up until now, but with Seth's feelings obviously growing just as strong for her as hers had grown for him, it was becoming a topic she could no longer hide from.

An hour later as Seth and Abigail waited for her at the bottom of the staircase, Ruby's heart beat quickly in her chest as she saw Seth dressed in the semi-formal black suit that he sometimes wore when they went to the theater. It fit his slim muscular frame like a glove, and with the crisp white linen shirt, black bow-tie, freshly polished shoes, and trimmed hair and mustache she thought that he looked devastatingly handsome.

Seth suddenly felt as if he forgot how to breathe as he watched Ruby almost float down the staircase toward him. He could not take his eyes off of her. She wore an ivory satin gown that molded to her curves perfectly. The modestly low-cut bodice was off the shoulders and had peek-a-boo lace along the cleavage and capped sleeves. The color complimented her skin tone, making it seem smoother and creamier than usual. Around her throat was a band of ivory ribbon with her favorite cameo pinned to it and a pair of pearl earrings on her lobes. Her hair, which she had decided to keep short for not only convenience but also to keep from being recognized, curled attractively around her face, framing it beautifully. By bringing more attention to her face which seemed softer and more feminine.

"You look stunning," he told her.

"Thank you. You look quite the elegant gentleman yourself," she said with an appreciative glance.

"I'll be the envy of every man there," he said, taking her hand as she reached the bottom step and placing a kiss on her fingertips.

"Why Mr. Grant, are you flirting with me?" she said in her best imitation of a southern drawl.

"Is it working?" he asked, grinning.

"Very much so," she said, her gaze glowing intensely, saying all that she dare not speak aloud

The sound of Abigail clearing her throat reminded them that they were not alone.

"We did mighty fine with that old dress. You look beautiful," she said to Ruby.

"Thank you Miss Abby for all of your help," Ruby said, walking over to Abigail and placing an affectionate kiss on her cheek.

"It was my pleasure child. Now you two have a good time and give Lucille my best," she said, walking them to the door.

Seth handed Ruby up into the carriage then walked around to the other side. "Why did my mother call that dress old? It looks brand new to me."

"It was part of an old wedding dress donated to the Auxiliary Committee by a wealthy patron during our clothing drive. The top layer was a beaded lace that was ruined and the ladies were going to throw it away. I thought the under dress could be saved. Your mother agreed and helped me."

"Well, the dress is as beautiful as the woman wearing it," he said appreciatively.

"Compliments will get you almost anywhere," she said, repeating the words she had said the night they had first made love.

"Almost?" he said, smiling at the memory.

"The night is still young," she said with a teasing grin.

Seth chuckled, "I think we'll be making our excuses early this evening."

When they arrived at the Wallace home Ruby thought for a moment that she might have misheard Seth previously when he told her that the Wallaces were an affluent Colored family originally from Michigan, for Lucille and Cornell could have easily passed for White.

"You are Lucille Wallace?" Ruby said in bewilderment.

"I see that Seth didn't tell you," Lucille said with an amused grin.

"Forgive me," she said, embarrassed at her rude reaction.

Lucille waved her hand dismissively, "I'm used to it. So many of our relatives are passing, but, in spite of them, Cornell and I fully embrace our Colored heritage and have never once considered deserting it. Now that we've gotten that out of the way," Lucille said tucking Ruby's arm through hers, "Let me get you something to drink."

They made their way to a table with several crystal pitchers and punch bowls.

"de Souza, that's a Spanish name, is it not?" Lucille asked, handing Ruby a glass of iced tea.

"Yes, it's my family's name," Ruby said.

"You have such a beautiful lilt to your speech, is Spain where you're originally from?" the older woman asked.

Sipping her drink, Ruby took a moment to answer, still hesitant to reveal too much about herself to anyone, "No," she said, gazing nervously around the room for Seth.

Lucille didn't fail to notice her discomfort. "Dear, you have nothing at all to fear here. You may speak freely about yourself without being judged or turned over to the authorities. Cornell and I are long time supporters of the Railroad and are very aware of Seth's most recent trip," she said to reassure Ruby. "As a matter of fact, our home in Michigan was a common way station for those traveling into Canada."

Ruby sighed in relief, "I haven't completely learned who I can trust, Colored or White."

"Personally," Lucille leaned in toward Ruby as if to tell her a great secret, "Neither have I and I've been here twelve years."

They both laughed out loud and Ruby knew she had found another ally in this new life of hers. They followed Seth and Cornell into the Salon and were soon joined by two other couples that had been invited to the dinner. Paul and Rachel Jackson, who owned a dairy farm and Henry and Carrie Walker who owned a tailor shop. Once dinner was announced, Seth took Ruby's arm and led her toward the dining room, but before they were able to step through the open doorway a soft female voice halted them.

"Seth Grant, is that really you?"

Ruby felt Seth tense and turned with him toward a woman coming down the staircase. She was a beautiful, exotic looking petite woman with a softly shaped, willowy figure, and jet black hair piled atop her head in perfectly corkscrewed curls that cascaded down her back like a silk waterfall. She had sleepy, doe eyes, a pert nose, soft, pink pouty lips, and a smooth, creamy complexion that reminded Ruby of Café con Leché, the milky coffee that was her father's favorite drink.

"Hello Olivia," Seth said without much emotion. "I had no idea you were back."

"Really?" she said doubtfully. "I ran into your mother over a week ago, she didn't mention it to you?"

"No. She probably didn't think it was worth mentioning," he said, although he wished she had.

Olivia's smile wavered a bit but she recovered quickly, turning her gaze on Ruby.

"And who is your friend?" she asked, although her interest didn't sound the least bit sincere.

Seth's hand went from Ruby's elbow to the small of her back, "Ruby de Souza, this is Olivia Wallace," he said in introduction.

"It's very nice to meet you," Ruby smiled, offering her hand in greeting.

Olivia's gaze changed from disinterest to disdain when she noticed the possessive way Seth's hand rested on Ruby's back.

"Charmed," Olivia said, ignoring Ruby's friendly gesture.

Ruby slowly lowered her hand. It was obvious the other woman had chosen to dislike her already. Ruby had a feeling that there was more to Seth's and Olivia's relationship than their parents' friendship.

"Seth and Ruby, what on earth is keeping you two?" Lucille said, walking out of the dining room.

Her cheerful smile faltered as she noticed her daughter standing there and the tense expression on Seth's face.

"Olivia, it was my understanding that you weren't feeling well and wouldn't be joining us for dinner tonight," Lucille said in irritation.

"It seemed all I needed was a short rest. Since I was feeling better, I saw no reason to stay cooped up in my room," she said, smiling prettily at Seth.

"Fine, I'll just have Sarah set another place for you. Now, why don't we join the others," Lucille said, pasting on her best hostess smile.

Olivia walked past them, making a point of brushing her full skirts along Seth's trouser leg. Ruby followed behind, curious at the drama unfolding before her. Lucille waited for the two young ladies to go in then smiled sadly at Seth.

"I'm so sorry," she said. "If I had known she was joining us I would have given you ample notice."

"It's alright, Lucille. I'll be fine," he said, smiling to reassure her. Hoping he could convince himself as well as her that he would be.

The food was delicious and the conversation was lively and entertaining, but the tension in the room was thick enough to cut with a knife. Ruby had seen surreptitious glances directed at Seth and Olivia by the other guests but, for the most part, the two ignored one another. After dinner, Lucille had coffee and dessert brought into the parlor where she opened a set of French doors that lead out into their garden to let in the fresh night air. The men took that opportunity to step outside to smoke cigars and discuss business.

Rachel Jackson sat beside Ruby, "It's so wonderful to hear that you'll be teaching," she said, picking up on the conversation they were having before dinner. "There are so few qualified young Colored people willing to teach."

"A teacher, how quaint," Olivia said sarcastically.

"And what do you do, Olivia?" Ruby asked, wanting very much to be cordial in spite of Olivia's snide comments.

"I'm enjoying my youth instead of wasting away working on a farm or in a stuffy classroom," Olivia said, insulting both Rachel and Ruby in one fell swoop.

"Olivia!" Lucille exclaimed in shock.

"You will have to forgive my daughter's manners ladies," Lucille said in apology, "She seems to have adopted the snobbery of the Europeans after spending the last four years in France."

"Mother, there is no need to apologize for me. I'm just speaking my mind. Have you ever been to Europe Ruby?" Olivia waved her hand dismissively before Ruby could answer her.

"Oh, now you must forgive my ignorance, I'm sure they didn't allow you off the plantation to go on a European tour, did they?"

The other women in the room gasped loudly.

"Olivia Margaret Wallace, I will not have you come back to this house belittling my guests that way," Lucille reprimanded.

Ruby reached over and patted Lucille's hand in comfort, "It's quite alright, Lucille, because Olivia is partially correct. Although they didn't own a plantation, the family that owned me did not take me on tours of Europe with them. In fact, this is the farthest I've traveled since they bought me off of the slave block over ten years ago."

Olivia gazed at Ruby with a satisfied smirk, "But, Olivia, in spite of what you may think of my life as a slave, I am not, nor will I ever be, ashamed of it because it has made me the strong, determined woman that I am today. I also learned not to hate, but to pity those who belittle others when they believe that they are more superior, for it is their own lack of security in themselves that makes them act that way."

Olivia's face turned red in anger. Ruby knew she had just made a bitter enemy and in at that moment, she didn't care in the least.

"Mother, I believe my headache is returning. I'm going to retire for the evening," Olivia said, standing and sweeping dramatically from the room.

"Ruby, I am so sorry. Olivia has become a different woman since returning from Europe. I have no idea who she is anymore," Lucille said in exasperation.

"It's alright. I have very thick skin Lucille, it will take much more than petty insults to wound me," Ruby said, smiling.

"Did you enjoy yourself?" Seth asked as they made their way home a couple of hours later.

"For the most part, yes, but I don't think Olivia and I will be meeting for tea anytime soon," Ruby said, chuckling.

"She seemed to behave well enough at dinner," Seth said, wondering what he could have missed.

"It was after dinner that her claws came out."

"I guess I missed that part of the show," he said with a disgusted sigh. "If I had known she was back in Philadelphia I would have declined the dinner invitation."

"I know you would rather not discuss what happened between you two but since she has chosen to direct her bitterness towards me, I believe I should know what I'm in for," Ruby told him.

"You're right," he said in resignation. "Four years ago, Olivia and I were engaged to be married," he blurted out thinking it was best just to come right out and say it.

"I see," Ruby had a feeling that they may have been involved romantically but she hadn't imagined it being as serious as marriage.

"Two weeks before the wedding Olivia took off without a word to anyone, including her parents. We were all worried sick until they received a short letter telling them she had met someone, was in Europe with him and to not come after her. A few weeks later another letter came, this time to me, explaining that she had felt neglected because I was more interested in breeding horses than being with her. She had met a French businessman while I was away purchasing supplies and horses for the livery. I had been gone longer than expected and I guess she couldn't wait for me to return," he said bitterly.

"It seems this man offered her a life I couldn't, a life of luxury, ease and attention. All I had to offer was love, hard work and a simple home. I knew it wasn't going to be enough from the very beginning but I thought that if she loved me, she would be happy," Seth shook his head sadly.

"Lucille and Cornell didn't spoil their children. Olivia was the only girl out of the five and her beauty got her a lot of attention. I believe that's what spoiled her. Knowing all she had to do was bat those eyelashes or pout those lips and men would fall over themselves trying to make her happy."

"Including you?" Ruby said.

Seth nodded, "When she directed all that beauty and charm in my direction, I couldn't resist. Olivia wasn't a bad person, she had a good heart and I know she loved me, I just think she loved having money and status more."

"That is a miserable way to live," Ruby said. "Because no matter how much money and status you have, you will never truly be happy if you're alone."

"If you had to choose between your family fortune and being with the man you love what choice would you make?" Seth asked.

"I would hope that I would never be in that situation but I would choose love over fortune. What is the use in having the fortune if you have no one to share it with?" Ruby said. She had seen what the love of money over family had driven her grandmother to do. She knew that she would never make that same mistake.

"I'm sure Olivia would heartily disagree with you."

"I'm not Olivia," Ruby said, smiling.

"No, you definitely aren't and that makes me very happy," he said, leaning over to kiss her softly on the lips.

When they reached the house, Seth walked Ruby to her bedroom door.

"Thank you Seth. In spite of Olivia, it was a nice evening," Ruby said.

"You're welcome. You made quite an impression on everyone tonight," he told her. He always enjoyed watching her socialize whenever they went out. She adapted so well to every occasion, whether it was a night at the theater with social elite or a small informal gathering with their friends, she managed to make anyone she spoke with feel comfortable.

They gazed at one another for a moment, neither wanting to say goodnight. Seth leaned toward her, kissing her once again, needing to taste her once more before the night was over. Afterwards he forced himself to back away.

"If I don't walk away now I won't leave at all," he told her.

Ruby nodded, reaching for the door knob. "Good night Seth," she said, walking into the room and closing the door behind her.

She stood leaning against it, listening and hoping he
would knock so she wouldn't have to continue being the strong
one. But there was no sound other than that of his bedroom
door closing. A shaky sigh escaped as she went about the task
of getting ready for bed, where she had to physically will herself
to fall asleep.

Some time in the middle of the night the sound of her
bedroom door opening and closing awakens Ruby. Sitting up,
she watches the shadowy figure of Seth walking towards her.
When he reached the bed, he stood over her as if waiting for
permission to continue.

"Tell me to leave right now and I'll do so."

Ruby took his hand, "I couldn't do that anymore than you
could stay away."

He sat beside her on the bed and took her in his arms,
holding her tightly, not wanting to let go, afraid she might
change her mind if he did. Ruby knew there was no turning
back. Her heart raced as she ran her hands up and down his
bare muscular back. The pants he had worn to the dinner party
were his only clothing.

"Make love to me Seth," she whispered into his ear.

He moved back just enough to look into her bright eyes then
kissed her like a man starved. Ruby returned his kiss with the
same intensity, their passion fueling a fire that refused to be
quenched. Reaching for the fly of Seth's pants she struggled
with the buttons as he fought his own battle with the small
pearl buttons on her night gown.

Having accomplished her task and growing frustrated with
the difficulty Seth seemed to be having she reached for the hem
and, sitting up on her knees, pulled the gown up over her hips
and torso, ripping the hem and neckline as she did so. She
reached for Seth just as he removed the only bit of clothing he
had, pulling him down on top of her. Seth realized she was just
as anxious as he was when she immediately wrapped her legs
around his hips. He obliged her by sinking himself deep within
her wet warmth. They groaned aloud in unison at the feel of
him inside of her.

Seth's strokes were long and swift and Ruby matched his rhythm enthusiastically. It didn't take long for either of them to climax. Seth covered Ruby's mouth with his own to drown out her passionate shout. Afterwards they lay tangled in each other's arms and legs trying to steady their rapid breathing and racing heartbeats.

"You don't know how many times I wanted to walk in here and do this. How many nights over the past six months that I stood outside your door when I couldn't sleep," Seth confessed.

"I think I have a pretty good idea," Ruby said knowingly.

"You too?" he asked, chuckling.

"It was torture not being able to at least lie in your arms." There had been so many nights when he had walked Ruby to her bedroom door, just like tonight, and she had desperately fought the urge to invite him in.

Seth pulled her closer so that she lay partially on his body. "*Você é meu amor, minha vida*," he whispered to her.

Ruby's heart beat erratically in her chest, "What did you say?"

Seth repeated it once again in her native Portuguese then in English, "You are my love, my life."

Ruby sat up, gazing down at him. She could barely see his expression in the darkness but she did see his broad smile.

"Where did you hear that?" she asked with a shaky voice.

"From you when we first made love at Caleb's."

"Oh," was all she could manage to say. She didn't recall saying those words.

"Did you mean it or was it just a cry of passion?"

"Seth, please don't do this," Ruby pleaded. She couldn't bear admitting her feelings to him. She refused to make promises she knew she couldn't keep.

Seth sat up, reaching over to turn on the oil lamp on the side of the table. Gazing back at her he reached out to stroke her face with his fingertips.

"I need to know because I meant it when I just said it." He knew he was taking a big chance by opening his heart to Ruby but he didn't care. He loved her and he wanted her to know it.

Ruby backed away from his touch, moving off of the bed, shaking her head negatively.

"I love you," he admitted with a smile.

"You can't," she told him, tears shining in her hazel eyes. Her heart ached from the pain of trying to hold back her feelings.

"I can and I do," he followed her off of the bed, slowly moving toward her.

"You know what my plans are. You know I can't stay," she said, desperately crossing her arms over her chest as if it would ward off his approach.

"I know, but I can't let you leave without telling you how I feel. I'll wait for you to do whatever you need to do. I'll be here when you've settled your past," he said, grasping her arms, gently pulling her towards him and placing them against his bare chest over his heart. The warmth of his skin and strong beat of his heart beneath her palms was like a rope pulling her into him, no matter how hard she tried to fight it.

"I love you Rubina Arinzé Domingues. Deeply and with all my soul," he said, smiling, happier than he could have ever imagined.

Tears of joy and sadness ran down Ruby's face, "Seth it's not that simple. I could be gone for several months, possibly years, I will not ask you to wait that long."

"You're not asking me," he said, wiping her tears away with the pad of his thumb.

"What if I don't come back," she said, her heart breaking as she tried to make him see that anything more between them than what they had just shared was not possible.

"What if my family does accept me? Takes me back with open arms? You can not expect me to leave them after having just reunited with them."

Seth's smile faltered for a moment, "We can deal with that if or when that time comes."

Ruby found herself wishing she had gone on to Canada and found work there until she made enough for her to go home to Brazil. But she had not. She had chosen to stay here, allowing her affection for Seth and her new friends to rule her actions. She had allowed herself to become too involved with a life that was supposed to be temporary. Now she was in too deep to pull herself out without hurting those she had come to care so dearly for.

"You never answered my question. Did you mean what you said when we first made love?" he asked her.

Ruby gazed into his eyes and saw such hope and love that she knew she didn't have the heart to lie to him. "Yes. I did."

"And now?" he asked, hoping he didn't sound desperate for her answer.

"Right now I can not imagine being anywhere but here, loving you."

He took her into his arms and held her tightly, "That's all I needed to hear," he whispered against her temple.

But would it be enough? Ruby wondered.

Eleven

Seth whistled happily as he worked with thoughts of Ruby permeating his mind. He had not been able to spend much time with her since they had admitted their feelings for one another. After that night it seemed everything was keeping them apart. He was either working late or she was with his mother at some auxiliary event, visiting the families in the area to meet the children she would be teaching and getting her little school room stocked and ready. Before they knew it, the school year began and she was the one working late or up and out early in the morning. They were living in the same house yet they had barely seen in each other in passing, let alone spent more than an hour together. Now they had finally found an opening in their schedules and were going to dinner at Thomas and Jenny's house, just a short walk from Grant's Smith and Livery.

Seth was expecting Ruby to arrive any moment so he wasn't surprised when a female voice called out in greeting as he was brushing down the last horse.

"I'm back in the stalls Sweetheart," he answered, setting the brush down and wiping his hands on his pants legs.

"You're just in time. I was getting ready to go in the back to clean up and change, maybe you can help me," he said suggestively as he stepped out of the last stall with a wide grin on his face.

"Hello Seth."

The grin faded as he gazed up to see Olivia standing in the doorway.

"What are you doing here?" he asked angrily.

"Just visiting a dear old friend," she said, smiling innocently.

"As much as I would love to sit and reminisce about the good old days with you, I don't have time," he said sarcastically, walking over to the pump in the corner and washing his hands.

"You not having time for me is the reason why we're not married," she said bitterly.

"No, you running off with another man is why we're not married. Now, if you'll excuse me, I have things to do. I'm sure you remember the way out," he said heading to his office towards the back of the stables.

Seth pushed Olivia to the back of his mind, replacing her image with Ruby's dark, exotic beauty. He had brought a change of clothing with him and had just changed his trousers and was reaching for his shirt when he felt a hand on his bare back. He knew by the touch that it wasn't Ruby. Olivia had followed him into the office.

He quickly turned around. "What the hell do you think you're you doing?" he asked angrily.

"You mentioned needing help getting dressed when I walked in, so I thought I would offer my services," she said, smiling seductively.

"I don't want what you're offering," he said in disgust, backing away from her and shoving his arms into his shirt sleeves.

"There was a time when you begged for what I had to offer," she said, halting his attempt to button his shirt by reaching into the opening and running her hand over his belly and following the line of hair leading into the waist of his trousers.

Seth grabbed her wrist. "Leave, Olivia, now!" He did not want Ruby walking in on them and getting the wrong idea.

"Seth, we used to be good together. You can't tell me that you don't feel anything when I touch you," she said doubtfully.

"I don't," he said, releasing her wrist and praying his body's response would not make him a liar.

"Am I interrupting?"

Seth gazed over Olivia's head to see Ruby standing in the doorway. He could only imagine what the scene before her must look like.

"No, Olivia was just leaving," he said, gazing murderously down at the other woman.

"I guess we'll just have to finish this," she paused, innuendo permeating the silence, "conversation some other time," she said, ignoring Seth's angry glare.

Olivia turned, walking slowly toward the door, her hips swaying seductively. Ruby stepped aside to let her pass.

"Enjoy him while you can for soon he will be mine," Olivia said to Ruby in French as she walked past.

"We shall see," Ruby answered back in perfect French, stopping Olivia in what she thought was her grand exit. She only paused for a moment before continuing on through the door.

"I forgot you spoke French," Seth said with a grin.

"Elizabeth's mother's family is from France. She spoke it fluently and taught me the language while I tried to teach her Portuguese. I picked up on the French much better than she did Portuguese," Ruby explained.

"I won't ask what she said but I do want to explain what you walked in on," he said hopefully.

"Nothing to explain, I heard enough to know that you didn't encourage her," she said, walking toward him. Once she stood before him, she began buttoning his shirt.

"You're not upset?" he asked.

She buttoned the last button and adjusted his collar, then, smiling up at him, "Not at all. We've been nothing but honest with one another. I trust that if you wanted to be with Olivia you would tell me," she said, smoothing his shirt over his chest.

"Well, I don't want to have anything to do with Olivia. You're the only woman I want to share my life and love with," he said, sealing his declaration with a kiss that left no doubt in her mind that he meant it.

Days later Ruby encountered Olivia once again.   The other woman was walking towards her as Ruby left the Vigilance Committee's office where she volunteered on Saturday mornings.

"Well isn't this a coincidence," Olivia said to another woman who was walking beside her.

"Hello Olivia," Ruby said, the greeting not sounding very sincere. She would have much rather walked past the woman without the least bit of acknowledgment, but it was obvious Olivia was not going to let that happen.

"You, know, I was just telling Bess here that I saw the most interesting thing in the sheriff's office today. It was a reward poster for an escaped slave named Ruby Elder," Olivia said looking innocently at Ruby.

"The funny thing about it was that the woman it described could have been you," she said, her expression changing to that of a cat that had just cornered a mouse.

"What do you want, Olivia?" Ruby asked calmly, not willing to show the cold fear she suddenly felt.

"What could I possibly want that you would have?" Olivia asked with a laugh.

"Say what you have to say, so that I can be on my way," Ruby said, her fear replaced by anger.

"There is no telling where information on this other Ruby's whereabouts could end up," Olivia said in a matter-of-fact manner.

"Is that a threat?"

It was obvious Olivia considered Ruby more of a threat in her attempts to get Seth back than she had first anticipated.

"Not at all. Consider it a friendly warning," Olivia said, deceptively sweet

"Thank you, but I don't think I have anything to worry about," Ruby said. She refused to be manipulated by this woman's games.

"Have a lovely afternoon ladies," she said, trying not to laugh at the look of embarrassment on Olivia's companion's face.

Ruby was furious by the time she reached Esther's house where she was helping her friend with a quilt.

"You know you have to tell Seth about this," Esther said after hearing about Ruby's encounter with Olivia.

"No. I can not start depending on Seth to solve all my worries. Besides, she's probably bluffing."

"And if she isn't?" Esther asked.

"Then I will deal with it myself. Right now I want to finish this quilt before that baby arrives," Ruby said, patting Esther's rounded belly.

"That wouldn't be soon enough," Esther said, chuckling. "I was barely this size the day I gave birth to Jessie. I've still got a few months to go and I already feel like I'm giving birth to a giant."

"Well, with Bishop as the father, I would not be surprised if you were," Ruby said, grinning at Esther's pained expression at the thought.

"So when are you and Seth jumping the broom and giving my children some playmates?"

"Esther," Ruby said in warning.

"Ruby, the man told you he loved you and that you were the only woman he wanted to be with. I don't know about you but that sounds like a marriage proposal to me."

"Let me get some more lemonade," Ruby said, picking up their glasses and heading out of the room.

Esther chuckled over Ruby's obvious attempt to drop the subject.

On her way home, Ruby thought about what Esther said and whether or not to tell Seth about Olivia's threat. She knew her friend was right, that she should tell him, but she had a suspicion that Olivia's bark was worse than her bite. Unfortunately, if Olivia wasn't bluffing and was fully prepared to turn her in to the authorities as a fugitive, then Ruby would have to leave sooner than she planned. Possibly with the next group the committee was escorting to Canada. Ruby decided that the best way to handle the situation was to call Olivia's bluff by acting as if she were not the least bit worried about it.

She would just wait it out and see what happens. Olivia reminded Ruby of her grandmother. If she judged her correctly, she knew that the other woman would take much glee in personally letting Ruby know what she had done just to see the satisfaction of bringing her down. That would give Ruby enough time to contact William Casey to find a place to hide until she could make her way to Canada. Eventually she decided that it was best not to tell Seth. He would only confront Olivia, which would possibly force her hand.

Olivia wondered if she'd gone too far with threatening Ruby. The other woman had done nothing to her accept unknowingly blocked Olivia's path back to Seth. If Ruby was out of the picture, Olivia knew she would have no problem winning Seth back. She only hoped her threat would work in running Ruby out of town before she realized Olivia had no intention of following through on it. She had decided that turning Ruby in was a very last resort. What she really needed was the opportunity to get Seth alone. She would seduce him, if need be.

It had not taken long for Olivia to realize she had made a mistake when she left Seth to run off to Paris with Philip. The Frenchman had promised her everything except what she truly wanted, which was marriage. Shortly after arriving in Paris he informed her that he had a wife and three children. She threatened to leave him, but he convinced her to stay by telling her that his marriage was an unhappy one. He didn't love his wife, he loved Olivia, and although by law he already had a wife, Olivia would be the wife of his heart. Olivia willingly accepted his explanation as well as the townhouse in the heart of Paris that he set her up in, her own small staff of servants and the best furnishings, clothing and gifts that money could buy.

She soon got used to spending the holidays and weekends alone because of Philip's obligations to his real family at their country estate. She refused to see the truth and lived blissfully and purposely unaware of Philip's other life until she overheard two women discussing the romantic holiday one of the

women's husband had planned for their wedding
anniversary that week and how much in love they still were
after ten years and three beautiful children. The woman had
been Philip's wife.

Olivia hurried back to her townhouse and waited anxiously
for Philip who was supposed to take her to dinner and an opera
that evening. When a note from him arrived explaining that he
had been called away on a family emergency and wouldn't be
able to see her until the following week, she decided she had
enough. She booked passage on the next ship out of France and
was gone by the time Philip returned.

Now she was home, trying to win back the one man she
should never have given up and she refused to let anything or
anyone stand in her way.

The next few months went by agonizingly slow for Ruby as
she waited anxiously to see what Olivia would do. It didn't
help matters that the other woman managed to show up at
every social event Ruby attended. Although Olivia completely
ignored Ruby, directing all her attention on the male companion
she had frequently been seen around town with, it was affecting
Seth more than he wanted. Despite what he told her, Ruby
believed that having left things so unfinished between them he
still harbored feelings for Olivia. He became more and more
distracted each time he saw her, particularly at times when her
escort was with her.

Olivia was fully aware of this and was using it to her
advantage. Ruby was obviously not as easy to manipulate as
she had thought considering she was still in town and on Seth's
arm. Seth, on the other hand was. Judging by the gazes Olivia
caught from him whenever she arrived with her male
companion, he was obviously jealous and jealousy was easier to
manipulate. Olivia had chosen her mother's upcoming birthday
party as the perfect moment to put the final stages of her plan
into motion.

The evening of Lucille Wallace's party would be an important one for Seth as well but it had nothing to do with Olivia. He could barely contain his excitement over what he planned for after the party. His mother was staying the night at Thomas and Jenny's caring for Thomas Jr. and their newest baby girl so that they could attend the party with him and Ruby. Seth's plan was for him and Ruby to stay at the party for a reasonable amount of time then escape as early as possible to come home for a quiet, romantic evening alone. Seth grinned as he wrapped his hand around the small box in his trouser pocket for the third time in the last half hour to make sure it was still there, and then made his way downstairs to wait for Ruby.

When she made her appearance Seth smiled with pleasure. The party was a formal occasion so he had asked a special request, which was for Ruby to wear the ivory gown she had worn the night of the Wallaces' dinner party. This time she added a pair of matching ivory satin gloves that went up the length of her fore arm, just past her elbows, and a pair of ivory satin slippers with a pointed toe and dainty heel.

"You're a vision of beauty," Seth said as she stood before him.

"Thank you. I see you have been to the tailor," she said, admiring the new, well-fitted tuxedo on his slim, muscular frame.

"A special occasion deserves special clothing."

"I'm sure Lucille will appreciate it," she said, straightening his bow tie.

"This isn't for Lucille." Grinning, he took her hand and led her into the sitting room.

"Since I'll be out of town next week and won't be here to celebrate your birthday with you, I thought we could make Lucille's birthday celebration yours as well."

"I know you didn't want anyone to make a big fuss about it, which is why I didn't tell anyone, but I couldn't let it go by without acknowledging that I'm very happy you came into this world 20 years ago. If you hadn't, I think I would be a very lonely man right now."

"Thank you," she said, placing a soft kiss on his cheek.

"I truly do feel blessed that you were brought into my life," he said, caressing her bare arm just above the top of her glove, then turning and picking up a jewelry box that she hadn't noticed sitting on the table.

"This is why I asked you not wear your jewelry tonight," he said, handing her the box.

Ruby hesitantly opened the lid then gasped in surprise, "Seth, you shouldn't have."

"True, but I did," he said with a grin.

Nestled within the box's velvet interior was an ivory pearl necklace with a small ruby heart dangling from the center and flanked by matching earrings. Removing the necklace from its case and stepping behind her, Seth placed it around Ruby's neck.

"When I first saw these, all I could think of was you wearing them with this dress." He locked the clasp, resisting the urge to place a kiss at the nape of her neck. He knew that if he did, they would not make it to the party.

When he walked back around her he smiled at the sight of the ruby lying nestled between her throat and the top of the dresses neckline. Then he noticed that she still stood gazing at the earrings that lay in the box.

"They would look much better on you than in that box."

"They're so beautiful," she said, gazing up at him with tears sparkling in her eyes.

"Not as beautiful as you," he said, taking the box out her hands and removing the earrings.

"May I?" he asked.

Ruby nodded. She was surprised at his gentleness in putting the earrings in her lobes and her heart felt ready to explode with all the love she felt for him at that moment. When he was finished, he took her hand and led her to a mirror in the foyer.

"They look as if they were made just for you," he said, smiling in admiration at her image in the mirror.

"Thank you Seth. This has already turned out to be a wonderful birthday," she said, her smiling gaze meeting his in the mirror.

"The evening is still young," he said with a secretive smile.

Gazing at him curiously, Ruby couldn't imagine what else he had in store for her.

Seth caught himself gazing across the room wondering what the hell was wrong with him. Ruby was a beautiful, vibrant, intelligent and loving woman who any man would be lucky to have in his life, yet he stood there wanting to pummel Louis Banks for looking so possessively at Olivia as they danced. He became even more annoyed when Olivia laughed at something Louis whispered in her ear then allowed him to lead her toward the garden doors.

Without stopping to think of what he was about to do, Seth excused himself from the group of men he had been conversing with and followed the couple. He caught up to them just as they were exiting the ballroom.

"Olivia, may I speak with you?" he asked.

Olivia turned, gazing at Seth curiously, "Seth, I believe you know Louis," she said smiling adoringly up at her escort.

"Banks," Seth said in greeting with a curt nod to the other man.

"Grant," Louis said with a humorous smile.

Seth's gaze fell back on Olivia, "May I speak with you," he repeated, insistently this time.

"Why of course," she said, looking as if she were truly concerned with Seth's behavior.

As soon as she excused herself from Louis, Seth took hold of Olivia's elbow, steering her through the garden doors.

"Seth, what on earth is the matter with you?" she asked after he let go of her arm.

"What's the matter with me? Do you have any idea what you look like in there hanging all over Louis Banks? Everyone in that room knows he's a fortune hunting gigolo. How could you not only allow yourself to be seen around town with him but behave so blatantly promiscuous?"

"Why Seth, I believe you're jealous," she said with a grin.

He chose to ignore her comment, not because it was ridiculous but because she was right and he didn't want to admit it.

"If you don't care how your actions affect your family's reputation then at least think about how it affects your own."

"I had no idea you even cared," she said.

"I don't," he said, sounding very unsure.

"Then why are we out here?" she asked, moving closer to him.

Seth knew that in some way he still cared for Olivia. That, in spite of what she had done, he still felt something for her, or at least for the Olivia he used to know. He gazed down at her, the light from the torches in the garden were lit well enough to show her face clearly. He saw the pout of her mouth and remembered how softly and easily they had yielded to his kisses. He began to wonder if they still would. Without considering what he was about to do, Seth took Olivia in his arms and brought his lips down upon hers. She hesitated for just a heartbeat before responding eagerly and passionately.

Although Olivia felt familiar in his arms, she didn't fit perfectly within them like Ruby did. She didn't touch his heart the way Ruby did with a simple gaze or smile. The realization of what he was doing quickly set in and Seth immediately began to regret acting so rashly, but before he could separate himself from Olivia the sound of someone clearing their throat interrupted them. He and Olivia both turned to find Ruby standing before them looking as calm as if she had just come upon two strangers.

"I'm sorry to interrupt but Thomas wanted to see you before he and Jenny left. When I went looking for you, Olivia's gentleman friend happily told me where to find you," Ruby explained.

Her calmness worried Seth more than if she had reacted by ranting and raving at finding them in each other's arm.

"Ruby, I'm..."

Ruby shook her head, raising her hand to stop him from saying more, "I know. You're sorry. Apology accepted. I'll wait inside while you finish your conversation, although I'm sure Thomas and Jenny will gladly take me home if you would like to stay."

"Damn it to hell," Seth swore as Ruby turned and headed back towards the house. He started to go after her but was brought up short by Olivia clinging to his arm.

"Where are you going?" she asked.

"Olivia, this was wrong, I shouldn't have allowed this to happen."

"Wrong? How could you say that? You obviously still feel something for me or we wouldn't be out here," she said confidently.

"Maybe I do, but it's not what it used to be. It's not like what I feel for Ruby."

"Ruby?" she said in frustration, "You care more about some Amazon darkie you've known for less than a year than you do about the woman you were going to marry?" she said in disbelief.

Seth shook his head sadly, "When did you become so bitter Olivia? What happened to the sweet, loving, giving woman I used to know?"

"I'm not the one that's changed Seth, you are. You're the one that was too busy to spend more than five minutes with your own fiancée. I could barely get you to come here for dinner with my family let alone spend an entire afternoon with me," she said bitterly.

"Now suddenly you have time to attend parties and dinners all over town with that woman. Running after her like some love sick dog when you didn't even bother to come after me when I went to Paris. I haven't changed at all Seth I'm still the same you just never took the time to look past the wrapping."

"Maybe you're right," he admitted, "But you knew how important it was for me to build my family's business not only for myself but for our future. The future of the children we talked about having, to afford the big house and social standing you wanted so much to maintain. I was doing it for us, Olivia, but you couldn't see that. You didn't have the patience to wait for me to do what I had to do for our life together. Instead, you ran off to a life you thought would be better. Well, you got the jewels and fancy clothes you wanted but it's obvious that it also made you a bitter and lonely woman," he said sadly, wondering what she went through while she was in Paris that made her this way.

Olivia saw the pity in his eyes and anger like she had never known boiled up within her.

"Go," she commanded. "Go to your precious Ruby. I don't need your love or your pity Seth Grant. I could have every man in that room wrapped around my finger by the end of the night."

Seth stood there gazing at Olivia for another moment, feeling responsible in some way for her becoming so bitter, but it was obviously too late to do anything about it. He turned and walked away, finally getting the closure he hadn't even realized he needed. With that chapter of his life over with, he could now start a new one with Ruby. That is, if she still wanted him after tonight.

Olivia watched Seth walk out of her life. She had lost him forever and she blamed Ruby for it. If Ruby hadn't come out into the garden, Olivia believed that her seduction would have worked and Seth would still be with her now.

"Well," she said, speaking out loud to herself, "If I can't have him, I'm sure as hell not going to let her."

And a plan she had refused to seriously consider before this moment made perfect sense now.

✷TWELVE ✷

Seth found Ruby speaking to Lucille with her wrap in hand making her excuses to their host.

"Ah, Seth, there you are," Lucille said. "Ruby tells me she's not feeling well. I hope you're taking her home right away."

"I told Lucille that there was no reason for both our evenings to be spoiled because of me. Thomas has offered to drop me off at the house," Ruby said with a weak smile.

Seth didn't miss the hurt and disappointment in her gaze.

"No need to worry Lucille, I'll take her myself. It was a wonderful party. Happy Birthday," he said, giving the older woman a hug and kiss.

He felt that once he explained to Ruby how much he loved her and that what happened with Olivia was a mistake then she would understand and they would be able to start anew.

"I'll save you both a slice of cake and deliver it myself tomorrow after church," Lucille said.

"Feel better dear," she told Ruby with a hug.

"Thank you again Lucille," Ruby said before turning and walking toward the entryway.

Lucille swatted Seth's arm as he turned to follow after Ruby, 'Whatever you did Seth Grant I would advise you to fix it. Ruby's a good woman and you would be a fool to let her get away."

Chuckling at Seth's surprised expression, she said, "I recognize the look of a woman disappointed in her man. Cornell has received it numerous times from me in 35 years of marriage. Just don't let it go too long before you apologize for whatever you did to cause that look," she warned him.

Other than the night sounds, Seth's and Ruby's ride home was a silent one. As soon as they left the Wallace home he had tried to explain what happened but Ruby told him she thought it best that they discuss it after they arrived home. When they did he assisted Ruby down from the carriage then led the horse and carriage around to the back of the house. He tried to figure out how he could possibly explain what happened between him and Olivia without hurting Ruby any more than he already had but realized that there was no easy way to do that. He told Ruby he loved her and that he no longer had feelings for Olivia, yet she walked out to the garden to find them in each other's arms. The only thing he could hope for was that she would forgive him.

When Seth entered the house he found Ruby in the sitting room and couldn't help but think about how different things had been in that room just a few hours ago.

Her gaze met his, "Before you explain, I would like to say something first."

Seth nodded and sat on the sofa across from her.

"First, I want to thank you so much for everything you and your family have done for me over these past months. I don't know how I will ever be able to repay you."

"Ruby, I didn't do anything but what I had to do," he said modestly.

"That's not true. You didn't have to take me with you on that journey. You didn't have to go with me when I had to separate from the group and you could have walked away the day you and Caleb brought me to the Vigilance Committee headquarters, but you didn't. Instead, you and your family welcomed me into your home and your lives and I will always be grateful for that."

Seth started to interrupt but she stopped him, "No, please let me finish before I lose the courage to say what I have to say," she pleaded. She felt as if her heart were shattering into a million pieces.

Seth saw vulnerability in her gaze that he had never seen before and it broke his heart. He nodded for her to continue.

I have come to care for your family as if they were my own. I have also come to care for you far more than I should have under the circumstances," she said, sighing heavily.

"You told me that when it was time for me to go, you wouldn't hold me back, that you would do so without a fight. Do you recall that?"

"Yes," Seth said hesitantly. He didn't like where the conversation was headed.

"It's time Seth. I have let this go on for far too long and before we get caught up in it any further I have to walk away."

"You're leaving for Brazil already?" he asked, hoping he had more time to convince her that this was the best place for her to be.

"No, not yet, but I think it's best if I found another place to stay until I do," she said sadly.

"There is a small house near the school that the church owns. They offered to rent it to me for a small fee but I had turned it down because I didn't want to leave here, but now I think I will take them up on their offer."

"When did you decide this?" he asked in bewilderment.

"When I found you and Olivia together," she said, not holding back the pain in her voice.

"Won't you at least give me a chance to explain?" He could tell by her expression that she had already made up her mind.

"There is no need to explain. I already have a pretty good idea about what happened," she said with an understanding smile that Seth felt he truly did not deserve.

"Then maybe you could explain it to me, because I'm not sure myself what happened," he said in frustration.

"I should have seen it coming but I had something else on my mind. Olivia made it known with our little exchange in French that day in the stables that she wanted you back but I thought nothing of it until I ran into her a few days later when she all but threatened to turn me in as a runaway if I didn't leave you alone."

"What?!" Seth shouted. "I'll wring her little neck," he said angrily, standing to leave.

Ruby grasped his arm, "Seth, no. It's obvious she was bluffing."

"How do you know? The authorities could be on their way here as we speak," he said worriedly.

"Because I believe she chose another plan, such as seducing you then arranging for me to find you two together." The image of Seth and Olivia's passionate embrace brought a tightness in Ruby's chest that she was sure would never dissipate.

Seth looked at her in confusion before realization quickly set in. "You mean what happened tonight was planned?"

"I don't have proof but yes, I think the whole scenario was set up."

Seth sat down. Taking Ruby's hands in his, "If that's true then you know there is nothing between Olivia and me. There's no reason for you to leave," Seth said hopefully.

"That's where you are wrong Seth. I do believe that before tonight you and Olivia had nothing to do with each other since her return, but I don't believe there is nothing between you. I've seen how you watch her whenever she's in the same room. It's obvious you still feel something for her, if not, she wouldn't have been able to get you in the position she did."

"Whatever was between Olivia and I died the day she left for Paris," Seth said, not truly believing the words himself.

"It's not just you and Olivia's relationship Seth, it's also me. I told you when we began this relationship that I could not promise you any more than what we had. I need to locate my family and it wouldn't be fair to you to let our relationship continue down the path it was heading," she said sadly.

Seth gazed at Ruby, wanting so much to tell her she was wrong. That what happened with Olivia meant nothing. That her determination to find her family didn't matter, but he couldn't because he would be lying. If there was one thing he and Ruby had it was their honesty with one another, he refused to begin lying to her.

"When will you be leaving?" he asked, trying to keep his rising emotions under control.

Ruby was also having a difficult time holding back tears, "Probably tomorrow afternoon. I'll speak to your mother in the morning before church services and the Reverend afterwards."

Seth nodded, "I'll help you take over your belongings."

"That's not necessary. I don't have much, just the one trunk. If you allow me to borrow the carriage I will return it when I'm finished."

"Please let me do this one last thing?" he asked, reaching over and stroking her cheek.

The tears she had managed to keep at bay almost broke free at the gentle touch, which had become such a familiar habit of his.

"Alright," she stood and headed for the doorway.

"Ruby."

She stopped and turned towards him.

"I'm sorry. I wanted so much for this birthday to be a special one for you," he said regretfully.

"It was special. I spent it with friends and someone I care very much for," she said with a small smile and touching the pearl and ruby necklace at her throat.

Seth nodded with a sad smile of his own.

"Good night Ruby."

"Good night Seth."

He watched as she made her way upstairs then, reaching into his pants pocket, wrapped his fingers around the small box that had been there the whole night. He took it from his pocket, opened the lid and gazed longingly at the small diamond ring. It took tremendous restraint for him not to run up the stairway after her. Tonight was supposed to have been the beginning of a new life together for them, now that life was over before it had even begun.

Ruby quietly closed the door to her room wondering how she had managed to get through that conversation with Seth without breaking down. Tears were running down her cheeks before she had made it half way up the staircase. Her heart was breaking and she had no one to blame but herself for being foolish enough to think that she could hold her emotions back and enjoy an intimate but uncommitted relationship with Seth.   Foolish to think she could just walk away and feel nothing.   Now here she was, weeping because she had given her heart to a man she knew she could not be with whether she was going to Brazil or not.

What happened tonight had made her see how selfish she was being in allowing Seth to continue pursuing her. Although she knew he still cared for his old love, she was still hurt by how easily he had fallen for Olivia's game.

Ruby allowed herself a few more tears then brusquely wiped them away and went about the work of packing the little belongings she had managed to collect during her time at the Grant's home.   Once she was finished she lay in the bed allowing the tears to come once more.   She would miss the warmth of this home and the two people dwelling within it more than she would ever admit.   What she would miss most of all is the companionship she and Seth had built during her stay. It was deeper and more binding than the few intimate moments they had been able to share.

As she cried herself to sleep, images of the dream Ruby had while she was lying sick those many months ago entered her mind. If it were truly a glimpse of their future like she wanted so much to believe then she and Seth would find a way to be together again.   Ruby held on to that dream to ease the unbearable pain of walking away from the man she loved.

Ruby and Seth adjusted to their new lives without each other by keeping busy. Seth worked day and night at the livery and when Ruby wasn't working she was with Abigail at auxiliary meetings or assisting the Vigilance Committee with the ever growing influx of fugitives arriving in Philadelphia.

On the rare occasion Seth and Ruby ran into one another, they were cordial, but distant. It was obvious to those close to them that they still cared very much for one another, but, in spite of Abigail's and their friends' best efforts, they continued to pine for one another from afar, neither of them wanting to cause the other more pain than they already had.

As fall turned to winter, Ruby spent more and more of her free time at the Vigilance Committee's office. It was a chance for her to lose herself in something meaningful and spend her free time productively as she worked toward forgetting Seth and saving enough money to leave for Brazil in late spring. If fugitives arrived while she was there she was ready to greet them with a friendly smile, warm, clean clothing and hot food whenever possible. It brought her such happiness to see the joyful expressions come over their faces when they realize that they had made it North or were just a river crossing away from Canada, or the Promised Land, as it was called.

Although she knew that joyous feeling well from her own experience, Ruby considered herself luckier than those who had to leave family behind in their escape. For them, the end of the journey was a bittersweet one. Many, just as their "Moses", Harriet Tubman had done, risked enslavement and death to go back for those they had left behind. All Ruby risked was her pride by searching a family who could refuse to accept her. She didn't care about the inheritance, or any of the trappings from a life she once took for granted, too young to know any better. All she wanted was her family, or at least what was left of it.

Thoughts of a family brought to mind thoughts of the Grants. They had become her family since arriving in Philadelphia and she missed very much being within the fold of their love. She still spoke with Abigail, Thomas and Jenny but rarely took them up on their invitations for dinner, afraid they would find an excuse to also invite Seth. Although Abigail made it a point to tell Ruby every chance she got how unhappy Seth was and that he was working himself to death. Just that morning Abigail had been so bold as to tell Ruby that she and Seth were being foolish and just needed to get off their stubborn hides and tell each other how they felt so that they could give her some more grandbabies to spoil.

Ruby had laughed but now she seriously considered what the older woman had said. Neither she nor Seth had told anyone why they had ended their relationship but she wondered if his mother was right. Maybe she was just being stubborn about her reasons for not taking a chance on a life with Seth. She wondered if it was possible to have Seth and still be able to find her family.

She gazed up from the list of new arrivals she had been recording for William Casey's ledger and realized it was later than she thought. From the look of the graying sky it was probably going to snow. She had a thirty minute carriage ride home so she knew she should leave now if she didn't want to be caught it. Ruby put the log book in the desk, locking it securely, and made her way down to the rectory where Still and a few of his volunteers were handing out hot meals to the fugitives that would be staying the night.

"Ruby, you're still here?" William said in surprise, looking at his pocket watch. "I thought you left hours ago."

"No, I wanted to make sure the log was complete," she said, yawning.

"Thank you. You were a very big help today with the new arrivals. It seems many travelers want to bring in the New Year as freedman."

"I wouldn't blame them," Ruby said, not able to hold back another yawn.

William chuckled, "Why don't I have one of the men follow you home to make sure you get there safely."

"No thank you. I'll be fine. Esther and Bishop are nearby. I'll stay there for the night if I feel too tired to travel home."

"I'll feel much better if you went straight there instead of trying to make it home."

"I may just do that. I'll see you in the morning," she said, heading out the door.

As she left the church she headed in the direction of Esther's and Bishop's townhouse then changed her mind. The cold air must have done her some good because she no longer felt so tired. It didn't make any sense to bother her friends unnecessarily so she turned down the road leading away from town to make her way home.

Olivia paced nervously in her room, the consequences of what she had done weighing heavily on her conscious and keeping her awake. She glanced at the clock on her dresser and wondered if there was enough time to put a stop to things before it was too late. It was already past midnight, for all she knew the slave catchers could have already been to Ruby's and was heading South as she stood there contemplating what to do next.

She sighed heavily, knowing she had no choice. It only took her a few moments to put on the riding suit she had worn earlier that day and make her way downstairs. She went to the stables, quickly and deftly saddled her own mare, a task she had thankfully learned from Seth years ago, then rode out as if her life depended on it.

Seth awoke to find his mother standing over him with a candle lighting the worried expression on her face. It took a moment for him to hear the loud knocking coming from downstairs.

"Get up son, something's wrong. Nobody in their right mind makes social calls in the middle of the night," Abigail said.

Seth nodded, reaching for the trousers he had thrown on the floor just a few hours earlier. He had been bone weary after spending the previous night and day at the livery with a foaling mare.

"Hold on, we're coming!" he yelled in irritation as they made their way downstairs.

Seth unlocked and yanked the door open ready to give their late night visitor a piece of his mind for waking them up at this hour but was shocked into silence at the sight of Olivia standing on his doorstep. Her long black hair was flying wildly about her head and shoulders, the collar of her riding suit lay open with the buttons done up in the wrong holes. She was breathing heavily and her face was flushed red. Seth heard a soft whinny and glanced past Olivia to find her mare standing on their front lawn munching at the grass.

"Seth, we have to go. We don't have much time," Olivia said frantically.

"Olivia, what the hell is going on? What are you doing riding around town in the middle of the night? Are your parents alright?"

"I'll explain on the way, but we have to leave now," she said, turning away from him and running to her horse.

As she attempted to mount, the mare snorted indignantly and shied away in protest, causing Olivia to fall on her face in the grass. As Seth hurried towards her she sat up, buried her face in her hands, and began weeping loudly. He knelt before her taking her hands away from her face.

"Olivia, what's happened?" he asked calmly.

"Oh Seth, I've done something terrible," she said between sobs. "I wouldn't blame you if you never forgave me."

"Well, you won't know if you don't tell me what it is that I won't forgive you for."

"But if we don't leave now, there may be no hope of stopping them," gazing at him as if that was explanation enough.

"Olivia, has anyone died or been seriously injured?" he asked, seeing that she was becoming hysterical.

"No, yes, I don't know," she sobbed.

"Why don't you let my mother take you in the house while I get your mare watered? She's not going anywhere right now after the way you must have run her over here." He nodded at Abigail who had followed him outside.

"C'mon child, let's get you a hot cup of tea and sit you by the fire," the older woman said helping Olivia up.

Olivia had not realized she was shivering from the cold until Abigail mentioned a fire. She had run out of the house without an overcoat and nothing underneath the light riding jacket but her undergarments.

"Tea would be nice, laced liberally with laudanum," Olivia said miserably.

When Seth returned to the house his mother was waiting at the door.

"How is she?" he asked

"Troubled. She keeps mumbling something about it being too late to do anything now," Abigail told him.

Seth sighed and followed his mother into the sitting room where Olivia wept silently into her tea cup.

"Alright Olivia, what's going on?" he asked a little more forcefully than he had before.

"I did something unforgivable Seth and if we don't get to Ruby's house to either stop them or at least get a search started it will be too late to help her."

"Ruby?" Seth said in confusion. "What does this have to do with Ruby?"

"I contacted the authorities and told them she was a fugitive slave," she admitted, refusing to meet Seth's gaze for fear of the contempt she would see in them.

"You what?!" Seth and Abigail shouted in unison.

Olivia flinched, "If the catchers haven't gotten to her house already, they will be soon," she said sheepishly.

Seth had never wanted to strangle someone as much as he did Olivia at that moment. The fact that she was a woman saved her from him laying his hands on her at all. Instead he stood and headed towards the stairs.

"Seth wait! Let me come with you!" Olivia cried.

He turned back towards her, his gaze heated with anger and disgust, "No, stay here and write down everyone you spoke with and what arrangements were made because if they have already taken her I'm going to need to get on the road before daybreak to start tracking them before they head too far South." He turned away again, taking the stairs two at a time.

Olivia had not missed the controlled rage in his voice.

"Child, what would make you do such a foolish thing?" Abigail asked angrily.

Olivia jumped, having forgotten the other woman was in the room.

"You wouldn't understand Miss Abby," she said sadly.

"I understand a whole lot more than you think. I also thought with Lucille and Cornell as your parents you would have more sense than this. Turning one of your own people in. You ought to be ashamed of yourself. Ruby has nothing to do with you and Seth's troubles. Whatever you two had between you was lost when you left with that White man," Abigail told her.

"Miss Abby, please," Olivia pleaded in distress.

"No. Out of respect for my son's feelings I've kept my peace about what you did, but the minute you involved Ruby, you involved me. That girl did nothing but what you should've done a long time ago, and that's to love Seth and accept him for who he is, not for what he could give her."

Olivia knew Abigail was right, which made her feel even more guilt over what she had done. She went back to weeping into her tea cup.

Ruby sat up in bed listening very intently for the sound of scraping that had awakened her. She had learned to become a light sleeper during her journey north, so the scraping at her front door had been like a loud knock to her sensitive hearing.

Easing out of bed, she went to close the bedroom door. Just as she reached it she heard the splintering of the wood as her front door was forced open. She quickly slammed the bedroom door shut but remembered, too late, that there was no lock on that door. She quickly grabbed the chair from the vanity table nearby and wedged it under the doorknob. She knew it wouldn't hold for long but it would give her enough time to escape through the window.

The intruders began banging against the bedroom door and Ruby didn't hesitate as she shoved open the window and quickly scrambled through. The frozen ground was ice cold on her bare feet but she didn't have time to think about that as she lifted the hem of her nightgown and took off at a run towards the church in the distance. Her small house was on church property and the minister and his wife lived in a house just behind the church. If she could make it there, or at least close enough for someone to hear her shouts for help, she knew she would be safe.

Memories of her kidnapping by slave traders as a child came vividly to mind. She had not doubt that those men were here for the same reason. Olivia had finally followed through on her threat but Ruby had no intention of going along willingly. She had not gotten this far just to be slapped into the chains of slavery once again. Her heart beat rapidly in her chest and her warm breathe came out as small plumes of smoke when it came in contact with the cold winter air. She was just a few yards away from the church when she was suddenly lifted up off the ground and dropped into the lap of a horseman. She landed on her stomach, momentarily knocking the wind out of her. Her mind worked feverishly to find a way out of the situation. She could push herself off of the horse but she knew that if she fell off the wrong way she could break her neck. At this point she didn't care. It was a chance she was more than willing to take.

Ruby shifted her arms, heaved herself up and brought her elbow down purposely in the rider's lap, almost bouncing off the horse's back. He howled in pain and drew the horse up short. As soon as the animal came to a stop Ruby pushed herself off. The rider attempted to grab a fistful of her hair on the way down but the shortened locks slipped right through his fingers. His attempt to stop her actually slowed her ascent enough for her to land unsteadily on her feet instead of her backside. She stumbled backwards for a moment then took off at a run when she regained her footing. Unfortunately, she was halted by the sudden appearance of a horse in her path. As she turned to run in another direction two other horses surrounded her closing off all escape routes.

One of the men dismounted, grabbing her from behind. Ruby struggled to escape his grasp but one of his beefy arms came around her throat, cutting off her air at the slightest movement. She had no choice but to stand still. One of the other men dismounted slowly, wincing in pain as he did so. Ruby concluded that he must have been the one she had unmanned in her attempt to escape. He walked over to her, grabbing her face roughly.

"You're lucky you're worth more alive than dead," he growled angrily.

Seth knew he was too late the moment he drew close enough to Ruby's house to see the splintered front door sitting wide open. Now the most he could hope for was that he would find their trail and catch up with them.

After spending a half hour searching the perimeter of the house to find out what direction their trail led he made his way home. From what he could tell there were at least three horsemen. He knew it would be foolish to go after them alone so he decided to stop by Thomas' then go home to stock up on supplies for the road. He just hoped his mother was able to get more information out Olivia to help with the search. If he had to talk to her himself, he wouldn't hesitate to strangle her this time.

Seth was saved from committing murder. Olivia had given his mother all the information she thought would be helpful then left so as not to have to face Seth again. He and Thomas decided to meet at the Vigilance Committee office to find out if there had been word through the railroad's network of communication of catchers in the area. Unfortunately, after having to get extra clothing and supplies, stopping by the livery to get a horse better suited for the possibility of a long journey then stopping to let Bishop and Esther know what was going on and leave instructions for what needed to be done at the smith and livery while he and Thomas were gone, it was almost two hours after daybreak before he got there.

When he arrived at the Committee's headquarters, William Casey was waiting for him.

"I saw Thomas' horse," Seth said after they greeted each other, "I assume he told you what happened."

"Yes and as soon as I heard I sent my eyes and ears out to spread the word and to find any information they could. I also made a list of friends for you to contact along the way," William said, handing Seth a slip of paper.

"Thank you Will. I'll send word to you whenever I can," Seth promised.

"Seth, there's something you should know before you go," William warned.

"Not long after Ruby left here last night a woman and man came in asking about her. Of course I told them I had no idea who she was but I knew they didn't believe me."

"How would they know to come here to look for her?" Seth said in confusion.

"It seems they were sent here but wouldn't say who sent them. The woman claims to be Ruby's great aunt," William said.

"What?!" Seth said in disbelief.

"I found it hard to believe also until the woman gave me her name. It's de Souza, the same name Ruby uses."

"Are you sure?" Seth asked.

"Yes. I ask her to repeat it, there was no mistaking what she said."

Seth didn't know whether to laugh or cry at the irony of the situation. Here Ruby had been concerned over how to go about locating her family and there's a possibility that they've shown up looking for her in the last place she would have expected.

"Do you think she's legitimate?" William asked.

"There's only one way to find out," Seth said. "Is she staying nearby?"

"Yes, at the Carson townhouse down the street."

Seth nodded, "Would you please let Thomas know I'll meet him out front," he said, heading for the door.

"Seth wait, what about Ruby. The trail could get cold if you wait too much longer," William said.

"If this woman is who she claims to be and has gotten this close to finding Ruby on a nonexistent trail then I'd be a fool not to seek her help in finding Ruby now."

❧ *Thirteen* ❧

Luciana and Amir were eating breakfast before they made their way back to the church to question William Casey again.

"Do you really believe he will tell us anything different today?" Amir asked doubtfully.

"No. I think Mr. Still is very good at what he does and is not foolish enough to tell us anything that could put their cause, or anyone involved with it, in danger," Luciana answered.

"Then why are you so sure he is lying about Rubina's whereabouts?"

"It was nothing he said or did. I would have believed him if it were not for a feeling I have that Rubina is close and needs us."

"Ah, the de Souza intuition?" he said with a grin.

"Yes, and it has not been wrong yet," Luciana said confidently.

They went on to discuss their other options in the likely event that William Casey told them nothing when their conversation was interrupted by a knock at the front door. Their gazes met in surprise. They had just arrived in the city late the previous day. The only people that knew they were there was the gentleman they had obtained the townhouse from and Mr. Casey.

Amir stood heading for the foyer, with Luciana following behind.

"Good morning Gentlemen. What can I do for you?" Amir asked the two men standing on the doorstep.

"Excuse us for disturbing you so early in the day," Seth said, "but I believe we may be able to help each other."

Amir's gaze perused Seth and Thomas' appearance before deciding that they didn't look as if they were there to do anyone harm.

"Luciana, these men claim that they may be able to help us with something," Amir said as he allowed Seth and Thomas to enter.

"Really?" Luciana said curiously, "Are you sure you have the correct house? We've only been here for very short time."

"Are you Luciana de Souza?" Seth asked.

"Yes and this is my nephew Amir. I am afraid you have us at a disadvantage though, for we do not know who you are."

So this was the cherished *Tía* Luciana Ruby spoke so fondly of, Seth thought gazing at the tall, regal woman before him.

"I'm Seth Grant, this is my brother Thomas and if you'll excuse my rudeness Miss de Souza but we don't have much time so I would like to get right to the reason we're here," Seth said.

"By all means Mr. Grant," Luciana said, wondering what these men could possibly want with them.

"I understand you're looking for your niece. I may be able to help you find her, but I have to be sure that you are who you claim to be," Seth said to Luciana, although there was no doubt in his mind. Not only did she resemble Ruby, but she and her nephew were just as Ruby described.

She knew when they arrived in this city that they were close to finding Rubina and now this man was claiming he could help them. The only way he could have known why she was there was if William Casey had sent them over. The hairs on the back of Luciana's neck rose in excitement.

"I understand. What do you need to know," she said, remaining outwardly calm.

"It's been over ten years since your niece was brought to America, why has it taken you so long to look for her?"

"We have been searching for Rubina since the day of her disappearance, unfortunately my sister's bitterness knew no bounds and we did not find out until recently where she was. Before then all we encountered were dead ends and false reports. Rubina is my heart, Mr. Grant. She and Amir are all I have left of my family and I do not care how long or how much money it will take, I intend to find her," Luciana said adamantly.

Something in Seth's gaze told her that it was the right answer but not the one he wanted to hear. She had a feeling he would have preferred if she and Amir had not come at all.

Hearing Luciana use Ruby's real name had felt like someone had hammered the last nail in the coffin of his and Ruby's future together.

"I have a question for you, Mr. Grant. Do you know where Rubina is?" she asked.

"I knew where she was up until last night when she was kidnapped by slave catchers. That's one of the reasons I'm here. We're on our way to look for her and could use your help."

"*Meu Deus*, we were so close," Luciana said in frustration. "Of course we will do anything within our power to assist you. Amir, you must go with them."

Amir nodded, heading for the stairs. Luciana grasped his hand as he walked by her.

"We've come so far, I can not lose her now. Find our Rubina," she said desperately.

Amir took her into his arms and held her close. "*Não preocupe a Tía, Deus é com nós, nós encountrará Rubina*," he whispered, reassuring her that they would find Rubina before placing an affectionate kiss on her forehead.

It felt so strange for Seth to actually see the people Ruby had spoken so lovingly of. They had never truly been real to him and he would never have imagined that he would meet them, so it was easy for him to put them in the back of his mind. Now here he was, in the very same room with them, and none of them had any idea where Ruby was or if she were unharmed.

"Mr. Grant, if I may be so bold as to ask what your relationship to Rubina is?" Luciana asked, interrupting Seth's thoughts.

"I brought Ruby North," was his only answer.

"I see," Luciana saw far more than Seth's words revealed.

"You mentioned asking for my help as one of the reasons you are here, what is the other?"

Because I love her more than my own life and I know that reuniting her with her family is the greatest I gift I could give her, was what Seth truly wanted to say. Instead he simply told her, "Because Ruby's reason for escaping north was to find her way back to her family. She risked her life to do so and I won't allow anyone to take that from her."

Luciana nodded in understanding, "Then I will be forever in your debt when you find her Mr. Grant," Luciana said sincerely.

Ruby huddled shivering beneath a scratchy, worn, wool blanket she had been given wondering if she would ever be warm again. It had been a few weeks since she had been captured and all she wore was the same nightgown she had on that night. The temperature had dropped considerably since then, snowing lightly for a day. Yet in all that time, the leader of her kidnappers refused to allow either of the other two men to give her anything but the blanket she now used, part of which she had to rip apart to make wraps for her feet to keep them from freezing.

Ruby had tried to escape twice during the first few days of their journey. The first time she had unmanned him with her foot to his groin when he attempted to rape her as she relieved herself in the bushes. She hadn't waited around to see if she had done any real damage, just took off running. She didn't get far and her punishment was his fist to her jaw knocking her unconscious. The second attempt was while her captors had slept. Although her wrists and feet were bound with rope, they had foolishly left her hands tied in front of her. It took her half the night but she managed to work the ropes around her ankles loose. She didn't bother with the ropes around her wrists, just ran once again. They hadn't caught her that time until late morning. Although she had gotten a few miles away from them she had been so anxious to escape that she hadn't covered her trail the way Seth had taught them all during their trek north. The leader didn't lay a hand on her that time. She could see in his eyes that he would have killed her if he had, something he wouldn't do considering they wouldn't get their reward if he did. Now when they stopped for the night they bound her hands behind her back, tying the rope to a tree as she was now, or they tied her hands and ankles together in a sitting position preventing her from moving her hands at all.

She hadn't tried to escape again. Not because she couldn't but because she realized she had to wait for the right time. She figured once they were further South, they would let their guard down a little. She allowed them to believe that they had won in keeping her from running again, but not that they weakened her spirit. When her gaze met with those of her captors it was as defiant as ever but she rarely spoke or did any more or any less than what she was told to do. To Ruby's captors she seemed resigned to her situation but still had her prideful nature, which they figured would be her master's concern, not theirs. All they had to do was deliver her to the authorities and collect their reward then she would no longer be their problem. Ruby knew that although she may have convinced the other two that she wouldn't try to escape again, their leader continued to watch her closely.

Ruby shifted trying to curl up in a ball, the need for warmth momentarily making her forget about the rope that tied her to the tree she leaned against. She winced as she felt the pull on her shoulders. The sound of a twig snapping nearby halted her movements. Gazing up she saw the leader coming towards her. Ruby sat completely still, watching him warily as he knelt down in front of her.

"I got a way you can keep warm," he said, leering lasciviously.

"I would rather freeze to death," she said in disgust. It had not been the first time he had made such remarks.

"If you weren't worth so much I'd give you a real good lesson in manners," he said threateningly.

Ruby didn't respond to the threat, she simply met his hostile gaze steadily with her own defiant one. He grabbed her face roughly, bringing his close enough to hers that she could smell his foul breath.

"You're too haughty for your own good. I don't see why anyone would offer so much to get you back. Bet you were some rich planter's bed warmer," he said with a sneer.

Still holding her face with one hand, he yanked the blanket off of her and grabbed one of her breast roughly, "Maybe I'll just sample some of this myself then sell you to the highest bidder. I could get twice as much as what your reward is worth by selling a choice little piece like you to a brothel."

Ruby's defiance faltered for a moment at the threat. Her captor must have noticed the fear in her eyes for he was smiling in satisfaction. Without another word he released her and made his way back to his bedroll near his sleeping companions.

Ruby's shivering was no longer from the cold so much as from the fear she had managed to keep at bay until now. She realized that if she were going to attempt another escape, she had better do it soon for she didn't trust that her captor would wait much longer to do what he had just threatened to do.

Seth gazed out at the darkening horizon, a storm was brewing. The oncoming rain would wash away all traces of the trail from Ruby's kidnappers that he, Thomas and Amir were following. They had lost track of them in Delaware after two days of snowfall, which had set them back two more days, the rain would set them back even further. Their only chance of saving Ruby was to high-tail it directly to Atlanta to head the catcher's off before they brought Ruby to the authorities there. If they didn't make it to Atlanta before them it wouldn't matter that the Elder's had freed her because when her captors find out they had captured her and traveled all that way and were not getting a reward, they may turn around and sell her to make up for their loss.

Seth sat down beside his fellow riders for a meal of dried beef and cold biscuits. They didn't chance lighting a fire for a hot meal or to warm themselves. It would alert people to their presence, something they didn't want since they were heading further South. Three Colored men on horse back traveling south would draw just as many questions as three heading north would. Seth and Thomas were both aware that although they all had certificates of freedom, it wouldn't matter to a greedy slave catcher patrolling the area.

"I think we should head out soon and travel straight through. We may need to head them off in Atlanta with a storm coming," Seth suggested.

"I agree," Amir said, gazing up at the sky.

"We're going to need to change horses and pick up more supplies. We may have to visit a few 'friends' along the way," Thomas said.

"You're referring to friends of the cause, correct?" Amir asked.

Seth and Thomas gazed at one another, not answering Amir's question.

"No need to worry my friends. What little I know of your underground transport system, I assure you, will not be revealed to anyone," Amir said with an understanding smile.

"How do you know so much about that? You've only been in America for six months at most," Seth asked suspiciously.

"It is amazing what information you can find out with the right price," Amir answered, shrugging.

"And you just happened to have the right price," Thomas said.

"That, and asking the right questions," Amir said. "I believe you know a Dr. Adam Clark?"

Seth nodded, "In a way."

"Word of our search for Rubina reached him. He pointed us in the right direction," Amir explained.

"You mean to tell me he told complete strangers what he supposedly knew of the railroad?" Seth asked doubtfully.

"Not exactly. He and Luciana sat behind closed doors for hours, I assume with her convincing him that she was who she said she was. Whatever bargain they came to for Dr. Clark to tell her anything is between the two of them," Amir said.

Amir gazed at Seth curiously. "I must ask. Why have you been so hostile towards me? I have only my niece's safety at heart. I would never do anything that would bring her to harm."

"I haven't been hostile," Seth said defensively.

"Yes you have," Thomas said with a knowing grin.

Seth gave him a withering gaze, sighing in resignation.

"It's not you, it's what you represent," he explained.

"Rubina's other life," Amir said as if reading Seth's mind.

Seth nodded.

"As a child, Rubina was very open with love and affection for her family but, like her mother, it was very hard to read what she was thinking. I can not imagine that trait having changed much in the life she has had to endure these past ten years. I can not tell you what decision she will make when she learns that we have been searching for her for as long as she has wanted to return home, but I can tell you that whatever she decides it will be the right decision for her. She has her mother's strong will and determination, she will not allow anyone to make her mind up for her," Amir said.

Seth knew what he was telling him. It didn't matter how much he cared for Ruby, it wouldn't make her stay here with him if what she truly wanted was to go home to her family. But he also knew that there was also the possibility that her family would not be able to convince her to return with them if she chose to stay with Seth.

A little less than a year ago Seth was confident about what he wanted for his life, which was to find his brother and to build Grant Blacksmith and Livery into an integral part of the Philadelphia commerce. Love and marriage were the last things on his mind. Now, within a matter of months, his future hung on the thread of Ruby's decision on about her future entailed.

❧ FOURTEEN ❧

Ruby knelt down in the muddy brush for a moment to catch her breath praying that the downpour of rain hid her tracks well enough to keep anyone from following her. Once she was able to breathe a little steadier she hiked up the hem of her nightgown, which was now a torn and soaked mess, and took off at run. Blood from cuts on the bottom of her bare feet soaked into the mud as it seeped through her toes but she didn't care. All she wanted to do was to get as far away as possible before her kidnappers realized she had escaped.

It had rained continuously over the past week and it seemed as if every house or farm the men stopped at to seek shelter turned them away. Not because they were against what the slave catchers were doing but because they didn't want to get involved in theirs or the abolitionists business. Most were small farmers who barely had the income to keep their farms going, let alone have slaves of their own.

They had been cold, wet and weary before they finally found someone to give them shelter for the night in his barn, but he had made the men promise to leave before dawn. Too tired to be overly concerned about securing Ruby they had simply tied her hands behind her back and bound her feet with rope then went right to sleep. Her agreeable nature since her last attempt at escaping had finally worked to her advantage, for Ruby had only feigned sleep. Sometime that night she had slowly began inching her way toward a sickle that lay nearby. She used its sharp blade to cut her hands and feet free and quietly crept from the barn.

Now she ran for her life, trying her best to cover any trail she left behind that the rain didn't wash away. She didn't know how long she had been running but by daybreak the rain had finally stopped, her lungs felt as if they were going to burst, and her feet throbbed in pain from the rocks and branches she had run over. But all of that was quickly forgotten when she spotted a house with a lone oil lamp burning in one of the lower windows.

"A safe house," she whispered.

Suddenly giddy with new found energy, she took off at a run toward the gated yard. She was reaching for the latch when the back of her gown was suddenly snagged from behind, drawing her up short of her goal.

"Noooo..." she cried angrily as she was yanked backwards. She began kicking, punching and scratching furiously trying to break free.

"Who's out there?" said a male voice from the direction of the house, followed by the click of a rifle being cocked.

As she continued her struggling, Ruby's captor raised his hand slapped her hard enough to render her temporarily senseless then encircled his arm around her throat, almost cutting off her air supply.

"What's going on here?" the other man asked, walking towards the gate.

"Go back in the house and mind your own business old man," the slave catcher said, pulling his handgun from his belt and pointing it towards the other man.

"You're on my property so this is my business," the older man said, glancing quickly at Ruby, "You alright?" he asked her.

Tears sprung in her eyes in answer to his question. The arm around her throat kept her from speaking. He seemed to understand and nodded in response.

"Don't interfere with the law mister. This woman is a fugitive," the slave catcher said, slowly backing away with Ruby.

The older man began moving forward, responding to the plea for help in Ruby's tear-filled eyes. A bullet whizzing past his head and lodging in the door behind him brought him up short.

"Next time you move, I won't miss. Don't bother following us. There are two other men waiting in the trees behind us who won't hesitate to shoot you," the catcher said.

When Ruby and her captor reached the copse of trees, his partners sat on their horses waiting, guns drawn. The look in their eyes told her that they truly would kill her if she even looked as if she were going to run. Ruby had to decide then and there if she was willing to risk a bullet in her back. The decision wasn't a difficult one. She didn't want to die.

She soon realized that death would have been the better choice when their leader began slapping her several times across her face with the back of his hands. Ruby fell to the ground in a daze, her face throbbing painfully. Before she had time to recover he yanked her up by the front of her gown, tied a rope around her wrists and led her to his horse where he tied the other end of the rope to the pummel of his saddle. When he was finished he turned toward her, grabbing her face roughly with his fingers.

"You wanna run so badly? Well you'll be doing plenty of it for the next few miles," he said, smiling sadistically.

Ruby was dazed, but aware enough to know what he intended and willed herself to stay steady when he mounted his horse. He set the animal at a steady trot for the first half mile, which, by some miracle, Ruby managed to keep up with, but when he increased the pace she began to stumble. It didn't take long before she was falling and had no way of slowing her descent. She was dragged on her side for another few feet before she felt the horse slowing down.

The man dismounted, walking back towards her. The pain from being hit and dragged and the pull on her arms was too much for Ruby to bear. She managed to stay conscious long enough to meet her captors gaze with one full of such burning rage and hatred that he stepped back as if it were a physical blow. His smile of satisfaction quickly disappeared as he realized that instead of breaking Ruby's haughty pride, he had only made it stronger. She refused to be broken.

Seth, Thomas and Amir made quite a sight as they arrived in Atlanta. Three Colored men riding into any southern town in the middle of the afternoon on horseback instead of in chains would draw much attention. They ignored the mostly hostile stares and headed straight for John Elder's law office. They had sent him a telegram a few days prior to expect them because they knew what commotion they would cause and wanted to make sure that the officials knew in advance who they were coming to town to see.

"Amir, please, come in," John said.

"These men are friends of Ruby who are helping with our search," Amir said, keeping the information of Seth's connection to the Underground Railroad and Ruby's escape to himself.

"Your telegram said that you had found Ruby but that there was a problem."

"Yes, we found out she was in Philadelphia but was kidnapped by slave catchers the day after our arrival," Amir explained.

John sighed heavily, "I blame myself for this. If I had just put my foot down with Elizabeth, Ruby would be safe right now."

"Mr. Elder, at this point it doesn't matter who's to blame. What matters is that we find Ruby," Seth said.

"Yes, you're right. Let's go to Elizabeth's home. We'll help in whatever way we can," John offered.

Ruby's entire body was in pain. Her face was still swollen and bruised, her arms still ached and she knew that at least one of her ribs was bruised from her fall while being dragged. They also had not given her any food and barely any water during the rest of the journey. Ruby knew it was to break her, but she refused to give them the satisfaction.

When they arrived in Atlanta, she had mixed emotions about returning. She felt relief that her current ordeal would soon be over and immense sadness that she would never see Seth and her friends in Philadelphia again or have the opportunity to find her family. She would be lucky if Elizabeth allowed her out of the house for fresh air, let alone give her the special privileges she had before she ran away such as day passes and unsupervised trips to run errands. She would never have the opportunity to escape again.

For more than ten years Ruby had managed to keep her hopes of returning to Brazil alive and in that one moment as she and her kidnappers approached the jailhouse they shattered like a dropped glass. It was near midnight and the streets were quiet. She sat in front of the leader on his horse, her feet and hands still bound and tied to the pommel of his saddle to deter her from trying to jump as she did the night they had taken her. He had nothing to worry about, Ruby was in too much pain and too weak to attempt anything but sit stoically in the saddle. Her one satisfaction in all of it was that she had stayed strong throughout her ordeal and although she had not earned her kidnapers' respect, they had come to an understanding. Other than checking the ropes around her wrists and ankles or taking her down off of the horse, none of them lay a hand on her again.

Ruby's only hope was that Elizabeth would come to claim her quickly and not make her sit in a jail cell for too long. She could endure ropes and confinement to the house, but she could not endure being locked up like a caged animal. It reminded her too much of her time in the slave pens when she first arrived in America.

The lead slave catcher sent one of the others into the jail to stake their claim on the reward for Ruby before taking her in. The man returned within minutes looking very disappointed.

"Nigger inside says that the sheriff is out till morning and the deputy is on the other side of town. We have to wait till he gets back to handle our business," he told them.

"Who's this nigger that told you that?" the leader asked.

"Says he works for the sheriff cleaning the cells and running errands."

The leader swore in frustration. "Tell him we're gonna make camp out back and to bring us some blankets, food and water," he told the other man.

After they made their way to a lot behind the jailhouse to make camp, Ruby was tied to a hitching post with the horses. Her tired gaze strayed from her captors to the back door of the jailhouse as a man with his hat pulled low over his face came out carrying a pile of blankets and a pot of coffee with three tin cups.

Although Ruby couldn't see the man's face, there was something familiar about him as she watched him cross the yard, handing each man a blanket. He spoke to the leader who looked over at Ruby then nodded hesitantly to the man. As the three slave catchers spread their blankets out and settled down with the coffee, the Colored man made his way towards Ruby. As he drew closer the hairs on the back of her neck raised when she realized what was so familiar. It was the way he walked. That bow-legged, assured gait only belonged to one person she knew. He squat down before her, handing her the blanket. When he raised his head he put his finger to her mouth to signal for her to keep quiet then stood, heading back towards the men around the fire. After assuring them that he would bring them some food right away he went back into the building.

The next few moments felt like the longest of Ruby's life as she waited for whatever would happen next. She still could not believe that Thomas was there, which would mean Seth was also nearby. Somehow they had found out what happened and came for her. The fact that Thomas had risked coming back south for her almost brought Ruby to tears but she held them back knowing that she was being watched closely by her captor. It would be suspicious if she began crying now after not shedding a tear during the entire journey.

"Damn, this coffee is bitter," the leader said, spitting out a mouthful and throwing the rest of what was in his cup into the flames.

"Yeah but it's hot and I've been fighting the chills ever since we got caught in that storm," said one of the others, pouring his second cupful.

Within moments the two that drank their coffee were yawning and complaining of being too tired to wait for the food they were promised and quickly fell asleep on their bedrolls. Seeing this, Ruby realized that the coffee must have been drugged, but since he only sipped it, the third man was still wide awake. Fortunately he didn't connect the bitterness of the coffee and how quickly his partner's had fallen asleep. With them asleep, his attention turned to Ruby and he stood making his way towards her.

"Looks like we got the whole night to ourselves," he said, kneeling in front of her.

Ruby didn't respond, she just continued watching him warily, not liking the tone of his voice or the lascivious grin on his face. She gripped the blanket Thomas had given her closely to her chest, but the man snatched it away with one hand, grabbing her tied wrists with the other, and held them above her head against the post she was tied to.

"After the hell you put me through, I deserve something to hold me over until I get that reward money," he said, grabbing the collar of her tattered gown and ripping it open down the front.

Ruby opened her mouth to scream and his mouth came down roughly upon hers, his foul breath sickening her to her stomach. She found the strength to struggle, but she was too weak from hunger and her injuries to do much damage. Where were Thomas and Seth? She wondered in fear.

"Let her go," a voice full of controlled rage said, followed by the sound of a gun being cocked.

As the slave catcher released her, Ruby began visibly shaking with relief. "Seth," she whispered.

"Now, back up slowly, with your hands up," Seth told the man.

As her captor did as he was told, a shadow fell over Ruby as Thomas came from behind the hitching post to untie her. As he helped her up she spotted more movement and gazed up to see another man tying up the two unconscious men by the fire, but with his back to her she couldn't see who it was. She was more concerned about seeing Seth, who was removing the leader's gun from his belt. She moved towards him but was halted by Thomas.

"You should wait," Thomas suggested.

"But Seth will kill him, I can see it in his face," Ruby said in concern.

"He needs to do this, let him handle it," Thomas told her.

Seth's way of 'handling it' as Thomas put it would only get him killed. Ruby knew that it wouldn't matter that Seth was there to help her, all that would matter to a southern judge and jury was that he had killed a White man and aided a fugitive slave. The only thing that kept her from ignoring Thomas was that she knew he wouldn't allow his brother to jeopardize his own life that way.

"What the hell is this?" Ruby's captor asked angrily.

Seth threw the other man's gun aside, "We're taking back what you had no right to take."

The man gazed over at Ruby who was leaning on Thomas for support, trying to hold her torn gown together.

"You're risking a lynching for her?" he asked, boldly turning to face Seth.

Seth pointed his revolver at the man's chest, "Move again without me telling you and I won't hesitate to pull this trigger."

"That must be a prime piece of dark meat there. Maybe, after you niggers are hanging from a tree, I'll just have to keep her for myself," the man said snidely.

Seth walked up to him, his revolver now pointing at the space between the other man's eyes. "If I find out you have violated her in any way, I will hunt you down and make you regret ever looking at her. Do you understand me?"

The man's cocky grin disappeared as he saw the deadly rage in Seth's eyes. "You won't get away with this. We'll be the ones huntin' you down. We know where to find her, remember?" he said with far more confidence than he felt.

"I'm willing to die for her, are you?" Seth said, pressing the gun up against the man's forehead.

He didn't answer, he could see that Seth meant what he said, but he wasn't willing to do the same. He made a vow to himself that if he walked away from this, he was getting out of the slave catching business and going back to highway robbery. It was a far less troublesome career choice.

Seth had seen Ruby's swollen, bruised face and pained expression as she moved. He truly wanted to kill this man but knew it wasn't worth it. It didn't matter that he had kidnapped a free Colored woman or that he had made threats to come after them. He was a White man and Seth was Colored, the law would not hesitate to either lock him up and throw away the key or more than likely hang him. He refused to lose his life and Ruby by being so foolish.

"Turn around," he told the slave catcher angrily.

"Look, I won't tell nobody you were here, I'll let you walk away without a word," the man said nervously, fear shining in his widened eyes.

"I said turn around," Seth repeated, not caring that the man thought he was about to kill him. His fear of death would insure that he won't come after Ruby again.

He kept the gun pointed at the man's head as he did what he was told. Seth knew he would probably try to run as soon as he could, but he wouldn't be given the chance. Seth brought the butt of his gun down on the man's head before he had completed his turn, knocking him unconscious.

Seth holstered his gun and, stepping over the catcher's prone figure, made his way to Ruby. She stumbled into his arms, tears streaming down her swollen face. He held her tightly, never wanting to let her go.

"I can't believe you're really here? How did you know where to find me?" she asked.

"I'll explain all of that later, right now I want to get you to Dr. Clark," he said in concern, gently touching her swollen face.

She nodded in agreement, "I don't think anything is broken but there is quite a bit of pain."

Just as he put his arm gently around her waist to assist her, the third man in their group who Ruby had forgotten was there, stood before her. Ruby felt Seth tense up beside her and gazed up at the tall man in curiosity.

"Thank you for helping to rescue me. Do I know you?" she asked.

"I believe you do," he said, removing his hat so that Ruby could see his face clearly.

Ruby hadn't realized he had spoken in Portuguese until she saw his face. His features were broader and more mature, but just as handsome as she remembered and her mind reeled at what his being there meant.

"Uncle Amir?" she said in disbelief, "Is it really you?"

"Yes," he said, his smile bright and wide just the way she remembered, tears sparkling in his dark eyes.

Seth's heart throbbed painfully in his chest as Ruby moved from his embrace toward Amir. When she reached her uncle, she raised her hands slowly to his face, as if she could not believe he was there unless she touched him. They stood there gazing at each other for another moment before Ruby collapsed against him weeping uncontrollably. Seth could only watch as Amir took Ruby up into his arms, carrying her as if she were the child she had been when they had last seen each other, and began walking towards the front of the building where their horses waited.

~*Fifteen* ~

Seth sat in Elizabeth Englund's garden on the stone bench he and Ruby had sat and planned her escape. Now, less than a year later Ruby lay in a room upstairs as a guest instead of a slave healing from the abuse she had received at the hands of her kidnapers and he was wondering if this would be the last time he would see her. He didn't even look up as he heard someone walking towards him.

Thomas sat beside him, "Dr. Clark just left. Ruby should be able to travel in a couple of days."

"That's good to hear," Seth said, distractedly.

"She's been asking why you haven't been up to see her. You're going to have to talk to her at some point before we leave."

"What am I supposed to say to her? I can never apologize enough for what she's been through because of Olivia's feelings for me," Seth said bitterly.

"She doesn't need your apologies, Seth, she needs your love. Tell her you love her. Tell her you want to marry her and give her another family in addition to the one she has," Thomas said.

"Her family," Seth said with a sad chuckle. "The family she has spent most of her life trying to find a way to get to and who has spent just as much time searching for her? I can't compete with that, Thomas. Do you honestly think she'll choose a life with me over one with not only them but with all the luxuries she could imagine at her fingertips? You heard Amir, She's an heiress. She has a fortune in inheritance from her father waiting for her in Brazil, not to mention being named the future Mistress of her family's sugar plantation. I'd be a fool to think she would want to live a quiet modest life with me over that."

"You know, to be the oldest one of us, you sure aren't too smart. If you'd take the time to stop feeling sorry for yourself you would see that she loves you and that it's possible for her to have her family and be with you."

"I risked my life as a conductor on the Railroad to find you and make our family whole again. She risked hers to find freedom and the opportunity to make her family whole. I won't ask her to give that up. It's too important to her," Seth said.

"So what are you going to do? Hide out in the garden for the next two days?" Thomas asked.

"No," Seth said with a sigh, "I'm leaving for Pennsylvania this afternoon."

Thomas shook his head sadly, "You're not going to even say goodbye to her?"

"It's better this way."

"Maybe for you it is," Thomas said standing up. "I'll go up and say goodbye then leave with you."

Seth watched Thomas head back into the house then gazed up at the window of the room Ruby was in. Unshed tears stung his eyes as he said a silent goodbye to her.

Ruby awoke from her nap to find Elizabeth sitting in a chair beside her bed. They gazed silently at one another, not sure what to say. They had not had a private moment to speak since Ruby had been brought there the night of her rescue almost a week ago. She knew that Elizabeth had freed her and had willingly offered her home for Ruby's recovery. She had been too overwhelmed with Amir's presence and then her Aunt Luciana's arrival a few days later. It had been an emotional week for her, one she didn't think she would ever get over the shock of.

"Thank you, Elizabeth, for all that you have done."

"It's the least I can do after what you've been through."

They were quiet for another moment then Elizabeth took Ruby's hand in hers.

"Ruby, I am so sorry for everything. If I hadn't been so selfish you wouldn't have gone through all this. It's my fault and I wouldn't blame you in the least if you never forgave me," She said with tears in her eyes.

Ruby squeezed her hand, "I do forgive you and I don't blame you for any of this. I know you weren't out to hurt me."

"You were my dearest and closest friend Ruby, I never wanted to hurt you, but I also couldn't find the strength to just let you go. I was afraid of being lonely without you nearby," Elizabeth explained.

"Even if it meant I would be unhappy?" Ruby asked.

"Yes, as long as I was happy," Elizabeth said sadly, "I'm ashamed of that. There is no excuse for what I did in denying you your freedom."

"No, but you have more than made up for it. If it were not for you then I wouldn't have my freedom and a family to get reacquainted with."

"Is there any way we can be friends again?" Elizabeth asked.

"I think we're off to a good start," Ruby said, smiling brightly and feeling freer than she had ever felt before.

She and Elizabeth spent some time laughing about their antics as children and acquainting themselves with what went on in each other's lives since Ruby left. They knew that they would never get back the closeness they once shared as girls so they began building a new friendship as women.

After Elizabeth left Luciana came to visit.

"You are looking much better," she said, placing a kiss on Ruby's forehead then sitting on the bed beside her.

"Thank you, it must be all the nursemaids I have," Ruby said, smiling.

"Having so many people who care for you is a good thing. I will be forever grateful that you were not mistreated during your time with this family," Luciana said. She was so thrilled to have her Rubina back.

"I have been very fortunate in having such good people in my life. I don't know what I would have done without all the friends I've made," she said.

"You miss your friends in Philadelphia?" Luciana asked.

"Yes, very much so, we became an odd little family during our journey north. I wish I could see them once more before we leave," Ruby said sadly.

"So you have made your decision about going home."

Ruby nodded, "I have to. You and Amir are my real family. I have been away from you for far too long."

"You know you do not have to leave right away. We can stay awhile longer, give you time to visit your friends again," Luciana told her.

"No, I've written them all letters explaining why I won't be returning for awhile, if at all. Its best that I go home from here, it will be hard enough saying goodbye to Seth, who I haven't seen him since they rescued me. It's as if he's avoiding me."

Luciana sighed, "Unfortunately, I have a message for you from him."

"From Seth? "Why is he not delivering it in person?"

"Thomas came up to see you earlier but you were asleep and he did not want to disturb you. He and Seth left for Philadelphia this afternoon," Luciana told her.

"Left? He left without saying goodbye? Why would he do that?" Ruby said in confusion.

"He told me to tell you that he is sorry that you had to go through such an ordeal and that if it were not for him that *bruxa pequena* Olivia, those were my words, not his, would not have done this to you," Luciana said.

"That's all?" Ruby asked in disappointment.

"No. He also said that he is happy to see you reunited with your family and that all he wants for you is to be happy living the life you choose,"

"The life that I choose? He never even gave me a choice. He just assumed which one I would choose without even speaking with me?" Ruby said in frustration.

Luciana took Ruby's hands in hers. She saw the hurt in her niece's eyes and felt her pain, "Do you know why he did that Rubina?"

"Because he thought it would be easier for me, but he's wrong."

"It was also because he loves you so much that he could not bear to see you torn between the life he wants to give to you and the one we offer you," Luciana said.

Ruby sighed heavily, tears sparkling in her eyes, "Maybe, but he obviously didn't believe enough in my feelings to find out what my decision would be," she said, hurt by the idea that Seth didn't trust enough in her feelings to talk to her.

"Have you ever given him reason to believe that you would make any other decision but to go home with us?" Luciana asked knowingly.

"No," Ruby answered honestly.

She knew that whenever Seth revealed too much about his feelings for her or it looked as if she were allowing herself to be too deeply involved with him, she made it a point to remind him that she was going home to Brazil and that a life in America was not in her immediate future. But now that her family had found her and had so readily accepted her back into their fold, she had been considering trying to find a way for her and Seth to be together but he left her with the only choice that made sense.

     ∾ ∾

Seth sat in his office in the back of the livery staring down at his account books and seeing nothing but a blur of numbers. He rubbed his eyes wearily then looked down at his pocket watch and realized he would be late for Sunday dinner. His mother would not be happy, especially since she specifically told him that morning not to be late because they were having guests. He really didn't feel up to being the charming host but he had been working night and day since he returned from Atlanta almost two months ago, rarely making time for his family and friends. Everything reminded him of Ruby. Late at night he would find himself standing outside the door of her old room willing time to turn back and for her to be on the other side waiting for him, but reality would quickly set in and he would go back to bed depressed and restless.

For days after he and Thomas had returned his mother made it a point to let him know what a fool he had been for letting Ruby go without a fight. She had no sympathy for the heartache he was so obviously suffering. She finally took pity on him when she came upon him on one of those nights that he had been standing outside Ruby's old bedroom. She no longer pointed out what a fool he was, although he knew she continued to think it. He decided it would probably be best not to incur her wrath and get home as quickly as possible, so he closed his books, locked up and made his way home.

When he arrived an expensive and fancy carriage he didn't recognize sat in front of the house. Whoever his mother had invited over was obviously wealthy. Probably one of the many benefactors her auxiliary committee was constantly wooing for donations. He sighed, looking down at his dusty boots, worn denim trousers and plain cotton work shirt that had become his uniform when working at the livery, and wondered if he would have enough time to go up and change. He opened and closed the front door as quietly as possible and headed straight for the staircase. He made it as far as the third step.

"Seth, is that you?" his mother said, walking out of the sitting room. "Where do you think you're going boy? You're already an hour late," she reprimanded.

"I'm sorry momma, I just thought it might be best if I changed before joining you."

"You look fine, now come on in here."

"Yes ma'am," he said with a tired sigh.

Following his mother into the sitting room, Seth tried putting on a pleasant smile, but his expression turned to shock when he saw who their guests were.

"Hello Seth," Ruby said, standing near the fireplace.

Seth couldn't speak. He could only stare at the vision before him. She was dressed in a burgundy riding suit that was obviously tailored to fit her curved frame perfectly with a golden colored silk blouse underneath that brought out the gold in her hazel eyes. Her hair had grown quite a bit since he had last seen her. It lay in soft, full curls framing a face which no longer held the gaunt, shadowed appearance her kidnapers had caused. She now looked vibrant, healthy and even more beautiful than before.

"Son, where are your manners? Don't you know how to speak?"

"You look well," was all he could manage.

"So do you," Ruby said, and she meant it. Even dressed in his work clothes Seth was still the finest man she had ever known. If anything, the clothing made him look even more masculine. It took quite a bit of Ruby's will power not to walk over and wipe away a smudge of dirt decorating his jaw.

Both continued to gaze silently across the room at one another. Neither sure what to say next.

"Abigail, weren't you going to give me the recipe for that wonderful pie you made this evening?" Luciana said, rising from the sofa.

"Yes, it's in the kitchen, just follow me," Abigail said, heading out of the room.

"Do you think they could have been a tad bit more subtle?" Ruby asked with a grin after her Aunt and Abigail left.

"Subtlety isn't one of my mother's best qualities," Seth said, smiling as well.

"My Aunt's either. They seem to be hitting it off quite well," Ruby said.

"When did you arrive?" he asked.

"Yesterday evening. I telegraphed your mother earlier in the week and asked her not tell you we were coming."

"That explains the secretive grin she's had all week. I thought you would be in Brazil by now."

Seth wasn't sure whether or not to be happy that she had not gone back and was standing in his sitting room turning his thoughts to mush.

"*Tía* Luciana has never been to America so she wanted to take advantage of the opportunity and go on a small tour."

Seth noticed that her accent, which had been barely noticeable, had thickened. Spending time with her family had obviously changed Ruby in other ways than the simple yet expensive clothing and jewelry she wore. Suddenly Seth thought of the ring he still had upstairs in his dresser. The simple ring that had been meant for her and could not compare to the finery she wore now.

"Why are you here?" he asked, hurt obvious in his tone. Their situation had changed so drastically and there was nothing he could do to change it.

Ruby heard the pain in his question and responded to it honestly, "To find out why you left without saying goodbye."

"Because you had what you've been wanting all of these years, your family. There was no longer a reason for me to stay."

If Seth's explanation sounded as weak to him as he thought, he could only imagine how it sounded to Ruby.

"I was not reason enough for you to stay? You traveled all that way to rescue me just so that I could reunite with my family?"

"No. I didn't want what happened to Thomas to happen to you. When I saw that you were safe under the care of your family, I came home," he said, trying to sound nonchalant about the matter.

"Nothing more?" Ruby asked, her intense gaze penetrating his, giving him permission to tell her the truth.

"What more is there?" Seth said, ignoring the voice in his head begging him to tell Ruby he loved her and couldn't bear letting her walk out of his life.

Ruby could see there was more he wanted to say but he refused to. Maybe she had been wrong, maybe he didn't care for her as she did for him.

"Do you love me Seth?" She felt compelled to ask even though she wasn't sure if she could bear hearing him say he doesn't.

"I care for you, I've never denied that," he said, his heart throbbing painfully in his chest.

"What if I told you that I love you and want to be a part of your life?" Ruby asked.

"I would tell you that you would be making a mistake and that it wouldn't be worth throwing your life in Brazil away for," Seth said, the lie almost choking him.

Ruby's heart felt as if it were shattering into a million tiny pieces that she would never be able to retrieve. The pain was almost physical but she managed to keep her composure.

"I see. Well, I should go get Aunt Luciana. We sail for Brazil in the morning and I would like to stop by Esther and Bishop's tonight before it gets too late," she said, walking over to the settee and picking up a burgundy riding hat with a jaunty black, turquoise and gold peacock feather on the side.

To Seth, she looked every bit the cool, sophisticated heiress she was born to be, giving him even more reason to believe letting her walk away was the best thing for both of them. She would have a life most Colored women could only dream of, he couldn't deny her that, no matter how much it broke his heart to do so.

"It was good to see you again, Ruby."

Ruby walked towards him, "You too Seth. Thank you for everything, I wouldn't be here if it weren't for your kindness."

Grasping his hand, she leaned forward, placing a soft lingering kiss on his lips. It took all Seth had not to take her into his arms, carry her up the stairs and lock her away until he convinced her she would be happier with him than with her family and their fortunes.

"Good bye Seth, be happy," she said before walking away towards the kitchen.

Seth stood there for a moment, still feeling the sensation of her soft, full lips against his, then quickly made his way upstairs to his room. Closing the door behind him, he thought of Ruby's words, "be happy." He knew that was impossible because his happiness would be boarding a ship to Brazil in the morning.

Ruby lay in bed unable to sleep, her conversation with Seth still on her mind. She could see in his eyes that he cared for her far more than he had admitted but something was holding him back. She sat up and lit her bedside lamp, deciding that reading would get her mind off of things. Just as she reached for the book on her bedside table there was a soft knock on her door. She gazed over at the door that separated her room from Luciana's in their connecting suite wondering if she should wake her. The two of them were traveling alone. Amir and Juan Carlos left for Brazil a few weeks after their reunion with Ruby to ready paperwork and other business matters for her return.

"Ruby, its Seth."

Her heart beat rapidly in her chest as she scrambled out of bed and rushed to open the door. Seth stood there, still dressed in his denim trousers and cotton shirt, only they were wrinkled and disheveled as if they had been slept in, his eyes were red and tired and his face shown signs of a day's worth of stubble. Ruby stepped aside to let him in and closed the door behind him. When she turned toward him, he stood in the middle of the room, gazing intensely at her.

Neither said a word as Ruby walked towards him, unbuttoning her nightgown and pulling it over her head. By the time she reached him, she stood before him completely naked. Seth seemed helpless as she began unbuttoning his shirt.

"Ruby, I don't know what to do," he said, pain and confusion in his voice.

"Shhhh," she said, placing a finger over his mouth. "I love you Seth Grant and no matter what happens after tonight, I will always love you."

Seth took her into his arms, kissing her as if he was a man starving and she was his only source of food. They made love slowly and passionately that night, exploring every inch of one another as if committing to memory, and then fell asleep in each other's arms.

Ruby showed no shame when Seth joined her and Luciana for breakfast the next morning and Luciana didn't show any surprise in seeing him there. She treated him as if he always sat at their table, talking to him about his business and future plans with the livery. Once breakfast was over and they were dressed, he tied his horse to their carriage and rode with them to the port where they were to board one of the ships from the Domingues Exports personal fleet of transport ships. Seth learned that was how Ruby and her Aunt had been traveling during their tour along the eastern seaboard of America.

This time Seth didn't leave before saying goodbye to Ruby. He waited on the dock with his arm wrapped around her waist, holding her close, while their personal carriage, horses and luggage was being loaded. Once it was time for her to board, the pain was almost too much for either of them to bear.

"You said to me once that you couldn't make any promises until you knew what your future with your family would be. Is that still true?" Seth asked.

"Yes, right now my future is with my family and the obligations I have to them," she answered. "I have an inheritance to claim and my father's business to learn before I can take over managing it from my Aunt. I can't say how long that will take or when I will be able to come back but I will be back," she said in determination. Ruby refused to believe that she and Seth were brought together only to be pulled apart forever.

"Then where does that leave us?" Seth asked.

"I love you with all of my heart, but..."

"You still don't want to ask me to wait for you?" he said, finishing for her.

Seth couldn't believe that she had come back into his life only to leave once again. He didn't know how he would bear it but he was determined to find a way for them to be together.

"No, as I said before it wouldn't be fair."

"I won't say goodbye, but I will say that I love you Rubina Arinzé Domingues, don't ever forget that," he said, taking her into his arms and kissing her for what might be the last time.

❧ EPILOGUE ❧

Sergipe, Brazil
Autumn 1860

Rubina stood on the veranda of the de Souza plantation gazing out at the field of sugar cane in the distance where heads bobbed and weaved between the canes and voices were lifted up in song as the now freed and paid workers cleared the fields for harvest. It was a scene she had never forgotten in all the years she had been away. It was eight years ago that she had first stepped foot back in her native country and she still found it amazing that she was home.

The first several months had been a time of adjustment for her and reacquainting herself to Brazil, then attending meetings with the managers of Dominguez Exports and the family's attorneys to claim her inheritance. At Luciana's insistence, Ruby had sat in on every business meeting, gone over account books and traveled on several voyages with the Dominguez transport ships, all in an effort to learn the family's businesses. The men had scoffed at a woman doing such things but they soon realized Rubina was very much like her Aunt and was intent on being taken seriously and showing them that she was just as capable of running her father's business as they were.

When one of her meetings took her to Buenos Aires for an extended period Rubina did something she had longed for ten years to do. She confronted her grandmother.

Luciana told Rubina that Maria had been sick for some time but it was still a surprise to find the beautiful, commanding woman who had once intimidated her now a withered version of her former self looking on fearfully as her long lost granddaughter stood before her. Rubina had envisioned this meeting so many times yet she felt none of the righteous anger she thought she would. She felt nothing but sadness for the frail, weak woman shivering beneath her covers. This is what her bitterness had brought her.

"Was it worth it?" Rubina had asked.

"It doesn't look as if you've suffered much. You should be thanking me." The old bitterness was back in her tone as she thought about the fact that she lay there with a weak heart, suffering alone, while Rubina stood before her looking as dark, beautiful and regal as Ifé had been.

Rubina read all of her grandmother's thoughts just in the way the older woman's gaze. It didn't take her long to realize that Maria would never change. That she would never be the grandmother Rubina wanted so much as a child.

"Maybe I should thank you for showing me that the only thing I missed by not having you in my life was sadness and heartbreak. Goodbye, Grandmother, I will not darken your doorstep again," Rubina had said, turning to leave.

"Wait," Maria had called out frantically.

"Yes?"

"Now that you are back, what will happen to the extra monthly allotments Luciana had arranged for my medicine and care?"

Rubina had sighed sadly, "Unlike you, my dear *Avó*, I would not abandon my family to suffer needlessly. You will continue to get exactly what father and *Tía* Luciana arranged, which is far more than you deserve," she had told her before walking out of the room.

True to her word, Rubina continued to provide financially for her grandmother until her death a little over a year after that visit but she never spoke to or saw her again. She felt no remorse or regret over their non-existent relationship because her grandmother had felt no remorse or regret over what she had done to her own granddaughter.

The one thing Rubina did regret was having gotten so caught up in proving herself capable of handling all that her inheritance had brought her that she had barely kept in touch with Seth. A year had come and gone before she realized that they had not even seen each other since that day on the dock. When it began to take her weeks to answer his letters his began arriving fewer and farther between until one day they stopped altogether. The last letter telling her that he could no longer go on this way. Since she could not seem to make a decision about their relationship then he was going to be the one to do it.

Rubina had been devastated, but she understood and didn't blame Seth for breaking off what had turned into nothing more than unfulfilled promises. They both had obligations not only to their families but their businesses that neither could just walk away from. She had made a choice and, in spite of how much they had proclaimed their love, she had never given Seth any indication that he had to leave his family and obligations to be with her. They had refused to ask that of one another. That was until one spring day when everything changed and Rubina's life once again went in a direction she would have never expected.

♏ ♏

Rubina was working in her father's old office in her childhood home where she now lived when her housekeeper announced that she had a visitor. She was speechless as she looked up to see Seth standing in the doorway looking even more handsome than she remembered. His hair and mustache were neatly trimmed. He was dressed in a chocolate color jacket and crisp white cotton shirt open at the collar with well-fitted fawn color pants that molded to his muscular thighs, and a pair of freshly shined brown leather riding boots. He looked every bit the proper gentleman caller. Her heart warmed and beat excitedly at the sight of him.

On his way there Seth had everything he was going to say to Rubina all thought out but as soon as he laid eyes on her his well-planned speech was out the window. She sat behind a large, ornately carved wood desk surrounded by open account ledgers. Her hair had grown out and it was pulled away from her face and hung down her back in thick unruly curls just past her shoulders. He could tell by her darkened skin that she spent much time out in the hot Brazilian sun. It gave him the impression of rich, dark chocolate and made her bright hazel eyes stand out even more. She stepped around the desk and Seth couldn't help but smile. She was dressed in a plain white lace trimmed blouse open at the collar and a pair of black riding breeches that fit her rounded hips and long legs like a glove and a pair of scuffed black riding boots. She was breathtaking.

"I see you haven't given up wearing pants."

Rubina had forgotten how casually she was attired. After her morning ride she had come straight to her office to work.

"I wasn't expecting anyone," she said, self-consciously reaching up to button her open collar.

"You look beautiful."

A flush of heat came to Rubina's face. She couldn't believe the sudden bout of bashfulness that overcame her, but it was quickly put aside as the realization that Seth was actually standing in her home hit her. She didn't remember moving but suddenly they both stood in the middle of the room in each other's arms.

"I can't believe you're here," she said, holding on to him as if her life depended on it.

"I had to come," he pulled away just enough to look at her face.

"I thought you had grown tired of waiting and given up on me," she said.

Seth chuckled, "I could never forget about you Rubina Arinzé Domingues," he reached up to touch her cheek.

"For the past year I've felt like I've been walking around in a fog because all I've been able to do is think about you, wondering if I'll ever get to hold you in my arms again."

Rubina smiled. "There were so many times I wanted to steer one of the transport ships I was on towards America just so I could tell you how much I missed you and that I never want us to be apart again," tears flowed freely down her face.

Seth wiped her tears away with the pad of his thumbs. "I'm here now and I'm not going anywhere anytime soon," he said, lowering his head and kissing her slowly and passionately. Savoring the taste of the full red lips he had dreamed so many nights about.

Rubina responded just as passionately, knowing at that moment, that she would not walk away from a life with Seth ever again. She would do whatever it took for them to be together.

ॐ ॐ

But there had been no need for Rubina to find a way for them to be together for Seth had taken care of everything. It seemed that she wasn't the only one he kept in touch with after she returned to Brazil with her family. Knowing of Seth's interest in horse breeding, Amir had broached him about becoming business partners. Grant Blacksmith and Livery would be working with Domingues Stables, which Amir had inherited from Rubina's father. It would be the perfect solution to his and Rubina's situation. A partnership with Amir would mean that he and Rubina could be together without having to give up either of their lives and he could build Grant's Livery back up to the successful business his father and uncles had dreamed of since they had been forced out of Haiti all those years ago. With Thomas, Joseph, the Grant cousins, and Asa there to run things in Philadelphia, there was no need for Seth to be there on a daily basis when he could be working with Amir to build up their stables.

Their partnership also gave Rubina the courage to step up and propose to her managers an idea she had been considering for some time. To expand Domingues Imports/Exports reach to the ports of America. They had offices in Brazil, Europe, Spain and the Caribbean but nothing in America. She knew with the waves of change happening in America this would be the perfect time to set up shop in the northeastern ports.

She and Seth had managed to make it work by splitting their time between two countries, spending six months of the year in America and the other six months in Brazil, which was why she was there now. Just as she and her parents had done when she was a child, Rubina and Seth always came back to the plantation for harvest.

Rubina closed her eyes as she stood looking out across the rows of sugar cane, taking a deep breath of sugar sweetened air. When she opened them two small children stood giggling before her on the bottom step of the veranda. She smiled down at her two youngest children, two year old Sela, with her chubby dimpled fingers and face, skin the color of caramelized sugar and thick black hair braided back in three neat rows resembling the rows of sugar cane in the distance, and four year old Seth Jr., with his father's chocolate brown complexion, squared, masculine face and deep brown eyes.

"*Vem a mãe, vem jogo com nós,*" he beckoned with his small outstretched hand.

"May we play too?" Seth said from behind her. He stood in the doorway holding the hand of their oldest child, six year old Ifé who was almost the exact replica of her namesake with exception of the Domingues bright hazel eyes.

With one hand holding their son's, Rubina placed her other in Seth's and felt a sense of joy like she had never known. For the first time in her life, Rubina felt her heart was finally and truly free.

ABOUT THE AUTHOR

Leslie Thompson is the owner of the independent publishing company Freedom of Love Press. Her love of African American culture and romantic fiction are the inspirations for her novels. Leslie Thompson is the proud mother of two children and currently resides in West Orange, New Jersey with her husband and son.

NOW AVAILABLE

SOON TO BE RELEASED
SPRING 2008